Mr. Darcy's Cousin

A Continuation of *Pride and Prejudice*

◆❖◆

Mariele Kirkby

2DW Books

PUBLISHED BY

2DW BOOKS

First Edition

Printed in the United States.

for Treva

in sunshine and in sorrow

Acknowledgements

Thank you to my long-suffering
daughters Lorna and Nicole,
to one special class who loved *Pride and Prejudice*,
and to Jen, my "average reader."

Chapter 1

"Miss De Bourgh? Are you here, Miss De Bourgh?" Mrs. Jenkinson's voice pierced the solitude of the morning somnolence that blessed the enclosed rose garden at Rosings Park. It caused the girl sitting with her face lifted to the pale sunshine to stand reluctantly and move back to the shade of a trellis tucked artfully between two of the purple plum trees that surrounded the secluded garden.

Hardly had she sat when her companion bustled through the arched entrance, carrying a thick merino shawl, a pink-striped parasol, and a heavy book with an embroidered marker placed squarely in the middle.

"Here you are, Miss De Bourgh! But really, dear child, you shouldn't expose yourself to the uncertain weather this morning."

Anne de Bourgh silently accepted the shawl that was tucked firmly around her shoulders.

"And you see, I have brought your parasol in case you should feel like a brief walk among the flowers. I daresay you won't . . . your mother told me at breakfast that you had a most troubled night, my dear. But if you feel like a little constitutional, here is your parasol to protect your skin." Mrs. Jenkinson's voice, high-pitched and, it seemed to Anne de Bourgh, never-ending, continued in a flow of mingled solicitude for Anne's health and admiration of her pale porcelain complexion, but the girl had become so accustomed to her companion's garrulity that she could acknowledge it with a barely audible murmur and a faint smile while pursuing her own reflections.

At the moment those reflections centered on the possibility of escaping luncheon with her mother, Lady Catherine de Bourgh. She had avoided breakfast simply by sending word by her maid Dulcie that she had passed a disturbed night and felt too unwell to rise. She could have remained in bed; Lady Catherine had long been resigned to the delicate health of her only child. But the sunshine had peeked through her curtains--golden and inviting after a long grey week of rain. That consideration, plus the fact that her mother would certainly send for Dr. Melchett if she had not arisen by noon, had resulted in her drinking a cup of hot sugary tea, dressing hastily, and taking herself and her sketchbook off to the rose garden for an hour of solitude before Mrs. Jenkinson realized she had arisen and tracked her down. Povey, Rosings' butler for the past three decades, had certainly seen her flit noiselessly out the side door, but Anne knew he would conveniently have forgotten by the time Mrs. Jenkinson inquired. *Dear Povey*, thought Anne.

Belatedly aware of silence, Anne looked up to meet Mrs. Jenkinson's expectant gaze. "I'm sorry," she murmured gently. "You were saying . . . ?"

"Only that I worry about your dear mother, Miss De Bourgh. She has had much to try her fortitude these last few months." *Including a useless invalid daughter*, Anne mentally added. "I fear that the news from Hertfordshire may yet prove too much for her."

Anne closed her eyes, needing no reminder of her mother's red-faced fury when news of her cousin Fitzwilliam's marriage to Elizabeth Bennet had arrived. Until the last moment, Lady Catherine had assured herself--and everyone around her--that Darcy would come to his senses. "He won't marry that encroaching little nobody. He is well aware of what he owes his name," Lady Catherine had reiterated. But he had married the little nobody and news of the nuptials had been brought to Rosings by a distressed Mr. Collins, Elizabeth's cousin. Anne had retired from the scene, knowing that her withdrawal would be interpreted as disappointed hopes, for Lady Catherine had planned from Anne's infancy for her to marry her wealthy cousin.

Once again aware of a pause in her companion's monologue, Anne smiled at her. "Perhaps you could read a few pages from Mr. Whitefield's sermons, Mrs. Jenkinson. I find your voice so soothing."

"Of course, my dear." Probably remembering Anne's "disappointed hopes," Mrs. Jenkinson patted her slender hand, happily opened the book at the marked page, and began to read in a high-pitched monotone, allowing Anne once more to sink into thought.

I hope Fitzwilliam will be happy with his "little nobody." And I hope she will be happy too. Anne had liked Elizabeth Bennet in the weeks Miss Bennet had spent at the Hunsford parsonage. Her lively manner had made the days that could sometimes seem endless pass much more quickly. It had been obvious that Anne's other cousin, Colonel Fitzwilliam, had felt the same. Anne smiled, remembering the evenings of music and stimulating repartee. Lady Catherine had not enjoyed the liveliness and animation that Miss Bennet had brought to conversations over the tea trays and dinner table, but Anne had relished the young lady's sparkling wit and unusual opinions. She had said little, having no desire to bring the familiar frown to her mother's face, but not much had escaped her. *Perhaps I was the only one who saw how often Darcy looked at Miss Bennet. Or how frequently--*

"--inside now, dear Miss De Bourgh?" Expert at deciphering the full meaning of a sentence from the last few words, Anne rose and strolled back toward the house, obediently clutching the smothering woolen shawl around her shoulders.

"But I have said enough on the topic. I shall not speak

upon it again," announced Lady Catherine for the third time that hour. Her glassy gaze focused on her daughter, seated nearly four feet away at the huge dining room table. Anne had once suggested that they might partake of luncheon at a table in the small drawing room. The result had been unhappy; Lady Catherine's condemnation of relaxing the formality due to the relict and daughter of Sir Lewis de Bourgh had occupied mealtimes for the next week, and Anne had never broached the subject again. "I have no doubt that Retribution in the guise of Sorrow and Repentance will soon teach my nephew the Duty he should have known."

Anne continued to rearrange her small portion in silence, idly counting the emphatically emphasized nouns in her mother's diatribe.

"How do you feel today, my dear? Are you at all feverish?" Lady Catherine abruptly changed the subject as she glanced at Anne's plate. Without waiting for a reply, she turned to Mrs. Jenkinson who was devouring a large portion of the game pie. "As soon as our meal is complete, tell Povey to send a footman--"

"I do not require Dr. Melchett's services, Mama."

"--to Tillman Place at once. I shall send a note to--"

Anne raised her voice sufficiently to be heard, and both her mother and Mrs. Jenkinson regarded her in patent surprise. "I am not ill, Mama. My headache is quite improved and I do not require Dr. Melchett's advice."

Her mother frowned. "I particularly wish you to be in good health by Thursday, Anne. We have guests arriving. You will wish to look and feel as well as possible."

Miss Jenkinson tittered excitedly, "Guests, Lady Catherine? But how exciting! May I ask--"

Ignoring the interruption, Lady Catherine continued majestically onward. "I think you will be most gratified when you know the names of the ladies and gentlemen who are to be honoured by a visit to Rosings Park. Perhaps you have formed some surmise, my dear?"

"No, Mama."

"*Other*s of our acquaintance have not known how fortunate they were to be welcomed to such an estate as Rosings. *Others* have not wished to take advantage of an alliance so brilliant that it would have set the *ton* in a stir. But we need not rely on *their* good wishes or their good sense. Indeed not!" Triumphantly Lady Catherine took a huge bite of pheasant, gravy, and carrots as Anne waited with her fork suspended in the air. She beamed upon her daughter. "On Thursday, my dearest, you will help me welcome to Rosings, Sir Crawford Daviott. Oh . . . and his mother, dear Lady Theresa and his sisters, Miss Daviott and Miss Susan Daviott. And some few others of his family. Is that not very pleasant news after our recent upset, my dear?"

Confused, Anne looked from her mother's face to Mrs. Jenkinson, to find that worthy lady smiling dotingly upon her. "Of course I shall be pleased to welcome them, Mama. But is this visit not very sudden? You have not previously spoken of it to me."

"I did not think the need for such a visit would arise, my dear. The sins of ingratitude and neglect of duty have never *before* belonged to the Fitzwilliam family. Nor, I must say, to the Darcys! But now we must bestir ourselves and look about us, Anne. You need not repine, my dear. Not when you have a mother to look to your interests."

With a satisfied little nod, Lady Catherine glanced at Mrs. Jenkinson. "Pray ring the bell for dessert. I fancy we may tempt Miss Anne to a few mouthfuls of fresh apple trifle!"

The Rosings ladies were accustomed to receiving such of their neighbors as were deemed acceptable visitors from two of the afternoon until half past three in the large drawing room. A handsome apartment, it could have held fifty with ease; the smaller west-facing drawing room might have seemed more appropriate to many hostesses, but Lady Catherine declared that the rightful consequence of Rosings could hardly be maintained in a room boasting no more than five windows; thus, at half past the hour of two, Anne sat in her accustomed place on a straw-colored damask settee, her sketch book on her lap secretary and her mind in a quandary.

What could Mama have meant by her remarks about the Daviotts? Why should I, in particular, wish to present myself at my best to these strangers? And what has Fitzwilliam's marriage to do with them?

Anne looked toward her mother, head leaning back in the throne-like green chair where she sat each afternoon, ostensibly absorbing the reflections of the ubiquitous Mr. Whitefield, but actually dozing stentoriously until some visitor arrived. Mrs. Jenkinson sat by the farthest window, her professed object being to alert Lady Catherine and Miss De Bourgh to the approach of a carriage. Anne was aware that her companion, too, enjoyed the benefits of a postprandial nap; indeed, many peaceful hours had passed with the older ladies nodding and Anne's pencils flying over the paper before her. But today her mind was too busy with apprehensive musings to attend her task.

. . . you will help me welcome to Rosings, Sir Crawford Daviott . . . we must bestir ourselves and look about us, Anne.

The only consolation to her mother's oft repeated assertion that Anne and her cousin Fitzwilliam Darcy would certainly marry had been the fact that the betrothal, existing only in Lady Catherine's mind, had prevented her from thrusting her daughter into the matrimonial market. Anne's delicate health had severely curtailed her presentation to the *ton*. Rosings had hosted no great ball to mark Anne's coming-out. She had, therefore, been spared most of the agonies that a deep natural reserve and a severe consciousness of her own shortcomings cast upon such festivities.

Anne had made her London debut and had been duly presented at a Drawing Room. Her attendance at several balls had been closely chaperoned by her mother, who had been determined to prevent a possible attachment to any young man

6

who might interfere with her plans for her daughter. Those plans had been overset by her nephew Darcy's marriage to a dark-eyed little "nobody" whom he had met on a visit to his friend Bingley. But now it seemed that her mother was looking to the future of Rosings and a possible alliance for Rosings' heiress. . . . *you will help me welcome to Rosings, Sir Crawford Daviott . . . we must bestir ourselves and look about us, Anne.*

Miserably Anne shifted in her chair. *Perhaps I misunderstood Mama. She may not have meant that Sir Crawford is coming to see me.* Her troubled thoughts were interrupted as Povey entered the room, cleared his throat, and loudly announced, "Mr. and Mrs. Collins."

Mr. Collins, the vicar of Hunsford, was a grave and stately man between five and twenty or thirty years of age, accompanied by the sensible young woman he had married. After fulsome greetings to each of the ladies, he advanced ponderously upon Lady Catherine, his patroness, seated himself by her side, and began at once to compliment her upon the beauty of the grounds. Charlotte Collins chose a seat by Anne as was their usual custom.

"Good afternoon, Miss de Bourgh. I hope I find you in good health today."

Anne smiled at Mrs. Collins whom she both liked and sincerely pitied. "Indeed, I am very well. As I hope you are also, ma'am?"

"Oh, very well indeed."

Anne knew from her maid Dulcie that Mrs. Collins was expecting a child in some five months, but such a subject was hardly suitable for polite conversation between the expectant mother and a young, unmarried lady. Their low-voiced conversation continued along the familiar lines of weather and gardening until Mr. Collins, cast into more than customary transports of delight, interrupted to call his wife's attention to Lady Catherine's latest pronouncement.

"Did you hear that, Mrs. Collins? Rosings is shortly to

play host to a baronet and his family. Sir Crawford Daviott! His family has long resided in Wiltshire at Daviott Hall. I am sure there is no one who has not heard of Daviott Hall. I had once the felicity of touring it with a party of college friends. The present baronet's father condescended to allow us to enter the hall even though the family were in residence. We were entertained to refreshments upon the terrace. The most excellent gooseberry tartlets! Indeed, I was so overwhelmed by such kindness that I could scarce swallow more than four or five! Sir Crawford Daviott! Indeed, Miss De Bourgh, nothing could be more suitable."

Mr. Collins beamed upon Anne. "My dear Miss de Bourgh, I do felicitate you. To have gained the attentions of a young man so distinguished. I can hardly find the words--"

"Thank you, Mr. Collins," said his patroness sharply with a quick look at her daughter's expressionless face. "Perhaps you will be so kind as to hand me my book of sermons? There is a point I wish to bring to your attention that you may use it to enlighten certain of your parishioners."

As Mr. Collins bent obsequiously over the book, eager for instruction, Anne's eyes met those of Charlotte Collins. In them she saw understanding and perhaps a little pity.

Anne was seldom alone. Lady Catherine held it unsuitable for a young lady of Anne's consequence to be unattended, so she was expected to go nowhere without the presence of Mrs. Jenkinson, Dulcie, or a footman. To find the solitude she craved, Anne was in the frequent habit of retiring to her bedroom on the pretext of a headache. Once there, she could dismiss Dulcie, who had been the nursery maid before graduating at Anne's request to the august status of Miss De Bourgh's personal maid. Had Anne remained long in London, her mother would certainly have hired a more accomplished lady's maid for her, but she had postponed that decision after an epidemic cold had given her the excuse to restore her daughter safely to Rosings Park. A deep affection resided between the plump, cheerful red-haired maid and her patently frail young mistress--deep enough that Anne could ask her to remove herself and not be found for several hours and know that Dulcie would obey and be ready to summon her when necessary.

That afternoon Anne sat beside her window, sketching the tiny speckled brown bird that flew from the crumbs on her windowsill to its nest in the oak. Usually she could immerse herself in transferring the flutter and whirr of the bird's wings to the stasis of a drawing, striving to convey the motion as well as the form of the swift little creature, but today her mind wandered until she flung the drawing from her. It would not join the hundreds of others, some full-page coloured drawings and some mere fragments, carefully laid in tissue and locked inside the wooden chest that had been her father's.

Today her stolen hours had brought no repose, and soon she must dress for dinner. Anne leaned over to rest her forehead on her folded arms, knowing she must steel herself to speak to her mother alone and dreading the interview with all her being.

A flood of memories submerged her consciousness. She remembered pleading to keep the puppy whelped by a stable dog. Eight-year-old Anne had been caught when her mother returned home unexpectedly early from the parsonage and heard her laughing as she raced around and around inside the stall where the puppy was kept. Ben Grouder, the assistant stableman, had been dismissed for allowing Miss Anne inside the stable and the puppy had vanished the same day. Anne's frantic pleas had availed her nothing but a week of meals in her room, overseen by Mrs. Jenkinson's terrified predecessor, who had also been dismissed from Rosings within the week as clearly unworthy of the trust she had been given. Lady Catherine had been at pains to explain to her tearful daughter that dignity and decorum were expected of Miss De Bourgh of Rosings Park.

Anne's mind drifted to a later memory when Miss

Fanny Brinstow, the daughter of a wealthy farmer, had accompanied her father to Rosings to inspect a horse for sale. Overjoyed at finding a companion her own age, twelve-year-old Anne had taken her inside the house to show her the conservatory. They had been drawing one of the rare orchids when Mrs. Jenkinson had found them and at once escorted them to Lady Catherine. Miss Fanny was restored to her father, and Anne stood in the Rosings drawing room, cheeks burning at her mother's reproach.

"You do not come of such common stock, Anne. In your veins runs the blood of two of the oldest and most respected families in England. You are a De Bourgh, and even more impressively, you are a Fitzwilliam. We do not lower ourselves to the level of a farmer's chit. You must trust me to know who it is suitable for you to befriend, my dear!"

The child had learned the lesson of obedience to a will far more obdurate than her own. If she did not come to think herself superior to nearly everyone else within her acquaintance, she could at least feign such belief behind a passive façade which the world mistook for disinterest or disdain. Secure behind her wall of silence, the young woman sought within herself for the peace and fulfillment available nowhere else since her father's death.

Inside, a small flame of hope for eventual escape from her mother's suppression of every natural impulse burned. But Anne knew now with a deep certainty that the doorway to escape was inching closed.

Lifting her head, Anne took a deep breath, straightened her shoulders and walked out of her room, down the long hallway, across the broad gallery punctuated by portraits of long-dead De Bourghs and Fitzwilliams, and stopped before her mother's door.

Chapter 2

Anne paused, mentally rehearsing what she would say, before tapping lightly on the heavy oak. After a full minute, her mother's dresser Herne opened the door a crack. "Miss Anne?" her voice rose in surprise as she stepped back into Lady Catherine's boudoir.

"I must speak to my mother, Herne." Anne met the woman's cold blue eyes.

"She is dressing for dinner, Miss Anne." Herne's rigid face expressed outrage at the proposed disruption of her ladyship's routine.

Making no reply, Anne walked over to one of the windows, shrouded even on this warm autumn day in heavy gold velvet. After a moment Herne disappeared into the adjoining bedroom and re-appeared in seconds with Lady Catherine, clad in an enormous violet dressing gown.

"Anne? Are you ill, child? I knew I should have summoned Melchett. You see that I knew best! Sit down at once. Herne shall instruct Povey to send a footman directly."

"I am not ill, Mama. I merely wished to speak with you. Alone, if I may."

A heavy frown appeared on Lady Catherine's face as a possible reason for Anne's unusual request occurred to her. An abrupt gesture swept Herne from the room as Lady Catherine turned uneasily to her daughter.

"I can think of no reason for this urgency if your health is sound, Anne. Perhaps you wish to thank me for my care in seeking out Lady Theresa Daviott? You need not. It was tedious to renew our acquaintance, to be sure, for a greater featherbrain it would be hard to find from here to Land's End!

So it was when we were girls together. Why, I recall that in the year of our come-out--"

"Mama, please tell me. Do we receive the Daviotts because . . . in the expectation of . . . "

Lady Catherine's frown grew as Anne floundered helplessly. After a moment she sat heavily on the velvet sofa and drew Anne down beside her. "I had wished to wait until their arrival. That would have been much more fitting. But you may allow your mother to be the first to felicitate you upon the honour you are about to receive, Anne. A very flattering offer indeed! Although certainly Sir Crawford is the more to be congratulated." Lady Catherine sniffed disdainfully. "The Daviotts are well enough, but a Fitzwilliam may look as high as may be for a husband. It is not every young man who may ally himself to the oldest blood in the land!"

"Oh . . . Mama . . . are you sure you have not mistaken the matter? I have not even really the acquaintance of Sir Crawford Daviott. I do know his sister . . . a little . . . for we attended an afternoon tea when she was presented. I did see him there but indeed, Mama, he hardly noticed me . . . "

"And pray, what need have you for his acquaintance, Anne? He is a very proper husband for you, I do assure you! Naturally your uncle and I have made all the necessary inquiries, and Sir Crawford has indicated to his mother that the match is to his liking."

"He cannot have the least partiality for me! We exchanged barely three words."

"I can only suppose that Mrs. Jenkinson has not properly monitored your reading, Anne! Where else would you get these trumpery notions? A *partiality* indeed! You are not some tradesman's daughter to tie her garter in public!"

Lady Catherine glared into her daughter's eyes, the same crystal grey as her dead father's and brimming with apprehension, and her voice softened. "I realize how grave was your disappointment at being so let down by your cousin Darcy, my dear. But you must surely realize that my hurt runs

12

as deep. Indeed, deeper! Why, my sister and I planned your betrothal even as you lay in your cradle. I have been at pains to find a means to allay the humiliation my nephew has brought to the family, and to give you, and Rosings, into the keeping of a gentleman worthy of the honour. No, child!" her ladyship's voice rose firmly as Anne reached out a hand in pitiful entreaty. "I trust I have taught you your duty well enough to know what your answer to Sir Crawford must be. There is nothing more for us to discuss. Now go and dress for dinner!"

Anne's eyes opened to an awareness of sunshine streaming through the double windows of her bedroom. Each evening before leaving her charge's room, Mrs. Jenkinson carefully checked that Anne's windows were closed with the blue velvet draperies drawn fully across them. And each night before taking the clothes and shoes Anne had worn that day away to be cleaned, Dulcie pulled the draperies open so that her mistress would awaken to the sights and sounds of nature.

Anne stretched, yawned and rose quickly to cross to the window nearest the big oak that towered over Rosings Hall. One of the squirrels who had been her companions since childhood was flitting up the trunk of the old tree toward his nest. Anne inched up the window that she and Dulcie had oiled to noiselessness and leaned out, her gaze following the squirrel's journey up the tree. It was the one with an endearing white splotch rising up one ear; he had figured in many of her sketches, thereby learning that the nuts and slices of fruit left on the limb nearest her window could be retrieved in safety.

Hearing her door open, Anne turned and saw Dulcie slide quickly inside the room. The girl's troubled expression brought yesterday's events flooding back. She sank down on the window seat, the joy of the morning draining away as though it had never been.

"Miss Anne, I told Mrs. Jenkinson you be no better this day than you was yestermorn. She bade me fetch a soothing tisane from Cook." Both girls eyed the greasy-looking liquid in one of the blue china cups on the matching tray. "Do you want I should pour it down the tree again and help you dress?"

"Oh yes, Dulcie, thank you." Both girls leaned out to watch the steaming liquid drizzle down the tree trunk. "I wonder if we might reach the hollow place in that limb? Perhaps Patchett would benefit from a soothing tisane."

Dulcie erupted into giggles. "Oh miss, the poor little varmint. 'Twould be more likely his death now, mightn't it? 'Tisn't Mr. Patch I'd like to dose with that nasty mess neitherways--it's that old Jenks." Dulcie turned to set the cup back on the tray. "What dress will you wear this morning, Miss Anne?"

"Oh, anything--something old, Dulcie. My Scotch cambric if it hasn't been thrown away."

"O'course it's not been done away with, Miss. When Mrs. Jenks said as how it be much too wore for you to wear, I hid it in my room special, for didn't I know it'd be wanted? I'll just run up and get it while you have your tea." She waited until Anne settled in the window seat to bring her the little tray with its pot, cup, and saucer, and poured for her. "And Miss?"

"Yes, Dulcie?"

"Might you not eat a bite or two of toast? There's still bramble jelly left . . . or pear butter, Miss?"

Meeting Dulcie's look, Anne smiled. "I'd love a slice. No, two slices, Dulcie--with bramble *and* pear!" she declared, just to see the soft brown eyes glow with pleasure. "And Dulcie?" Already at the door before her mistress could change her mind, Dulcie turned.

"May I borrow your old brown pelisse this morning?"

"O'course, Miss. I'll bring it with the dress."

Three quarters of an hour later, Anne, clutching her folding easel and box of colours and warmly dressed in clothing more befitting her maid than the young mistress of Rosings Park, waited in the hallway as Dulcie peered down the stairs.

"All's clear, Miss." As Anne started past her, Dulcie whispered hesitantly, "Miss Anne . . . where might you be going? 'Tis likely a morning her Ladyship might send for you with visitors coming and all. And if she does . . ."

"I'm only going to the small apple orchard beyond the kitchen gardens, Dulcie. If you need me, come to the edge of the gardens and whistle. I'll hear you."

Dulcie watched her mistress race down the steps as lightly as Patchett might have done. Povey emerged from the small drawing room into the corridor leading to a side door near the back of the house, but he did not acknowledge Anne's presence, nor she his. On her many early morning journeys out into Rosings Park, Anne was invisible to the servants to whom she had never spoken a harsh word. They had long since learned that any kindness or consideration their employment might yield would only be forthcoming from the young mistress. There were not many services they could perform to make her lot in life easier to bear, but they could fail to notice her frequent adventures into the parklands of Rosings, and this, they faithfully did.

Humming softly, Anne carefully erased a line and frowned in concentration at the huge clump of fairy caps in front of her easel. Their blooms would be gone with the next hard rain, and Anne was determined to capture their hues for her sketchbook first. It was not the flowers that her fingers found so difficult to reproduce. Delicate lavender grew into deepest purple in the heart of each blossom and nothing, Anne thought, could be more graceful than the tall stems stretching upward toward the sky.

It was the woolly yellow and brown worm inching its way up the stalk whose image eluded Anne. No matter how she tried, it seemed . . . *flat* . . . once its likeness was transferred to the page. Anne frowned, trying to discover what the round bristly shape on the paper lacked. "I have captured the woolly's shape and his color," she murmured softly, "but his . . . his *warmness* is not here."

"Perhaps his warmness would be easier to depict if you moved him into the sunshine," a voice observed from behind the small hummock on which Anne sat.

"Oh!" The sudden movement occasioned by Anne's surprise left a dark mark across the top of her drawing and caused the stranger to exclaim in equal dismay.

"Forgive me, ma'am. You were so enrapt in your task that I hesitated to disturb you to make my presence known." Anne's wide grey eyes met the stranger's, also grey but of darker slate colour bordering almost upon blue. He smiled ruefully and his cheeks creased attractively as he took a step backward and removed his hat. "I fear that I should have gone on my way without interrupting a Muse at work. But I so wanted to see the outcome of her hard labour."

Anne rose, her heart pounding, to stand between the stranger and the page clamped to her easel. For years only Dulcie had ever seen her work, and even that notice was paid only in passing. She regarded her mistress's absorption in her sketches as a way of filling empty hours, an escape from the dreadful boredom of Rosings, a trifling hobby that would be abandoned soon in the press of marriage and motherhood. The closeness between the two had certainly never hinted to Dulcie that Anne saw her art as far more than a way of whiling away the tedious stretches of days at Rosings.

Seeing the girl still standing wordless and tense, the stranger said gently, "I fear I've frightened you, coming so suddenly upon you with no notice. I'm Lieutenant Philip Collins, the brother of the vicar of Hunsford. And you, I believe, must surely be Miss De Bourgh. I'm on my way to the hall now. We are to be introduced at luncheon today. I hope you will forgive my forwardness in anticipating that honour."

"I . . . I am indeed Miss De Bourgh. You are . . . I must welcome you to Rosings, Lieutenant Collins. Your brother and Mrs. Collins are frequent visitors, sir."

Again Lieutenant Collins' eyes crinkled in a smile and the drollery in his tone was evident. "Of that fact, Miss De Bourgh, I can assure you I'm quite cognizant. William's letters to me are nearly equally divided between advising me how to make my way in the Service . . . and extolling the glories of the De Bourgh family of Rosings Park."

Even as the words left his lips, Lieutenant Collins regretted them, fearing the young lady might resent his humor at the expense of her mother and home, instead of sharing his amused appreciation of his brother's exaltation of all things De Bourgh. Instead, Anne de Bourgh's eyes met his in a moment of shared amusement before she replied demurely, "Mr. Collins is, indeed, our strongest advertisement of the glories of Rosings, Lieutenant. We are most obliged to him."

Hoping to further ease his unexpected companion's disquiet, the lieutenant allowed his gaze to wander past her to the drawing. "Might I now be permitted to see your representation of the gentleman who is even now fast escaping, Miss De Bourgh?"

Anne turned to see the worm diligently making his way into higher grass. "Oh . . . certainly," she replied hesitantly. "But . . it is only a sketch, sir. Hardly worth anyone's time." She reached out to remove the page from its clasp, only to be stopped by her companion's swift motion. Lightly but firmly, he laid his hand on her wrist, the action seeming somehow impersonal for his eyes were fixed upon the drawing before his intent gaze.

Anne waited, conscious of her heart racing, either from the unaccustomed masculine touch or the equally unaccustomed exposure of her work to strange eyes. Comments made when she had first begun to draw in earnest echoed in her memory. *Such a nice little effort, Anne. Let us hope you will improve upon further instruction from a drawing master.* And later: *How . . . striking, my dear. But hardly what one would want to frame for one's drawing room. I do not know that your time may not be spent to better effect with harp tuition . . .*

By the time Anne emerged from the schoolroom, she had learned to hide her drawings and watercolours away in her room, guarded from harsh criticism or insincere flattery in their wooden fastness.

Now she stood watching the stranger's thin tanned countenance, so nervous that her stomach clenched and she regretted the toast she had eaten to pacify Dulcie.

The trespasser did not hurry in his examination of the drawing, even squatting to regard it more closely. "I can hardly find words, Miss De Bourgh, to describe the pleasure your drawing gives me. At least no words that will not forcibly remind you of my brother." Again his white teeth flashed. "Such an exact depiction that an onlooker could swear this flower grew at his very doorstep. And yet so much more than mere accuracy. I feel this fellow's determination to scale that stalk even as I feel the flower striving ever upward. It relishes the sun's glory, does it not? But knows the winter is surely coming, just as the worm does. You may not feel you have captured his *warmness*, Miss De Bourgh, but you have certainly depicted his perseverance."

Anne had not breathed since his perusal began and now she inhaled so sharply that she gasped. "Oh . . I . . . I am so surprised that you should perceive my intent, sir. At first I merely tried to portray the flowers soaking in the last of the sun's warmth. But then, this little fellow came and overset all my plans."

Even as she stumbled for words to express her astonishment at his understanding, a sharp whistle pierced the stillness of the orchard. "Oh, I must go. Excuse me . . " Frightened eyes, fringed by long lashes, met his as Anne began to gather her pencils. Quickly, Lieutenant Collins unfastened the drawing and handed it to her, watching as she wrapped it in tissue, rolled it into a compact circle and stowed it away in her drawing box.

"Might I be of assistance in carrying your belongings

18

back to the house, Miss De Bourgh?"

"Oh no! No. You see . . . Lieutenant, may I beg a favour of you?"

"Certainly, Miss De Bourgh. I am quite at your service."

"Please say nothing of our conversation this morning." Anne met his surprised look pleadingly, her pale cheeks becomingly flooded by a wild-rose colour. "You see . . ." Another whistle marred the silence and, seeing the girl's confusion, Lieutenant Collins promptly handed her the easel, now neatly folded, and the wooden box.

"Don't disturb yourself, ma'am. I quite understand. I shall look forward to luncheon with considerably more pleasure than I first anticipated." He was answered only by a smile. It seemed to start in her eyes, merely a sparkle in their crystal grey depth, before the corners of her lips curled upward, and her slender face was suddenly transfigured by warmth and charm. Thoughtfully, he watched the slender grey-clad figure dart through the apple trees and disappear among the hedges at the orchard's border.

His older brother William had described Miss Anne de Bourgh as a paragon, the beautiful, refined, and accomplished daughter of a noble line, clearly destined to adorn the highest ranks of the aristocracy. His younger brother Henry, who had visited William and Charlotte in the spring, had dismissed her as a bread-and-butter miss, inordinately proud, and lacking any attraction beyond the vast inheritance that would one day be hers.

Neither description seemed to Lieutenant Collins to befit the shy girl whose embarrassment and pleasure at his moderate praise of her sketch had been so obvious. *No, she is not beautiful*, he thought, *until that smile lights her face. Then a man doesn't remember whether she is or not.*

Back at Rosings Hall, a breathless Anne struggled into a green-striped dress, helped by an equally breathless Dulcie.

She was not remembering the warmness of a brown worm, whose elusive essence would usually have occupied her artist's eye and mind. She was not thinking of her mother's likely annoyance that luncheon had to be held back until Miss Anne felt like arising. She was not even dreading the advent of Sir Crawford Daviott, though it was his specter she had sought to banish by staying over-long in one of her favorite refuges in the park. She was wondering if she might be seated beside Lieutenant Philip Collins at the luncheon table.

"I find myself almost unable to appreciate the excellence of this fine ham, your ladyship," remarked Mr. Collins as he accepted a second large slice. In an aside to his brother, who was seated beside Lady Catherine, with Mrs. Jenkinson upon his right, Mr. Collins delivered his fifth encomium upon the meal thus far. "All the pork served at the Hall is raised upon the home farm, my dear Philip. There is no finer to be had anywhere in Kent. Indeed, perhaps in the width of the country. I am sure you have not had better, even upon all your travels."

Upon his brother's assurance that he certainly had not done so, Mr. Collins returned his attention to his hostess. "But as I was saying, your ladyship, I am distracted by the knowledge of your condescension in sending your carriage for us. It was quite unnecessary, I assure you. Mrs. Collins and I take weekly enjoyment in our walks from our humble abode to Rosings. Do we not, my dear?"

Charlotte Collins glanced up from her plate to reply tranquilly, "So we do, Mr. Collins. The ride was most agreeable, but I look forward to walking home, for the grounds are in great beauty even though the autumn advances."

Lady Catherine bowed her head in regal acceptance of the tribute. "As you say, Mrs. Collins. I daresay there is not another park so well planned and carried out within carriage distance. I would hesitate to tell you what Sir Lewis de Bourgh laid out, all told, to assure that Rosings Park would retain beautiful prospects from March through October."

Lady Catherine paused to glance at Lieutenant Collins. "I understand that you had already set out before the carriage arrived to take you up this morning, Lieutenant?"

"Yes, your ladyship, that is so. I did not wish to miss the natural loveliness that my brother had so eloquently described to me."

His hostess directed a supercilious smile at the lieutenant. "And were your expectations met, sir?"

For a moment Lieutenant Collins' eyes rested upon the shining silver head across the table before he replied deliberately, "They were exceeded, your ladyship. I can only assure you that any expectations I had formed of the beauty of Rosings were more than exceeded."

Lady Catherine smiled complacently. "Pray pass me the bay jelly, Mr. Collins. Anne, my love, you are looking quite pink. Are you sure you are not feeling feverish?"

Chapter 3

The following morning Anne was again awakened by sunshine strained through the leaves of the sheltering oak tree, but she did not at once arise and rush to the window. Instead, she stretched out on the big feather mattress before pulling the covers up to her chin and closing her eyes again. The dreaded occasion on which she would be presented to Sir Crawford as a possible . . . as a *likely* bride was only two days away, but Anne's thoughts were upon Lieutenant Philip Collins.

The Collinses and their guest had remained all afternoon at Rosings; Mr. Collins, as could usually be relied upon, had monopolized Lady Catherine's attention while Mrs. Collins and Mrs. Jenkinson maintained a subdued conversation which had usually stilled if anyone approached. Anne knew they were probably discussing such absorbing topics as midwives, wet nurses, and christening gowns.

That had left Anne to entertain Lieutenant Collins, a task which would normally have appalled her. She had known few young men, other than her cousins who had seemed to accept their aunt's estimation of Anne's health and usually left her to her own devices. A mutual fondness existed, but Lady Catherine's ubiquitous match-making tendencies had prohibited Darcy and Fitzwilliam from speaking often to Anne.

During the six weeks she had spent in London, Anne had met several young men whom she felt she might have liked to know better. However, Lady Catherine had insisted that Anne remain beside her at the few very select entertainments they attended. Any partner who claimed Miss De Bourgh's hand had to brave her mama's stern looks to procure it and return her immediately to that lady's awe-inspiring aegis. Thus, the conversations that might have led to friendship with any of the young gentlemen of the *ton*—or even more than friendship—had never had a chance even to begin, and Anne usually felt herself at a complete loss when called upon to converse with a young man.

To her relief, neither she nor Lieutenant Collins had needed to search for a topic of common interest. Almost immediately he had requested permission to view Anne's drawings, and with a murmured excuse to her mother, Anne had brought down a portfolio of watercolours and one of pencil drawings. They had conversed very little, which was no more than the others expected. Lady Catherine had long made clear that Anne could have little of interest to say to visitors; the burden of their entertainment, like so many others, must rest upon her mother's shoulders.

Eventually, Lady Catherine had accompanied Mr. and Mrs. Collins and Mrs. Jenkinson into the conservatory to explain the plans her gardeners had developed for forcing fruit superior to that of any other house in the county. She had assumed that her daughter and Mr. Collins' brother would follow them upon the tour.

Turning to Anne instead, Lieutenant Collins commented quietly, "You don't seem eager to share your quite extraordinary talent with others, Miss De Bourgh. Including those close to you."

"Oh . . . it would not please my mother, sir. She believes that females should occupy themselves with the requirements of their house and family--that they should do their duty in whatever sphere of life God saw fit to place them."

"Might not God have seen fit to bless you with an unusual talent designed to bring pleasure to others?"

Anne blushed. "You are very kind. But the answer, sir, is no. My mother would find any open display of my work abhorrent--unbecoming to a well-brought-up young lady.

23

Besides, she would have demanded far more of me in my duty to Rosings than she has . . . had I not been in delicate health."

The lieutenant regarded her thoughtfully, at a loss to identify the puzzling nuance of her final remark. He could have believed that the pale and silent young lady who had sat opposite him at luncheon did not enjoy robust health. Nor had the companion who mutely handed him watercolour drawings to examine contradicted the universal tales of her constant *malaise*. But the girl he had seen in the orchard that morning, humming happily as she studied a furry brown worm, had belied that image, and his curiosity made him say, "You seemed to feel very well when I encountered you earlier, ma'am."

Anne smiled, but instead of replying, she asked him earnestly, "You possess a discerning eye, sir. Would I be far wide of the mark to ask if you are yourself an artist?"

Lieutenant Collins laughed. "Miss De Bourgh, I certainly am not, if declaring myself an artist places me in the same class of taste and accomplishment as you. But I have had the good fortune to learn from two true artists in my life. One was at school--a drawing master whose passion for art informed my early years and greatly influenced my tastes. Then when I was aboard my second ship for some months, I was befriended by the purser who, I think in another sphere of life, might have become as well-known as Mr. Constable or Mr. Turner. Why, after he left the service, his work was reproduced in books of nautical engravings which enjoy some popularity. In fact, I possess one of them. If you are kind enough to invite me to tea tomorrow, I shall bring it to show you."

Anne's shyness forgotten, she leaned toward her companion, listening with eager interest. "Indeed? I naturally have no knowledge of what life must be like onboard a ship of His Majesty's Navy, Lieutenant, but I wouldn't have been disposed to think it a place where one would have the leisure to pursue such an interest as art."

"There are certainly times of furious activity, Miss De

24

Bourgh, and even ones of peril. But there are also many vacant hours to be filled. Why, half the belongings a man takes aboard, if examined, would turn out to be books, or perhaps wood to be carved, or a chess set--or brushes and canvas and paints, in my case."

"And so you learned from a . . . a purser, you said?"

"Hiram Reese . . . I owe him a considerable debt. I had learnt something of perspective, but it was his instruction that enabled me to make my paintings lifelike . . . as much as my talent would permit."

"Were your subjects those at hand? The sea and the ship and perhaps the men aboard? Or did they spring from memory or imagination?"

"They were, Miss De Bourgh, in part a reflection of the scenes directly before me. I also carried pictures in my mind. When we were at liberty for nearly a month in Lisbon, I roamed the streets and the countryside around it, my sketchbook in my hand. I've not much talent in drawing, certainly not nearly as much as you have, but I would try to reproduce the most salient details of scenes which I wished to put on canvas later."

"I should so like to see some of your paintings," Anne said wistfully.

He flushed faintly. "I hope you will not think me too much of a coxcomb when I tell you that I carry some of them about with me. I wished to allow Charlotte and William to choose—"

"Anne!" Lady Catherine's voice held a tone of sharp reproof. Anne straightened at once. She had been unaware that she had leaned closer to Lieutenant Collins in her absorption in his conversation. Now she became abruptly aware of their proximity--of his long-fingered hand resting near hers, of the force and directness of his blue-grey eyes, even of a peculiarly masculine scent in her nostrils. Her eyes met her mother's where she saw a mixture of surprise, reproof, and concern.

"Yes, Mama?"

"We have missed you, Anne. I require you at once! And I am sure Lieutenant Collins will prefer joining his family in a walk in the garden to sitting here. Why, the room has become quite stuffy!"

Under her companion's gaze, the expression of interest which had lent a most becoming animation to Anne's features was replaced by the passivity normally to be found there. Her glance held no friendliness or, indeed, any expression beyond the merest civility. With a murmured excuse, she stood and walked away, leaving the lieutenant to follow the ladies of Rosings onto the lawn, where an inspection of late blossoms in the herbaceous borders was proposed.

Anne lay in bed on the day before the all-important guests were to arrive at Rosings, her thoughts entirely occupied by yesterday's *tête-à-tête* with Lieutenant Collins. He had seemed to be genuinely struck by the skill and imagination of the drawings she had shown him. She had said little, wishing to draw no attention to their conversation or its focus, but within her had surged a happiness seldom felt. He *liked* her work. He *admired* her aptitude. Anne supposed it was in the hope of his approbation that she had taken the totally unprecedented step of showing her drawings--that, and the fact that he was a stranger who would be gone in a week. Besides, he had not spoken to the others of their earlier meeting. Surely that omission had merited some degree of trust.

A gentle scratching sounded at Anne's door, Dulcie's inquiry as to whether or not her mistress was ready to rise. This morning Anne ignored it. She was not ready for anyone's company, even Dulcie's.

Waiting for several minutes, Anne pushed back the covers and did something most unusual. She walked through her bedroom into the adjoining dressing room and stood before the tall cheval glass there. *How do I appear to other people?* Anne wondered. *How will Sir Crawford be struck by my*

26

appearance? And she was unable to suppress her next, surely ridiculous, query. *What did Lieutenant Collins see when he looked at me yesterday?*

Anne examined her image as though taking stock of a stranger. She saw a very fair girl, her hair so light as to seem silver, so long that it nearly reached her waist. It was fine hair and difficult to manage, which was one of the reasons her mother favored pulling it back into a plain arrangement on the crown of Anne's head. At seventeen she had experimented with a less severe style, but Lady Catherine had frowned at the wispy curls Dulcie had cut to fall at Anne's temples. *You do not need to depend for attention upon the tricks and artifices other young ladies must practice, Anne. Miss De Bourgh may look as high as may be when the time comes to settle her preference. Not that we shall have to look far!* And Anne's hairstyle had reverted to severity.

Pushing back the straight silken fall of silvery-pale hair, Anne examined her features. She saw wide-set grey eyes, well-opened, but not *distinguished*, Anne thought. Not *striking*. She thought of Miss Elizabeth Bennet's dark eyes, which she had much admired. Clearly, Anne remembered with a small, amused quirk of her lips, her cousin Darcy had admired them also. Part of their beauty had come from the thick dark lashes that surrounded them. Anne's lashes were thick, but not nearly dark enough to show her eyes to advantage. Some ladies used cosmetics to achieve that appearance, Anne knew from below-stairs gossip that Dulcie had related to her.

But what could she use to achieve such an effect? Boot black? Surely not. And besides, what possible pretext could she use to secure such a thing? Suddenly Anne turned and scurried to the fireplace in her bedroom, which had been lit last night in spite of her protests. Mrs. Jenkinson had insisted, citing the light rainstorm that had drenched Rosings and then passed; the girls had followed Anne's usual policy of pretending to acquiesce and then extinguishing the fire once

Mrs. Jenkinson had retired. Thoughtfully, Anne took an edge of her nightgown and rubbed it across a sooty, half-burned log.

Returning to the mirror, she cautiously rubbed the cloth lightly across an eyebrow and the lashes of one eye and peered at the result--which was startling. Quickly repeating the process on her other eye, Anne surveyed herself again. Her eyes seemed to leap out at the onlooker now, like shining pools, fringed by darkness. The dark lashes and dark irises together seemed to highlight the clear grey depths of her eyes into a striking prominence. *One could hardly go about with soot rubbed into one's lashes, but perhaps Dulcie could . . .*

Her small straight nose was *passable*, Anne decided-- nothing out of the ordinary but perhaps that was a blessing. She recalled Miss Daviott's nose quite clearly as long, beaky, and distinctly curved at the end. Her mother Lady Theresa had referred to it with pride as the Membray nose, pointing out in one of her interminable, rambling monologues that, of the younger generation, only dear Augusta had been blessed with the distinguishing mark of Lady Theresa's own family. Anne had been thankful to be left thus undistinguished, and meeting Miss Susan Daviott's dancing brown eyes, she had known her sentiments were shared by the youngest member of the family.

My mouth? Anne first pursed her lips and then smiled into the mirror. Her mouth was perhaps more than passable. It was a small mouth, but not thin, Anne thought. Her lower lip was full while her upper was heart-shaped; when parted they revealed even white teeth. The notable lack of colour which characterized her complexion did not extend to her mouth. *I do not smile enough*, Anne thought as her lips curled upward to give warmth and animation to her features. *But so often there is nothing to smile about.*

Perhaps it is my paleness that makes me appear plain. And that, Anne reflected as she continued her inventory, *is more my own fault than ought else.* During her childhood, Mrs. Jenkinson had been zealous in following Lady Catherine's mandate that Anne's delicate skin be always protected from any

28

insalubrious weather--wind, sunshine, even the mildest of breezes. By her teens, Anne's escape from her mother's constant solicitude had been illness. Its simulation had provided blessed hours of solitude in which she could read books from the Rosings library smuggled to her room by Dulcie, sit at her window and watch the constant changes in Nature as evinced by the oak tree and its denizens--and most of all, perfect her skill in drawing and water colour. Even when she began to venture outside on small odysseys whose object was finding more challenging flora and fauna for her pencils-- even then Anne had very carefully covered every inch of her skin. A blooming complexion would ill support her claims of poor health.

Pallor is a defect that may be remedied, Anne thought, resolving to discard her bonnet for part of the time she spent in the park. *But in the meanwhile . . .* Beside her bed was a basket of flower petals which Dulcie kept replenished from spring through autumn, when it was then filled with pine cones and other aromatic offerings of Nature. It was the work of a minute for Anne to sift through the basket and find the petals she was searching for—the last of the season's bright pink peonies. Her mother would not have the flowers on the vast table in the dining room because if one dropped it would stain the snowy tablecloth. Returning to the mirror, Anne rubbed the fragrant petals across her cheekbones until a gentle colour rewarded her.

There, she thought. *I do not look so odiously plain after all.* A different girl seemed to regard her from the mirror, a girl with shining eyes and a rosy glow. But her face was not the only aspect of femininity by which a girl was judged. Indeed, from Anne's stealthy reading she sometimes thought it was not even the major one, at least for gentlemen. For a moment Anne's fists clenched on her voluminous white cotton night-gown before she reached resolutely for the hem, drew it swiftly over her head, and dropped it on the floor.

Determinedly, although with a natural colour

superseding the flowers' stain, Anne studied the body now revealed. *I am not generously formed. There is no getting past that.* The voluptuous curves that seemed to characterize her favorite fictional heroines did not magically appear in the cheval glass. *But there* are *curves,* Anne thought. Her breasts were small but they rounded upward into delicate pink nipples. Her midriff was slender, curving down to a truly tiny waist that swelled into a small but rounded bottom and long, slender legs.

It is the clothes Mother chooses for me that make me look so flat, Anne reflected. The straight, stiffened fabrics favoured by Lady Catherine, made up into dresses modestly high at the neck and never extending less than half-way down Anne's forearms, masked every curve. *And that too is something that might be remedied. If I am to be married, I may choose my own dresses. And they will look nothing like the ones I wear now. I will choose the colours to suit myself, and I will have none of the ones Mama makes me wear.*

A louder scratch at the door caused Anne to snatch up her nightgown and pull it hastily over her head before crossing into the bedroom to admit Dulcie. *Perhaps,* Anne thought, *Sir Crawford is more personable than I remember. Perhaps he is kinder and more gentleman-like.* But it was not Sir Crawford's face she was picturing as she opened the door.

It is foolish of me even to go to the orchard today, Anne scolded herself as she slipped through a gap in the hedge and started downhill toward the shady corner where she had established her easel yesterday. *I can stay scarcely an hour after lingering so long this morning.*

Nevertheless, she settled herself with yesterday's drawing on the easel. No furry brown worm presented himself for study so she contented herself with perfecting the background behind the tall purple flowers. *I shall make the apple trees hazy . . . only a suggestion of their trunks perhaps . . . gnarled and bent from their load of fruit each year . . . .*

Gradually she sank into her normal state of happy absorption, but some part of her was unsurprised when a voice spoke behind her.

"I come bearing a gift today in hopes of pardon for interrupting your labour, Miss De Bourgh." Anne's shy smile turned to delighted laughter as she turned to greet Lieutenant Collins and saw what was extended to her on a drying apple leaf.

"Oh thank you!" Anne reached out a hand and reiterated "No . . . truly" when the newcomer laughed and would have tossed the leaf away. "I had looked for my subject earlier, but he was disinclined to sit for me today."

"I make no doubt that he was only shy in the presence of a lady. Let me find him a comfortable seat and perhaps he will condescend to stay. Let's see . . . it was this leaf, was it not?"

Together they established the brown woolly on a leaf at least approximating his position in the drawing, and Anne looked up to find an arrested expression on the lieutenant's face. Seeing her questioning expression he flushed slightly. "Forgive me . . . it is only that you look different today. But I suppose it is merely the magic ladies work with a different bonnet or a new pelisse."

No, it is the magic ladies work with a smudge of soot and a wisp of flower and an old yellow dress soft from many washings. The thought brought a sparkle of merriment to Anne's face that melted the stiffness she would normally have shown. "Perhaps it is only that I feel so . . so . . . uplifted today. I thought the rain would surely stay, but here we sit in the sunshine. Is that not reason enough to be content?"

"I cannot answer for everyone, Miss De Bourgh. Most people, I believe, require more cause for content. But I assure you that I find myself very pleased with my lot this morning."

Anne's lashes dropped to shield her eyes as colour rose in her cheeks, and Collins realized that he had embarrassed her. *How strange,* he reflected, *that the heiress of Rosings Park*

31

should find so mild a compliment disconcerting when she must have a host of suitors. "I feared you might not venture out today, you know. I thought the wet grass and chillier air might dissuade you from finishing your drawing."

"I am not so frail—nor so easily dissuaded from my object," Anne replied gravely, even as she wondered if finishing the drawing of the fairy caps had truly been her purpose this morning. *But even if I did hope to see him this morning, what harm can there be? He is the vicar's brother, after all. And there are so few people that I can talk to about my drawing. Indeed, there is no one.*

Watching the changing emotions flicker across her face, Collins said gently, "And now you are sad."

Solemn grey eyes lifted and met his with a curiously childlike trust. "For a moment. I was thinking of my father. This orchard was one of the places he used to bring me when I was small—to this very place, in fact."

As remembrance lit Anne's face with happiness, her companion thought again how pleasing her aspect became when her lips curved upward into a smile. "He'd swing me up to a limb in one of the apple trees and then pull himself up. We'd sit there quietly never uttering so much as a word until Nature's people ventured out again."

"Nature's people?"

"Oh yes. You might not realize, Lieutenant, that there are dozens of pairs of eyes upon us right now. Rabbits and moles and squirrels. Pheasants and woodcocks and countless songbirds. Perhaps even the red fox who lives over the hill has ventured so close this morning."

The lieutenant glanced around them. "If so, I wish we could coax him out to make my acquaintance."

"We could not do that, I'm afraid. Master Fox knows too well the danger that people present. But I was here one winter evening near dusk, and he suddenly appeared just where that little copse of beech stands. He stood there looking at me with his golden eyes for what seemed far longer than the few

32

moments it must actually have been. It felt as though we were frozen in time. I hurried home and I was able to complete a watercolour of him by noon the next day. It is still one of my favourite studies."

"Have you drawn them all, Miss De Bourgh—all of Nature's people?"

"Most of them. If one sits very quietly and moves only a hand, they may linger long enough to enable one to get a few quick strokes down on paper. Or sometimes I don't try to draw them at all as long as they are content to stay. I just sit quiet and try to . . . to absorb their . . . their *being*." Anne blushed as she realized the seriousness of her tone, and glanced self-consciously at her listener, but Collins seemed interested in her description.

"I should like to see your drawings of . . . of Nature's people."

"Then I shall hunt out the best of them. My most favourite of all is a wood mouse who crept right up to me one day. I had left the remains of my breakfast under a stalk of blooming clover, and he quite lost all fear as he sat clutching the crust and enjoying the jam on it."

Remembering the little creature and his frenzy of enjoyment, Anne smiled again, her eyes glowing with pleasure.

Philip Collins thought suddenly, *William had the right of it, after all. She* is *beautiful--just not in the way of young ladies in silken ball gowns, flirting for the pleasure of it and fluttering their fans and uttering languid sighs. She is as shy as the woodland creatures she loves and rather like one of the flowers she draws--only just beginning to bud and not likely to be noticed by uncaring eyes, but truly lovely when one takes time to see her.*

Realizing he had been standing speechless for a long enough time to make the young lady look quizzically at him, Lieutenant Collins asked diffidently, "Would it distract you to have me sit quietly and watch you draw? I promise to do nothing to frighten away any of your shy subjects who might appear. I feel Fortune has favoured me yet again with a third master from whom to learn!"

Anne laughed and glanced mischievously up at him. "Now you seek to flatter me, sir! But it will not distract me even if you do not sit quietly. I often talk to myself as I draw. Indeed, my realistic Self argues vehemently with my . . . my imaginative Self with distressing frequency."

Lieutenant Collins seated himself close by Anne's side instead of behind her as he had intended. "And who is winning the argument this morning?"

"I think you may discern the answer for yourself if you look at the trees I have shaded into the background, Lieutenant."

The two heads, one fair and one dark, bent close over Anne's drawing as a small woolly brown worm crawled away, unnoticed.

◆ ❖ ◆

Chapter 4

On Thursday in the forenoon, the Rosings ladies sat in the large drawing room, Miss De Bourgh and Mrs. Jenkinson occupying themselves with needlework, Lady Catherine with informing them of exactly how the Daviott visit would be conducted and assuring them of the degree to which they would enjoy it. Most of her strictures were aimed at her daughter, who sat, pale and silent, with nothing more to contribute than an occasional "Yes, Mama." Anne had made an abortive attempt to occupy herself with her sketchbook, but her mother had instantly taken the activity amiss, declaring, "Not today, Anne. You will soil your dress with the pencil lead."

Now she eyed her daughter with satisfaction. "You would scarcely credit what your outfit cost, first and last, but I do not mention it, my dear. You may be sure our guests will expect no less! And a lady's hands are most gracefully occupied with embroidery."

Anne, therefore, sat with an oval of embroidery in her hands and a knot forming inexorably in her stomach. It seemed to her that she had been perched on the sateen settee for hours, unable to relax for fear her mother would once again trumpet her famous pronouncement that a lady's back never touches the chair on which she sits. Her admirably straight back ached, her hands ached, her head was beginning to ache, and she could not help reflecting on the last time she had sat there, so comfortably conversing with Lieutenant Collins. *Is there a hope that I received the wrong impression of Sir Crawford? I was not truly attending on that occasion. Perhaps he will prove to be as kind and pleasant and interesting as--*

Mrs. Jenkinson abruptly shot straight up in her seat, her cheeks blazing with excitement. "I hear the carriage, Lady Catherine! I am quite sure that I do!"

I am going to be sick. On the carpet. On my dress. How angry Mama will be. How disappointed in me. Perhaps if I go quietly upstairs now, they can say I was too ill to come down.

But it was too late. Povey had already announced the visitors, and Anne stood with her mother and Mrs. Jenkinson to receive them. Lady Theresa Daviott was as Anne remembered her, tall and stick-thin. Her hair, an improbable bright gold, was swept into what seemed a bird's nest of swirls and tucks, and her lace-trimmed yellow gown seemed more suitable to a garden party than a trip into the countryside--and more appropriate for one of her daughters than herself. Her amiable flow of commonplace never ceased, even when greetings were being exchanged.

"Theresa, how very good it is to see you and how happy I am to welcome you and your son to Rosings! Oh, and the young ladies to be sure--and the rest of your family." The two ladies touched cheeks, their eyes meeting with something of the satisfaction of two generals congratulating each other on the successful first skirmish of an important battle.

"Anne, you remember Miss Daviott," her mother pronounced. A tall, thin, anemic-looking blonde pressed her cheek lightly to Anne's and murmured an adenoidal greeting over the determined monologue of Lady Theresa.

"--looked forward to a drive through the lovely, lovely countryside of Kent for the past weeks, my dear, although Augusta does sometimes feel the movement--"

"And Miss Susan Daviott." The kiss felt more sincere this time and it was accompanied by a hug from the shorter, slightly plump, and also blonde younger sister. Anne met her twinkling brown eyes and felt marginally better.

"--recommend a good dose of Dr. Skinner's Stomach

36

Powders prior to leaving although it never seems--"

Anne saw that the expression of roguish humor in Miss Susan's eyes had not changed. She was next introduced to Mr. and Mrs. Powell, Lady Theresa's cousin and wife, and then to a young curate, Jeremiah Coulville, also a cousin. The Powells were a nondescript pair who looked awed by Lady Catherine's regal greeting while Mr. Coulville's gloomy expression never altered. Anne curtseyed to each of them, repeating the same stiff words of greeting until finally she heard the only introduction that mattered.

"And certainly you remember Sir Crawford Daviott." Her mother's voice sounded almost coy, and Anne turned stiffly to greet the large figure who had strode last through the doorway.

"Just giving orders to assure myself the horses will be seen to properly. Always do, you know. Miss De Bourgh, most pleasant to see you again. Thought of you many times since our meeting in London." Instead of bowing, Sir Crawford ambled forward with a hand outstretched. In the sudden stillness, Anne realized that even Lady Theresa had ceased talking. Hardly aware of what she did, but very aware of eight pairs of onlooking eyes--nine if she counted Povey-- Anne extended a hand which was punctiliously kissed by Sir Crawford.

Anne would have answered his greeting, indeed the memorized words were on her lips, but she was unaccountably seized with a desire to giggle when his luxuriant mustache brushed the back of her hand. *It feels exactly like Patchett's tail*, she thought hysterically. *It looks rather like it too.* And so she remained silent for an awkward moment until both her mother and Lady Theresa launched into speech at the same time and Povey and two maids entered with the tea trays.

"--treat myself to a week in the country air." Sir Crawford now occupied the settee with Anne, who had still not managed to regulate her mind enough to converse sensibly.

Not that her silence seemed to matter to any particular extent. Sir Crawford seemed well equipped to carry the conversational burden for them both, leaving Anne struggling to banish the image of the settee suddenly splintering under his considerable weight and catapulting both of them onto the thick-piled carpet amongst shattered china. She doubted even that disaster would cause his mother to cease talking for more than a minute.

The settee was too small to seat both of them in comfort and not even pressing herself into the side of the upholstery until a spring sharply announced its presence could keep her more than an inch from Sir Crawford's thickly-muscled thigh.

"Wouldn't normally know how to occupy myself here since I brought no dogs or guns, of course. Fine country for hunting, Kent. Or so I have been told. Friend of mine has a hunting box here. Do you hunt, Miss De Bourgh?"

Anne thought of Patchett and his numerous family, of the fox and its kits whom she had sketched on four consecutive mornings last spring, of the fat partridges with their wings surprisingly iridescent in the sunshine of Rosings Park. "No, sir. I do not."

"Ah then, perhaps that is a skill you might enjoy acquiring. Assure you that I have known ladies' hands quite as adept at making a good kill as any man's." As though to prove his point, Sir Crawford lightly touched one of Anne's folded hands. His fingers looked like nothing so much as fat sausages, overstuffed to bursting, and their heat was repellent. However, it was impossible for Anne to withdraw any further from his touch than she already had. "Sure that your late father's gun room could supply the necessary, Miss Anne." Anne stiffened indignantly at the familiar use of her name. "Borrow a dog or two from a neighbor if you keep none and off we'll be for some sport! Fine way to spend a morning or two, eh?"

"I do not often rise before eleven, Sir Crawford. I sometimes have difficulty sleeping." Frantically Anne seized the familiar excuse like the hand of an old friend.

"Why then, no reason we could not make an afternoon of our sport, is there? We must let you get your beauty sleep, mustn't we? Although clearly you need none! You will find me most amenable to your pleasure." He leaned closer and Anne met his protuberant brown eyes. The pressure of his hot fingers increased, only now they had progressed down her wrist and she could feel his thumb slide into the palm of her hand. She stood hastily and picked up her saucer and cup with a clatter.

"My tea has grown cold. May I procure you another cup, sir?" Without waiting for a reply, Anne walked to the table behind which Mrs. Jenkinson was pouring and handed her both cups, asking her to re-fill Sir Crawford's and take it to him. With a murmured excuse to the entire party, she fled upstairs.

Luncheon proved to be far more of a trial than tea had been. Anne was placed at the foot of the table with Sir Crawford on one side and Mr. Coulville on the other. She made several attempts to converse with the latter, partly to escape Sir Crawford's attentions and partly for the sake of courtesy, but Mr. Coulville concentrated fiercely upon his food, devouring large portions of every dish offered, and answered in monosyllables. That dangerous streak of mirth once again arose in Anne as she speculated on what her marriage would have been like if Mr. Coulville had been the prospective bridegroom. She visualized long days of total silence between them, she sketching and he--well, chewing perhaps? Composing a sermon on all the seven deadly sins except gluttony? With servants so inured to silence that the maid would scream and faint from the shock if the master so much as commented upon a ragout.

Anne had plentiful time for foolish thoughts, for Sir Crawford had no difficulty finding topics upon which to discourse. He told Anne at great length of Daviott Hall; by the end of luncheon, she felt she could have drawn its outline and principal rooms. He dwelt with loving detail upon the new stable block he had just caused to be built and upon the latest acquisitions to occupy it, earnestly describing their bloodlines, the features which had justified his expense upon them, the many angry gentlemen he had out-jockeyed in acquiring them, and supplying her with the exact amount he had laid out for each.

"Not a stingy man, I assure you, Miss Anne. If I see something I want, then I purchase it. But only the finest, mind you. You will not find Sir Crawford Daviott being taken in!" He launched into a long anecdote about a curricle for sale, his acumen in detecting a flaw in its undercarriage, and exactly what he had said to its owner.

Stifling more than one yawn, Anne was careful to keep her left hand in her lap throughout the long repast, for Sir Crawford's tendency continually to be tapping her forearm to emphasize his points repulsed her. He never withdrew his hand until it had touched her skin, and it took only a few such gestures for Anne to resolve to remain out of reach. She could manage the meal without lifting her glass to her lips.

Nearly an hour later than usual, the company rose and walked out into the hallway leading to the drawing room. Anne looked longingly at the stairs. Escape was forestalled immediately.

"Miss Anne, might I impose upon you to show me the gardens? Been told they're all the crack, I assure you." Sir Crawford's brown eyes met hers. *They look like boiled chestnuts*, Anne thought. *And he sounds as though he is reciting a lesson off by rote.*

"Many of the plants are past their beauty now, sir, since we are so far advanced toward the autumn."

"No matter. I am sure enough remain that I may form an impression of them."

"An excellent idea, Anne! You know that you like to walk after luncheon to recover your spirits." If Lady Catherine could actually be said to titter, she tittered. "I assure you, Sir Crawford, Mrs. Jenkinson must have toured the gardens with her charge almost daily! How pleasant for Anne to have a new companion on her daily walk." There was no gainsaying her mother's hand upon her shoulder, but Anne paused at the door to look backward.

"Would not Miss Daviott or Miss Susan Daviott wish to accompany us?" Augusta seemed not to hear Anne's invitation, but Susan moved forward, only to be stopped by a firm look from her own mother.

"Oh, no, my dear! Susan never walks after a meal. It gives her dyspepsia." Susan stopped in her tracks, trying to appear indisposed as Sir Crawford possessed himself of Anne's arm, and she was drawn inexorably out the door amid Lady Theresa's distressingly exact description of dear Susan's bilious tendencies.

The afternoon had turned cool, tending once more toward rain, and Anne thought she had seldom seen less auspicious weather for displaying the natural beauty of Rosings to a visitor. Acutely conscious of Sir Crawford's bulk unnecessarily close to her side, she led him more or less at random to the section of the garden closest to the western side-door. "We call this the purple garden, Sir Crawford. It is very pretty indeed in the springtime, for the irises and the crocuses and the hyacinths do make such a show. But now I fear there is little of beauty to be seen."

"Quite out there, Miss Anne," the baronet responded promptly, his eyes fixed boldly on her face. "Assure you that I find much of beauty to admire."

The inflection of his voice and his heated glance made his meaning clear, but Anne could only think, *How foolish he sounds. He can see nothing beautiful in me.* She had not dared to attempt any of the subtle enhancements with which she and Dulcie had experimented in the face of her mother's certain inspection before the visitors arrived. The dress that had been

41

chosen for her to wear was an unbecoming pink, so bright that it blanched her face to total pallor, and not one tendril had been allowed to escape from the intricate twist of hair at the back of her head. Most of all, Anne's lips were so stiff that it took an actual effort to move them into a smile. *It is not my beauty he admires at all. It is the estate that surrounds us. And most of all, it is the nine thousand pounds a year that will be mine someday. No--not mine. It will be my husband's. It will be his to do with as he pleases just as--*

At this point, Anne realized that Sir Crawford was waiting in some impatience for a reply to the gallantry with which he had just presented her. She could not now recall what his last words had been, and as the pause lengthened to awkwardness, he gestured toward one of the many arbors built into the grounds. "You are unwell after the excitement of the morning, Miss Anne. Let us sit while you compose yourself." Once again, Anne nearly giggled. *He thinks I am so over-whelmed by his attentions that I shall have the vapours.* Struggling to maintain her composure, Anne allowed herself to be seated beside him.

She sat as stiffly as a statue on the bench as he heaved himself down beside her, the wood groaning under the sudden weight. He turned slightly to face her and she was presented with the sight of his olive coat strained tightly across his chest and even tighter across the considerable protuberance of his stomach beneath. Hastily, Anne lifted her eyes to his face. Encouraged, he leaned closer and the aroma of the roasted onions that had accompanied the sirloin of beef wafted over her. Smiling complacently, Sir Crawford allowed his right arm to stretch along the back of the bench until his fingers lightly brushed Anne's shoulder. "What a handsome estate this is, Miss Anne." Recollecting himself, he hastily added, "Nearly as handsome as its young mistress!"

Anne murmured a response as she watched his eyes move from the massive outlines of the house, rising tall and graceful against a leaden sky, across the acres of carefully tended gardens, and on to the park stretching beyond the artful cultivation. It seemed to Anne that there was a degree of self-satisfied possessiveness in his gaze, and abruptly Anne thought of Sir Lewis, who had loved Rosings and its people, not from pride of lineage so much as from the sense of responsibility that he had felt for them. For her kindly and respected father to be succeeded by a man such as the one who sat so smugly on the uncomfortable seat beside her filled Anne with an unconquerable repugnance.

"I should enjoy touring the entire estate," Sir Crawford remarked meditatively, unaware of the hot surge of resentment that rose in his companion's breast.

When she didn't answer, he glanced at her. "Do you ride, Miss Anne?"

"Not often," she managed to respond as she fought to subdue the anger and anguish battling for place within.

Sir Crawford nodded as though he found her answer no more than he had expected. "Saw a nice little phaeton in the stables," he continued serenely. "Just the thing for a tour. Perhaps we could arrange it for tomorrow. How much of the place could we see in an afternoon?"

Unsure whether the hot tears she was suppressing were the result of misery or rage, Anne remained silent until he glanced at her in inquiry, shifting his heavy body closer.

"I don't know what my mother has planned." The stiffness of his companion's demeanour finally seemed to make an impression on the baronet who genially shifted the subject to his favourite topic of conversation.

"You've not traveled in Wiltshire, your mother tells me, Miss Anne?"

"No . . . I have not had that pleasure."

"Then you will surely wish to hear about it. Let me tell you of some of our chiefest attractions. Rival those of Kent, I do assure you. Hope it won't be long until I shall be able to introduce you to them myself. Never been one for fussing and furbelows, you know." Anne could only assume that his final remark referred to their wedding, which already seemed settled in the baronet's mind.

As Sir Crawford began a lengthy description of the natural wonders of his native county, Anne sat rigidly upright, reflecting that she must present a positive exemplar of her mother's beliefs about ladylike posture. *The scent of onions . . . the feel of hot fingers close to my skin . . . clothes constricting an ever-increasing girth . . . the glories of Wiltshire and Daviott Hall . . . I might live another fifty years. So might he. How shall I bear it?*

Chapter 5

After her protracted "walk" with Sir Crawford in the grounds, Anne was permitted to retire upstairs to rest before dinner, which was to be a magnificent affair. Several neighboring families had been invited, making up a group of six-and-twenty, Lady Catherine had announced with satisfaction. At the last moment, a single gentleman had sent his excuses, citing mumps as the condition preventing him from enjoying one of Rosings' notable dinners.

"Mumps!" Lady Catherine had exclaimed. "How very peculiar. And most inconsiderate of him. Now had it been the influenza, I could have understood. Or even gout. My dear father suffered from gout to the extent that he was forced to throw crockery at the servants to relieve his suffering. But mumps!" Rather than have uneven numbers, Mr. William Collins had been invited at the last moment to replace the inconsiderate guest. Of course he could not be included without his wife, and so she and Lieutenant Philip Collins had likewise been included in the guest list.

It was that last addition, confided to her by Dulcie, that held Anne frozen before her mirror minutes after Miss De Bourgh should have been downstairs greeting her guests as they entered the large drawing room.

"Oh miss! Lady Catherine has sent up twict to see what be keeping you. She'll be ever so put out! Let me settle your scarf--"

"No. Dulcie, hand me the little casket of powders we made."

"Miss! We was just experimentin', you said. Just to see, you said. Your mother--"

Anne met Dulcie's eyes in the mirror, and the maid gave up the battle. Not for nothing had she known Anne for most of her twenty-three years.

"Very well, Miss. Set down and let me do it. The heavens forbid we mark your dress."

Ten minutes later, Dulcie opened the door and Anne walked through it, a gauzy dark blue scarf arranged negligently over her shoulders and silver slippers peeping from beneath the pale blue pastel gown that Lady Catherine had ordered made for the occasion. She had favoured a brighter hue, but for once Anne had triumphed. Both the scarf and the slippers had been purchased by Dulcie in London at Anne's behest, and neither, Anne thought, would meet with her mother's approval. But she could hardly order her daughter back upstairs in front of thirty-odd guests. Drawing a deep breath, Anne reached the newel and began to descend the stairs just as Povey appeared at the bottom, clearly commissioned by his mistress to accept no demur in bringing Miss Anne downstairs. As she reached the bottom, the old man stared at her, unsure of the reason for her altered appearance. A rosy color suffused her face, and her grey eyes seemed to sparkle. The dark spangled scarf provided a startling contrast to her blonde hair, piled high on her head with silvery curls gleaming at her temples. Startled into saying, "I've never seen you in such looks, Miss Anne. Complete to a shade," Povey was even more unsettled when she laid one small velvet-gloved hand on his arm and squeezed it gently. Standing even straighter than usual, the old man escorted her to the door of the drawing room.

Mr. and Mrs. William Collins and Lieutenant Philip Collins had been among the first of the Rosings guests to arrive. To do otherwise would show the grossest lack of appreciation for Lady Catherine's condescension in inviting them, Mr. Collins had lamented as he hurried his lady and his brother in their preparations. An invitation that had arrived mere hours before the occasion in question had dampened neither Mr. Collins' gratitude nor his eager expression of it.

At five minutes before time for dinner to be announced, Lieutenant Collins was standing beside Miss Laetitia Troubridge, a stout well-grown young lady of no more than seventeen, listening to a fluttering recital of her sensations upon receiving an invitation to dine at Rosings.

"This is the first time we have been honoured by an invitation from Lady Catherine, Lieutenant, although we moved to the district more than a year ago. But, la!" She fanned herself vigorously, glad she had not given in to her mama's insistence that she wear lace panels in her low-cut décolletage. *Really such a handsome gentleman*, she thought as she simpered up at him. "Mama says that Lady Catherine don't do nearly as much entertaining as was done when Sir Lewis was alive. This is a special occasion, as you might say!"

"Indeed?" Her listener's brows rose inquiringly.

"Oh, my yes! I assure you the entire neighborhood is expecting that an announcement of Miss Anne de Bourgh's engagement will be made tonight." The young lady eagerly imparted all the gossip she had heard about the impending nuptials while at the same time wondering just what her listener's expectations were. *But never mind,* she thought. Her mama was almost certain to have found out already.

Wishing himself back at the parsonage where he would have preferred to spend the evening reading, the lieutenant became aware of a lessening of the laughter and chatter of the room and glanced up. Anne de Bourgh was standing in the doorway. Realizing herself the cynosure of most eyes, she glanced about her and smiled shyly. Her attention was immediately claimed by the young man to whom he had been introduced upon his arrival, Sir Crawford Daviott. He advanced upon her and offered his arm, just as Povey, after a nod from Lady Catherine, announced dinner.

Lady Catherine was led in to dinner by her neighbor Sir Clement Calverly, a small red-faced man who came barely up to her ears. Miss De Bourgh followed with Sir Crawford.

Lieutenant Collins gallantly led Miss Troubridge into the large dining room, an impressive sight with all the leaves in a table loaded with gold-rimmed china, heavy silverware, crystal flower vases, and an enormous epergne which, to the lieutenant's startled eye, resembled nothing so much as several snakes writhing together, but turned out to be an untalented silversmith's lavish representation of ivy growing up a copse of trees.

He found himself seated between an elderly lady for whom everything had to be repeated at least twice and a flirtatious young matron named Mrs. Priddy. He did his duty both to his dinner, which was excellent if rather prolonged, and his dinner partners, but his attention strayed continually across the table. Miss De Bourgh was seated two places up on the other side and seemed to be in both unusual looks and spirits. She resembled an ice princess, he thought, in her pale blue dress, her blonde delicacy thrown into high relief against the deep red silk of the wallpaper behind her, and the dark blue scarf that completed her evening attire. There was a most attractive colour in her face; he wondered if the change in her appearance was due to pleasure in Sir Crawford's company and felt an unaccountable depression at the thought. What, after all, was the heiress of Rosings to him? William had also boasted to him of the intended alliance between the Daviotts and the De Bourghs. Most people would find it unexceptional enough. So too should he. It was foolish to wonder if Miss Anne de Bourgh would find contentment in marriage to a man who had struck him as a bluff, overfed sportsman without an ounce of sensibility or a rational thought. Apparently he was the heiress's choice. It was foolish to imagine her as a butterfly too easily crushed by careless or cruel hands.

The ladies retired to the drawing room after dinner. On such social occasions in the past, Anne had been accustomed to vanishing discreetly into the background, but this evening she found herself still the center of attention. Everyone, it seemed, had heard rumours of a possible engagement. Everyone was eagerly speculating on such details as likely settlements and the frequency with which the young couple might be expected to reside at Rosings. Naturally no lady was so vulgar as to ask outright, but conversation with Anne abounded with leading questions or comments until she was heartily grateful when the gentlemen made their appearance. If another lady brought up the subject of Wiltshire, she felt she might scream.

In the midst of the chatter that arose when the cloud of dark-coated gentlemen mingled with the bright-gowned ladies, Anne heard her mother's voice rise above the rest. "I have a small surprise tonight," announced Lady Catherine, and for one dreadful moment Anne thought her mother intended to announce her engagement before the prospective bride and groom had even spoken of it. But then the hearty, almost masculine-sounding voice continued, "A space has been cleared in the long gallery and musicians await us there. Miss De Bourgh and I offer this addition to Rosings' usual hospitality in honour of our special guests, Sir Crawford Daviott and his family. Sir Crawford--pray lead my daughter upstairs."

Minutes later Anne found herself opposite Sir Crawford as the musicians struck up a quadrille. The two began to dance and other couples joined them on the floor, perhaps eight or nine. In other circumstances Anne would have been overcome with embarrassment at the unusual attention paid her, but tonight she moved, danced, and even spoke, feeling that she was enveloped in a particularly long and complex dream. Surely Anne de Bourgh was upstairs in her room, pouring over the latest volume of Wordsworth which her cousin Giles had been kind enough to procure for her. She could not be the girl in blue dancing with a man whose very glance filled her with revulsion. She could not be waiting for an offer from him. Soon she would wake up to discover the she had fallen asleep in her favourite window seat with the candles guttering beside her, her book forgotten in her lap.

Her next partner was Mr. Horace Priddy, the son-in-law of a neighboring landowner. His finicky manner of dancing would have amused her on any other occasion; on this one, she found matching her steps to his small precise ones to be an intolerable strain. Her mood was not improved by the sight of his flirtatious young wife moving too close to Lieutenant Collins as they passed by in the dance.

When Mr. Priddy returned her to her seat, she saw that Lieutenant Collins was waiting there and for the first time, Anne felt like herself again. Mr. Priddy was gone with a murmured lisp of thanks, and the lieutenant looked at her, rather unsmilingly Anne noticed, and said, "Might I have your hand for whatever dance is next, Miss De Bourgh?"

As he spoke the strains of a familiar country dance began and Anne replied, "Lieutenant . . . could I prevail upon you to sit this set out with me instead? It is very warm and I am . . . a little tired."

It was not fatigue he saw in her face, Collins thought, so much as strain. He certainly could see no hint of elation or joy in it. "I will be delighted. In fact, I thought I might impose upon your good nature, Miss De Bourgh. You may recall asking me what type of subject I paint. Not knowing special entertainment of this nature would be offered, I brought a few of my canvases. If there is somewhere--" He broke off, glancing around the dimly lit gallery.

"Of course. Shall we retire to the small drawing room, sir? I have been so eager to see your work."

Lieutenant Collins smiled ruefully. "I fear you're like to be disappointed, ma'am. But I shall be glad of your opinion."

Anne glanced across the gallery and saw that her exit would be obscured from her mother's view by the dancers. Quickly, she led the way down the gallery, through an archway, and downstairs to the little drawing room where generations of Rosings ladies had sat on sunny mornings. Tonight it seemed to be a blessed oasis of peace and sanity in the midst of Anne's nightmare. With a murmured excuse, Lieutenant Collins left to retrieve his paintings, returning in moments.

Anne seated herself on the sofa with the gentleman beside her and eagerly received the first of the rolled canvases, a view of an island seen from aboard a ship. The colors were vivid, but the most striking aspect of the image was formed by bold dark strokes delineating the ship's riggings, through which it was clear the artist was looking.

The girl said nothing to her companion but her approbation was clear in the upward flash of her shining grey eyes. Gently laying aside the painting, Anne picked up the next, a study of a child's face. A ragged little boy with an infectious grin and speaking black eyes proudly held out a fish he had caught. Anne smiled back at him before turning to the third canvas, a line of dolphins arching up out of the sea. At first their shining skins seemed silver but then she became aware of a hint of pink . . . of turquoise . . . of purple. When she looked directly at the creatures, no color but grey was evident, but as soon as she glanced at the lines of a ship depicted upon a distant horizon, her eye became sure once more that the dolphins were flashing with iridescent colour.

"Oh---" Instinctively, Anne's hand went out to grasp Lieutenant Collins' wrist, in much the same place as Sir Crawford had earlier touched her. But Anne did not notice in her excitement, and if her companion did, he certainly did not seem inclined to recoil. "Oh, Lieutenant! How *did* you manage this effect? It is exactly what I have tried to achieve on several occasions with a rainbow that appears with some frequency over the lake here on a warm summer day after a storm. But I do not paint often enough to claim proficiency in oils, and I have never succeeded in conveying merely the *impression* of the colours!"

"Ah, that's a trick which I owe to my old friend Reese. You may recollect that I mentioned him to you?"

"Oh yes, indeed I do!"

"Well, Miss De Bourgh, he taught me a trick in the mixing of paint. It's a delicate process, but if one can manage it successfully, it can usually be relied upon to lend just the evanescent touch which some subjects demand."

"You were too modest about your talent, Lieutenant." Anne looked accusingly up at him, candlelight glinting in her silvery blonde curls. "Why, you led me to believe you were practically a novice, yet here I find paintings that anyone would be proud to have upon their walls!"

"Now it is you who are too kind," he responded playfully, but he found it difficult speak lightly. He was too conscious of her physical presence beside him, drawing him to her with the mixture of innocent friendliness and warm desirability that was rapidly becoming too disarming for him to resist.

As they continued through the dozen rolled canvases, neither of the two was aware of time passing. The music drifting into the room from the gallery above ceased, began again, and ceased again, and still they spoke eagerly as they studied the powerful, deeply colorful paintings, so different from Anne's own style.

"Miss Anne." A gentle voice spoke from the open doorway. Looking up, Anne saw Povey and rose quickly.

"Miss Anne, your mother has been searching for you . . . as she did not see you among the guests in the gallery." The thoughtful old eyes rested briefly on Lieutenant Collins. "I told her that I fancied you had torn a lace and that you must have sent for Dulcie to come to your room to help repair it."

"I'm sorry, Miss De Bourgh. I have thoughtlessly distracted you from your guests."

Already on the way to the door, Anne paused to smile at Lieutenant Collins over her shoulder. He stood with the candelabra's light full upon him--hair unfashionably long and glinting with a hundred different tints of gold and brown, eyes looking more blue than grey in the light, and that smile that creased his tanned cheeks so attractively. "It was no distraction, Lieutenant, or if so, a very welcome one. I gained so much more pleasure from talking to you than I would have from a country dance. Seeing your paintings was a very great honour. Thank you."

Then she was gone. He heard her silver sandals tapping swiftly down the oak-floored hallway toward the stairs. Povey, face once more impassive, turned to Collins as he stowed the canvases in their leather satchel, his hands a trifle unsteady. "Might I trouble you for a few words, Lieutenant?"

Collins looked up at the butler in surprise. "Certainly."

"Thank you, sir." Povey gently closed the door.

Fortunately Anne reached her seat just as the music from a set was dying. Sir Crawford forestalled her mother in approaching to speak to her and soon bore her off to the refreshment table that had been set up near the gallery's far exit onto a balcony. The maid curtseyed as they approached. "What may I pour for you, Miss Anne? Sir?"

"Wine. The red. Miss Anne? Join me in a glass?"

Eyeing Sir Crawford's face, which appeared even ruddier than it had that afternoon, Anne wondered if the dancing had brought the flush to his fleshy cheeks or if others trips to the refreshment table had preceded this one. From the maid's swift warning glance, she deduced the latter. "Only rataffia for me, please." Anne smiled her gratitude for the un-spoken warning. "Thank you, Betty."

"Shall we find a quiet place to sit, Miss Anne?" Without waiting for her answer, he steered her through the open doorway onto the south balcony. Expecting to find other guests taking the air of an unusually warm evening, Anne stopped short when she saw the empty expanse stretching before her, lit only by the wavering moonlight and a faint illumination from within.

She turned to her escort. "Sir Crawford, I do not think it proper for us to sit here alone."

"I have your mama's permission to speak to you in private this evening, my dear. Excellent place, this. Romantic, you know. Girls like such things, eh?" he boomed jovially as he closed the door firmly behind him.

Turning to Anne, who stood numbly clutching her untouched glass, Sir Crawford removed it from her grasp and, drawing her forward, set it and his now-empty wine glass on the parapet.

The moon's rays combined with light shining through windows from the gallery to provide enough illumination for Anne to see Sir Crawford reach up to pull irritably at the neckcloth whose intricate folds constricted his thick neck.

Taking an audibly deep breath, Anne's companion launched into what sounded yet again like a speech he had learned off by rote. "Miss Anne, it cannot have escaped your attention how much I admire you. I was struck by your--by your beauty and ladylike deportment when we met in London. Such grace." He had not released Anne's hand and his grasp tightened now as she tried to withdraw it from his grip. "Heard so many people speak of you with the highest admiration. Including Mama and my sisters. I traveled into Kent with the express purpose--with the express intent--"

He has forgotten the next line, Anne thought with irrepressible humor, even as she felt ready to sink with embarrassment. *Should I prompt him?*

"--with the intention of seeing if you could possibly be the paragon I remembered." Nearing the end of his oration, Sir Crawford's words picked up both speed and expression. "Miss Anne, I realized at once that my memory had not deceived me. Indeed, seeing you has only increased my ardor. Will you do me the incomparable honour of becoming my wife?"

Finally managing to wrest her hand from his grip, Anne wondered how it could feel like a block of ice after lying encased in velvet in his sweaty clasp for at least the last five minutes. She searched desperately for words, wondering why she had not prepared an answer for this address which had been clearly imminent, and finally managed to stammer out, "Sir Crawford, I do not . . . I cannot . . . indeed, sir, your request is so sudden--"

"Nonsense," he objected, sounding much less like an actor in a play. "Don't be missish! Lady Catherine must have prepared you for my offer!"

"Oh indeed, Mama did mention . . . but . . ." Knowing she must have sounded detestably coy, Anne backed away from him as she spoke, turning slightly so that the light from the window behind them cast a glow over her silvery hair and white shoulders.

"By Jove," her cavalier muttered feelingly, "what I said was no more than the truth. I had thought you a lifeless little stick but seeing you now--"

Before Anne could retreat or even begin to reply, he caught her slender arms and pulled her close to him. Anne felt a surge of panic as she heard her lacy shawl tear. Then her body was pressed against his, and his mouth descended on hers. His lips felt wet and hot and fleshy and his mustache's luxuriance seemed likely to stifle her. His open mouth pressed down on her closed one, and Anne felt a sharp pain. Struggling to free herself, Anne felt his hands tighten into a vise-like grip on her upper arms, and then his tongue forced its way through her lips. This indignity galvanized her; she managed to strip the gloves from her hands. Forcing them up to the hands holding her arms immobile, she dug her fingernails into their hairy surface with all her strength.

With an oath, Sir Crawford released her, and Anne stumbled backward, striking her leg sharply on a stone statue and nearly overturning it. Seeing him stride purposefully toward her, Anne cried furiously, "No! No, I will not marry you!" Straightening herself, she tried to speak with what composure and dignity she could command although her voice shook. "I feel su-sure we should not suit, sir. I am sorry you have had this long journey for naught!"

"So you wish to play the innocent, little bird? Not too innocent to enjoy a tryst with an admirer earlier in the evening, were you?" Anne stared at him, uncomprehending. "Thought I hadn't noticed that fellow dangling after you? When you belong to me, those little games will cease, my dear."

"Did you not *hear* me? I said that I refuse your offer, sir!"

"And I say that the little bird will sing a different tune after a talk with Lady Catherine. This match is settled, Miss Anne, and considering you are three and twenty and unwed, you should be damned glad of it. Think I'm not aware you were thrown over by your high and mighty cousin, do you?"

Sir Crawford's voice grew angrier as he spoke. Seeing him take another step toward her, Anne turned, her heart beating so furiously she was breathless, but felt his hand on her arm before she could move. He swung Anne's slight body around to face him. Seeing his reddened face looming over hers, Anne was straining desperately away from his wine-sodden breath when a calm voice spoke from the darkness of the doorway. "Miss De Bourgh?"

Both Anne and Sir Crawford turned to see Lieutenant Collins silhouetted against the light from the gallery. "I believe your mother is calling for you," he said gently to the terrified girl. Behind her, she heard Sir Crawford take a deep, angry breath before releasing her. "You must pardon her, sir," he continued, and though he did not raise his voice, the note of command was like the crack of a whip.

"Thank you, sir," she replied, clenching her hands to force steadiness into her voice. "I shall go to her directly." Anne walked swiftly away, limping slightly from the blow to her leg, but not toward the door back into the gallery. Instead, she sped swiftly to the balcony's south edge where another door opened into the gun room. Praying it was not locked, Anne grasped the knob, felt it turn, flung herself inside, and slammed the door behind her. Her frantic fingers found the key which she turned until she heard the satisfying click of the lock. In darkness, she felt her way hastily across the room, let herself out into the empty corridor and ran limping toward the backstairs that lay just around the next turn. Thankfully, she passed no servants. *They must all be occupied in the front of*

56

the house, she thought in relief. Two minutes later she was in her room, heart pounding, with the door locked behind her. Only then did she allow the tears to come.

Dulcie, summoned by Povey to Anne's room, was outraged. Surveying the blood on her mistress's cut lip, the torn shawl, and the swiftly-forming bruises on Anne's arms, Dulcie exclaimed in horrified surprise, her accent reduced by fury to near unintelligibility. "I've now't seen t' like, Miss Anne. A reet sackless brute an' no argufying! Marry up with him? Why, I'd as soon see ye lyin' a-corpse. Oh, what I wouldna gi' ta turn him o'er to John Jacob for a lesson," she spat, referring to the burliest of the Rosings footmen.

Anne sat quiet under Dulcie's ranting and ministrations, hardly hearing the words as her mind raced. *I cannot marry him. Tonight was bad enough--but only think of how much worse it would be if he were my husband.* Anne's shudder was enough to draw from Dulcie an unaccustomed gesture. She leaned down to hug the other girl's shoulders for a brief moment. Anne rested her head on Dulcie's shoulder, fighting hysteria, as a knock sounded at the door and the two pairs of eyes, soft brown and clear grey, met in the mirror before Anne straightened and stood, her legs trembling so fiercely that she wondered if they would hold her. Neither of them doubted from the knock's reverberations who stood on the other side.

Lady Catherine was already scolding as Dulcie opened the door. "And why pray, is this door locked? I see no reason for locked doors in this house. We are not some rooming house in Cheapside, I hope." Her eyes went swiftly to her daughter and her frown deepened at the sight of her bruised and tear-stained face, so starkly white even in the dimly lit room. "You may go, Dulcie."

For an instant the little maid hesitated as though she would defy the command, but a quick motion and a warning look from Anne sent her from the room.

"Why are you not downstairs helping me entertain our

guests, Anne? Surely you realize that your absence will have been noticed. Do you want to set the neighborhood in an uproar of gossip?" Concern softened her mother's exasperation for a moment when the girl stood mute. "Are you taken ill?"

"I am not ill, Mama. I . . . Sir Crawford . . . I had a talk with Sir Crawford which upset me. I would have returned to the ga-gallery, but I was not in such condition as to be seen by guests." Anne struggled to control her voice.

"I am well aware that you had an interview with Sir Crawford. Anne, what were you thinking of to refuse him? Have I not made clear the lengths to which I went to solicit that offer for you? Had we not reached an understanding as to what your answer must be?"

"I cannot marry him, Mama!"

"Cannot? *Cannot* marry him? Nonsense! Do not talk such fustian to me! You know I have the greatest dislike for these Cheltenham tragedies! Of course you can marry him. What possible reason do you imagine you have found for refusing an offer so eligible?"

Anne swallowed hard, fighting the familiar sensation of trying to stand resolute against a will stronger than her own. She struggled to steady her voice before she answered. "Mama, you do not know . . . he . . he embraced me, Mama!" Anne's fingers went to the bruises on her arms. "And . . . and he kissed me. It was . . i-it . . . " Anne removed the handkerchief she had pressed to her lips and met her mother's eyes, struggling for coherency against the sobs which she was determined to suppress.

For a moment Lady Catherine's eyes rested on her daughter's swollen mouth and then she sighed. "My dear, you have very little knowledge of the world. You must allow yourself to be guided by those who have your interests at heart. Sir Crawford did admit to me that his ardor inspired in him more attention to you than was seemly. Certainly you had a right to be shocked."

Hearing the gentler note in her mother's voice, Anne

58

looked up hopefully. "But you will find that all men have such tastes, which ladies certainly do not share. To some degree, these passions are . . . necessary. I have made every effort to protect you against such attentions, Anne, but you surely know that the daughter of this house has a duty to it. When you have provided an heir--for the Daviotts but also for Rosings, you must remember, Anne . . . well then his attentions will doubtless find other . . . objects. And he will leave you to go about the business of your house and your children. That is the way of the world, my dear, and it will not change for all your protestations."

Anne stared uncomprehendingly at her mother. Slowly, she shook her head. "You cannot . . . Mama, you cannot have understood. It is impossible that I should marry a man like Sir Crawford. You—surely you cannot *wish* him to follow in Papa's footsteps here at Rosings. I know that you cannot!"

As Lady Catherine stood listening to her daughter's plea, an expression which Anne knew well formed upon her face--an affectionate expression, but also an obdurate one that held all the condescending knowledge of a woman of the world, speaking to a foolish child who must be directed to see where her benefit lay. When Anne saw the familiar steely look in her mother's eyes, hope died within her and she sank slowly back into her chair.

"What is impossible, Anne, is that you should foolishly let pass an offer so advantageous to our consequence. I will not be made a laughingstock among our entire acquaintance, nor will I allow you to refuse a young man whose birth and breeding make him an entirely eligible *parti* for you. I will leave you now and hope a night's counsel brings to you a clearer knowledge of your duty. But understand, Anne--I will not be defied in this. Sir Crawford will be your husband-- within the month. I have already drafted the notice to be sent to the *Times*." Lady Catherine paused for a moment, and Anne thought she would continue, but then her lips tightened and she turned to walk away.

Pausing with her hand on the doorknob, she said coldly, "I will explain to our guests that you felt too unwell to come back down." Her eyes met her daughter's as she continued, "Let's have no lying a-bed in the morning. I shall see you at breakfast when I'm sure you will be quite recovered. "

Anne was still sitting frozen by her mother's words when the door clicked closed behind her. After a moment she twisted around on the window seat to stare out at the inky night, but the darkness had no comfort to offer her.

Chapter 6

Anne lay awake far into the night, a candle burning on the table by her bed, hardly daring to close her eyes. As soon as she did, she again saw Sir Crawford's shape looming over her on the moonlit balcony. She heard the sound of his rasping fervor, smelled his hot, wine-scented breath. Worst of all, over and over, she felt his wet, fleshy lips pressing against hers and the intrusion of his tongue.

In addition to the vivid memories, darkness brought worse imaginings--of what it would feel like to lie helplessly in the darkness beneath Sir Crawford's heavy, straining body in this very house. Anne had no clear idea of what went on between married couples that resulted in babies nine months later, but she had been raised in the country. She knew enough to feel ill to the very quick of her soul at the thought of sharing a marriage bed with a man like Sir Crawford Daviott.

Toward dawn she dozed a little, only to be awakened by Dulcie's scratch at the door. Before she could answer, the little maid had slipped inside. Glancing at the clock, Anne saw that it lacked five minutes of seven; she looked at Dulcie in confusion, for Lady Catherine had informed her guests that breakfast would not commence until half past eight, due to the unusually late hours they all had kept.

"Miss Anne! 'Tis sorry I am to wake you so long before 'tis needful, but I thought mayhap you'd wish to read this afore you have to go downstairs."

Anne sat up straight as she reached for the small folded paper Dulcie was extending to her. Wondering what it could possibly be, she was suddenly fearful that Sir Crawford had renewed his importunities in this form. She swung her legs off the bed, standing with difficulty for the leg she had bruised was throbbingly painful. Sinking down on the window seat, she opened the note.

> *Miss De Bourgh,*
>
> *Forgive me if I assume too much in writing to you. I could not but see the distress you suffered last night. My brother has informed me that Lady Catherine de Bourgh is set upon your betrothal to the man--for I cannot name him "gentleman"--who was the author of that distress.*
>
> *I am hardly more than a stranger to you, but I can not see a lady in such a situation, with no father or brother to turn to, without offering whatever aid is within my power to give.*
>
> *Perhaps you do not stand in need of such assistance as I am disposed to think--however, if I may indeed serve you, please meet me this morning as early as you may in the orchard that we might discuss what assistance I may offer. I shall remain there until noon unless I hear otherwise from you.*
>
> *I have told Povey of my intention to offer you such service as is within my power to perform.*
>
> > *Your obedient servant,*
> > *Philip Collins*

Anne read the scrawled words twice before their sense sank into her troubled mind. Pushing her tangled hair back from of her face, she blinked at Dulcie's anxious freckled countenance. "I don't . . . Dulcie, where did you get this?"

"From Povey, Miss. The gentleman asked for him at the kitchen door this morning. He told Cook as how he'd lost something from his pocket in the drawing room and asked for Povey. Then he give him that note for you."

Anne said nothing, remembering the events of the

previous night. *What in God's name shall I do? I cannot stay here if I refuse to marry Sir Crawford. Mama will make my life unendurable. And I truly would rather be dead than be his wife. But how can Lieutenant Collins possibly help me?*

"Miss?" Anne's eyes met Dulcie's questioning ones. "Do you want I should bring you some tea?"

"No." Anne swiftly made up her mind. "I want you to help me dress. Something heavy and warm, Dulcie." Her eyes went to the window where a faint drizzle of rain had returned the landscape to grey. At least no one else was likely to be out taking the air before breakfast. "And bring me your cloak, please. Quickly!"

When Anne reached the bottom of the steps, Povey was waiting for her. Meeting the old man's troubled eyes, Anne motioned for him to accompany her into the morning room where she closed the door before turning anxiously to him.

"Miss Anne, I hope I did right in sending the lieutenant's note up to you. But he has seemed to me most truly the gentleman, and you must have someone to help you."

"To . . . help me?"

"Thomas was on the balcony last night, Miss Anne. Lady Catherine stationed him there in case any of the guests wanted the torches lit or food carried outside."

Povey's eyes met Anne's.

"He saw?"

"Yes, Miss. He had just nerved himself to come to your aid when Lieutenant Collins came outside." Quietly, Povey extended to her the gloves she had worn the previous night, wrapped in the mangled silk scarf. "He picked these up for you after the gentlemen went back inside. He was sorry he did not move to help you more quickly. But for a footman to come to blows with a guest--"

A shamed flush rose to Anne's cheeks. For a moment she could think of no reply. But Povey had been one of her earliest friends at Rosings. He had quietly extricated her from difficulties in an apple tree when she was no more than five, had taken upon himself the blame for an armchair ruined by a heedlessly held paint brush, had stood many times between her and the consequences of her mother's exalted expectations and inevitable disappointment. "Thomas could not have helped me." The girl's shoulders rose and fell as she took a steadying breath and continued, "My mother insists that I marry him, Povey."

"Does Lady Catherine know--"

"Yes . . . I told her what happened on the balcony. Exactly what happened." Their eyes met in perfect understanding. "She is determined that I shall marry him in any event. I . . . . I don't know what to do, Povey. There was a time when I would have turned to Aunt Elinor, but she has been very unwell this summer. I cannot cut up her peace by involving her in such unpleasantness with Mama. I have no other friends to turn to for help."

"I think Lieutenant Collins will stand your friend, Miss." Anne looked at him in surprise. "Unless I miss the mark, he is a man to be trusted--a man of your father's stripe. Go now and see what help he has to offer you."

"And Miss?"

Already at the door, Anne turned. "Yes, Povey?"

"I am your friend, Miss Anne. As is nearly everyone who serves this house." Tears blurred Anne's eyes as the old man reached out to pull the rough woolen hood more closely about her face before he opened the door.

Collins had been waiting for nearly an hour by the time he saw Anne's hurrying form moving toward him at the orchard's edge. As she neared, he saw how heavily she favoured her left leg; he fought down a murderous anger as he moved to meet her, but it darkened his eyes to bleakness and she hesitated as she lifted her face to him.

Forcing down the rage, he smiled at her. "Good morning, Miss De Bourgh. May I suggest that we talk beneath

64

the shelter of one of the big trees in the wood? I promise you'll be quite safe." His eyes flickered beyond her shoulder and Anne knew he was wondering why she had come unaccompanied, defying all precepts that guided the behavior of a young lady.

Quietly, she answered the thought instead of his words. "I could not bring Dulcie. If my mother sends for me, she must be there to come and warn me. Besides . . . I am not afraid, sir."

Collins knew as well as Anne the grim punishment that might follow her breach of propriety. When he had spoken to her here before, the meetings had been, at least to the casual eye, accidental. The vicar's brother had simply stopped to speak to the young lady of the house on his way to call. But a deliberate meeting, so early in the morning in the rain that had now begun to beat down steadily, conducted in the wood--there would be no mercy if it were discovered. He had liked Anne de Bourgh for her love of beauty which he shared, for her joy in the creation of art, and for the sweetness of her spirit. Now he felt a distinct admiration for her courage in defying society's dictums in order to avoid entrapment into marriage with a man quite unworthy of her.

Sir Crawford's rank and consequence are a matter of indifference to her, in comparison with his character, Collins thought in amazement and knew that his impulse to help the friendless girl had hardened into determination.

Silently, he extended his arm and supported her toward the wood, feeling her dependence on his strength at every step. When they had reached shelter under the boughs of an enormous oak, so old that it might have stood in Cromwell's day and before, he removed her sodden cloak and folded it in upon itself to make a seat for her. She smiled and shook her head. "I believe the forest floor will be dryer, Lieutenant . . . and just as comfortable." He joined her as she sank gratefully down upon a cushion of leaves many seasons old, tucking her legs beneath her skirts and leaning back against the huge trunk.

Meeting her steady grey gaze, Collins searched for words to begin. "I noticed that you were limping last night, Miss De Bourgh, and still today, I see. Were you seriously injured?"

"No . . . it is only a bruise." Unconsciously Anne's hand sought her upper thigh. She saw that the lieutenant's eyes were on her cut lip and blushed.

"Sir Crawford did not . . . hurt you in any other way?"

"He did not, sir. Had you not arrived, I don't know what might have occurred, but as you did, no damage was done."

Again silence fell. Taking a deep breath, Collins began again. "Miss De Bourgh--"

"I think, Lieutenant Collins, it would be as well if you use my name." She blushed redder but met his eyes bravely and was rewarded by the softened expression on his face.

"Then Miss Anne . . . is my brother correct in his assurance to me that Lady Catherine will not alter her intention to wed you to Sir Crawford?"

"He is quite correct."

"Have you told your mother of the treatment you received at his hands, Miss Anne?"

"I related the whole to her last night."

Collins stared at her in disbelief. "My mother is of a most unyielding disposition, sir." Fleetingly, she glanced up and then away. "I have never known her to admit error or to change her mind unless circumstance forced such alteration. I assure you that she will not do so now. She feels that Sir Crawford is an ideal husband for me, and she has a reason for wishing me to be wed soon."

"But . . . what did she say when you spoke to her? How could she justify your marriage to such a brute? Surely, the heiress of Rosings does not stand in need of the financial advantage such a match would bring. Indeed, I would have thought quite the opposite."

"I believe perhaps you are correct, and Sir Crawford's

family will be the one to benefit from an alliance with our family. My fortune is certainly his object. As for what my mother said . . . she told me that such passions on the part of gentlemen are *necessary* . . . that I will not have to bear with them after I produce an heir . . . that my duty should direct me to marry the husband who has been chosen for me by those who know more of the world than I."

"She told you that such passions are necessary," he repeated incredulously. He paced a step or two away to stare out over the gloomy, rain-sodden prospect before them. "I don't know when I have heard a more outrageous observation, Miss Anne." He turned back to her impetuously, but moderated his tone when he saw the shame in her eyes. "And your reply? Did you refuse to accept his offer?"

"I did, Lieutenant. But . . . I do not think I can stand against her for long."

"Surely if you are adamant in your refusal--"

"You do not understand what she is like. Everything I care for will be taken from me. My drawing materials . . . my books . . . even Dulcie. I have had to fight to keep Dulcie with me, for my mother wanted to hire an experienced lady's maid from London--a more *genteel* one, she said. She will do that now. She will feel that Dulcie encourages me in defying her. And she will never cease berating me--from the time I rise in the morning until I retire, she will remind me that I have failed in the chief duty of a daughter of our house. Every day I will be told again how lacking I have shown myself to be in gratitude to her, when her only care in life has been for me and my happiness. And it will not be for just a month or even a year. I will inherit a sum of money sufficient to support me, apart from Rosings and its income, but not for over a year. And even then, she . . . I . . . " Anne was staring past him, her face empty of expression. Then her eyes met his and he saw the desolation there. "Why do I try to tell you? You are a man. You cannot know the strictures of the life I lead. Men can just . . . go. They can earn their way . . . choose their path in life.

For women, life holds no such choices."

After a moment, Anne stood with difficulty, leaning on the tree. "Lieutenant Collins, I thank you for listening, but I do not believe there is any way you can help. That you *wish* to do so elicits my deepest gratitude." Her smile wavered. "Forgive me for embroiling you in my difficulties."

Rising also, he stretched his hand to stop her as she turned away. "Wait, please. Miss Anne, is there no one . . . no member of your family . . . no good friend who would give you shelter if you decided to leave Rosings?"

"No. No one." He found the soft voice unbearably pitiable. "No one has ever defied Mama and they will certainly not do so for me. Hardly anyone knows me, Lieutenant. I have spent most of my life here at Rosings where I have met very few people. Mama seldom took me with her when she visited until a year or so ago."

"*No one* has ever opposed Lady Catherine's wishes?"

"Only Fitzwilliam. He did not truckle under to Mama." Anne laughed with real humor in her voice. "If he had, this occasion would not have arisen. I would be Anne Darcy by now."

"Ah yes, I recall William's mention of that affair. Mr. Darcy is your cousin, isn't he?"

"Yes, the son of Mama's sister for whom I was named. Mama and my Aunt Anne Darcy intended us to marry, but instead Fitzwilliam fell deeply in love with your cousin, Miss Elizabeth Bennet. It was their marriage, I think, that infuriated Mama to the point of insisting on my immediate betrothal. She wants to show Fitzwilliam, you see, that I had no trouble finding a bridegroom suitable for my station--even if he has jilted me."

Collins regarded her face thoughtfully, noting the humor sparkling in her eyes even in the midst of her distress. "You don't appear to be wearing the willow for him, Miss Anne."

Anne smiled. "Oh, I am not. I had no more desire to

wed my cousin than he had to wed me, even though I have always been fond of him. I thought of him as the brother I would like to have had. As children, we were the best of friends. I so anticipated his visits to Rosings, for I had few playfellows, and Fitzwilliam loved the birds and animals as much as I did."

"And you were not hurt when he became engaged to Miss Bennet?"

"No, indeed. I liked her very much. I think she is one of the liveliest and most charming people I have ever met. I wanted Fitzwilliam to be happy, and I was very pleased for him when he married Miss Bennet and took her to Pemberley, whatever anyone else thought of the match."

"Could you not go to them for help, Miss Anne? If, as you say, your cousin does not stand in awe of Lady Catherine-- and I am sure that his affection for you equals yours for him-- would they not allow you to live at Pemberley until your mother can be brought to see reason? You would be safe there, and surely the gossips could make little of your visiting your married cousin."

Anne stared at him, completely still for a long moment. A sigh parted her lips, and he saw hope in her face for the first time since they had taken shelter together under spreading branches.

Unconsciously, Anne held out her hand, and he caught it comfortingly between both of his in a warm clasp. "Pemberley! I never thought of that--of asking Fitzwilliam to help me. But I don't know if Miss Bennet--I mean Mrs. Darcy--would want me there. Perhaps she would not. I could not show her the admiration I felt for her because Mama disliked her so very much."

"Do you truly think your cousin would refuse you aid in this desperate circumstance?"

"No." Anne's eyes were filled with an immense relief and a rising excitement. "No, I know that he would not. I do not even believe his wife would want him to refuse. She seemed to me most amiable, and I do not believe Fitzwilliam would have married anyone who is less than kind. But, Lieutenant, how could I possibly reach Pemberley? Why, it is several days' journey."

Lieutenant Collins' cheeks creased in the mischievous smile that she found so endearing. "That is my problem, Miss Anne. I told you that I'd do my possible to help you. Did you doubt me? Why, we of His Majesty's Royal Navy are not to be found lacking!"

Anne's smile matched his at the teasing note in his voice, and she began to speak, but he shook his head in a decided negative. "No, there is no need to thank me and no time either! You need to be returning very shortly to the house. Now listen carefully, Miss Anne, to our plan of campaign. If you trust me, there's no reason we cannot bring this off."

Chapter 7

It was well past nine o'clock when Anne slid unobtrusively through the side door. She knew that Povey would be helping serve breakfast to Rosings' guests, but Dulcie was rushing toward her down the hallway as she entered. Swiftly, she ran to Anne and grasped her arm. "This way, Miss Anne. Hurry!"

Following her up the back stairs, Anne felt a hysterical giggle bubble up inside. It seemed to her that she had spent the entire morning listening to a succession of worried voices telling her to hurry. She and Dulcie passed a footman on the stairs and then a thin woman with a haughty air whom Anne didn't recognize. She looked questioningly at Dulcie when they had passed her, and the maid hissed, "Dresser to Lady Theresa. Hurry, Miss Anne!"

By the time the two girls reached Anne's bedroom, every sensation in her body seemed to be centered in the painful bruise on her leg. Dulcie swiftly peeled the cloak from her shoulders and began to unbutton her wet dress.

"Has my mother sent for me already?"

"Yes, Miss, near twenty minutes ago. Povey told her you was tired and didn't wish to come down to breakfast, and oh miss, he thought she were going to come up here her own self! Whatever would I have told her?"

"Why didn't she?" By now, Anne was shivering violently and Dulcie drew her to a seat in front of the roaring fire and began briskly to rub dry her hair.

"Povey told t'ole bes--told Lady Catherine that he'd see you come down so's she wouldn't have to leave her guests. I was just on my way to try and find you, Miss Anne."

"It's dry enough now, Dulcie. Put it up." As the maid began to pull her damp hair back into a sleek chignon, Anne instructed her. "I'll be back upstairs within the hour. Be sure that you are here, for I need to talk to you and it must be this morning."

Dulcie held her dress as Anne stepped into it. "Oh, Miss, your petticoats is still damp-like. We must change them. You'll catch your death belike."

"They'll do. Fasten the dress, Dulcie--and don't let Herne or Mrs. Jenkinson send you off on any errands. Make some excuse if she tries. In fact--go into the dressing room and close the door. Don't answer if they call." Anne flung off her mud-encrusted boots as she spoke and slid her feet into dainty slippers. After a quick glance in the mirror, she pressed her cold hands to her cheeks for a calming moment. "Do you remember telling me once that what you would wish for most in the world is adventure?"

"Yes, Miss." Her maid gazed at her wonderingly.

"Well, I think you are about to get your wish." Leaving Dulcie wide-eyed and full of questions, Anne walked sedately down the steps to breakfast.

As she entered the dining room, re-arranged to accommodate both the Daviotts and guests who had spent the night at Rosings before traveling home, Anne was conscious of several pairs of penetrating eyes upon her.

Povey, who was dexterously shifting a chafing dish to make room for a sizzling platter of sausages, kidneys, and bacon at the enormous sideboard, looked relieved to see her, as did Lady Catherine. Underlying the facade of civility maintained for the benefit of her guests were both anger and worry, Anne guessed from a glance at her mother's countenance. She would be consumed with apprehension that her daughter's uncharacteristic rebellion might thwart her carefully laid plans to secure her a bridegroom the world would envy, while struggling to show no signs of her incredulous anger at Anne's ingratitude for her pains.

Sir Crawford was seated with his sisters on either side, but he was not eating with the gusto which had characterized him on the previous day. Anne's fleeting glance at him revealed heavy reddened eyes, and she wondered just how much wine--and other spirits--he had imbibed last night. He muttered a good morning to her, but otherwise did not distinguish her entrance, a forbearance for which Anne was devoutly grateful.

Mrs. Jenkinson rose immediately, begging Anne to take her seat beside Lady Theresa. "Please allow me to prepare a plate for you, Miss De Bourgh. I know just what you will like. Some toast, I know, and tea. Dulcie always makes it much too sweet, does she not?" She continued to chatter as Anne seated herself by Sir Crawford's mother, who had interrupted her monologue to Mr. Priddy only long enough to smile sweetly at Anne.

"--sure that dear Dr. Briscoe did all that was possible to save him. Indeed, he studied under Dr. Robert Graham, and *he*, you know, was a physician to the late queen. He was most assiduous in bleeding my husband twice a day, assuring me that his malign humours--"

Against the soothing background of Mrs. Jenkinson's recital of the culinary delights Anne was shortly to enjoy, Lady Theresa's thorough description of her husband's final days, and the animated chatter of Mrs. Priddy, whose flirtatious remarks were failing to coax Sir Crawford from an apparent fit of the sullens, Anne reviewed what Lieutenant Collins had referred to as their "battle plan."

I can do this, Anne mentally affirmed as she took a sip of the bitter tea that had been set before her. *What can Mama do to me in a single day? She cannot eat me. And I am not alone.* Mr. Coulville happened to look at Anne at that moment and was so startled by the brilliance of her smile that he failed to move quickly enough to secure the last apple muffin. *I am not alone. I have a friend, and he will help me.* The smile widened as she remembered the expression of grim determination with which Dulcie had shut herself into the dressing room and the kindness in Povey's hands as they had pulled up her hood that morning. *No--not a friend--I have friends!*

As more guests arrived for breakfast, some began to drift away, as did Anne, hoping to slip unobtrusively back upstairs. She reckoned, however, without Sir Crawford, who caught up with her at the foot of the stairs. Anne saw him, but mounted three steps before turning around; she liked the sensation of looking down on the disgruntled baronet instead of up at him.

"Miss Anne, may I be so bold as to request the favour of a few moments?"

"I must go upstairs and change, sir. I have spilled some tea down my skirt." Anne gestured toward the stain, deliberately made moments ago.

"When you come back down then? Imperative that I speak with you." His tone spoke more of command than entreaty. *What an annoying man he is*, she thought indignantly. But open defiance was no part of the plan, so she inclined her head politely.

"Where may I find you when you return?"

Anne sighed. "In the small withdrawing room. Povey will show you where it is. Now . . . pray excuse me." Without a backward glance, she ran up the stairs, limping only slightly, and into her room where she pulled open the door to the dressing room to hiss "Booooo" at Dulcie, whom she discovered carefully dusting and cleaning every item on her dressing table.

"Oh, Miss, you didn't half scare me. And Herne come knocking at the door twict. But I set quiet as a mouse in here just as you told me." Dulcie grinned impishly. "Weren't she bullin' when she left the second time!"

"Good." With her eyes sparkling, Anne grasped both

Dulcie's hands and pulled her to the window seat. "I need you to do three things today, Dulcie. And you must keep all three of them secret, except from Povey."

Eyes fixed on her mistress' face, Dulcie listened intently, gripping her hands together in her anxiety to understand.

"We must find a way to get my large trunk from the box room to the dressing room here without attracting notice. Can you think of a way?"

The girl was silent for a moment and then her face brightened. "I could ask one of the visiting menservants to help me, Miss. They'll think naught of it. I'll just say 'tis needed. An' I have the very one in mind . . ." A saucy smile curved Dulcie's lips and Anne smiled back.

"When you have it here, pack my best clothing in it. But Dulcie . . . " Anne's eyes met the maid's squarely. ". . . I need you also to bring a valise here and pack it with clothes enough for five days, if you can. The plainest, most serviceable clothing I have. And soap and my toothbrush and combs and my blue brush . . . and . . . oh, you will know better than I what to pack."

Confused, Dulcie nodded.

"I will not be taking the trunk now, so put nothing in it that I might require on a journey. It is only a blind. And you must pack a valise for yourself, Dulcie. Take anything that is dear to you. I have no notion when we might be back in this house again."

"Yes, Miss," the tremulous voice agreed.

Anne looked at the other girl closely and then spoke softly, "Dulcie, I should have asked you first if you wish to accompany me. I am going to my cousin Darcy's estate in Derbyshire--Pemberley. It is some distance and we must go by stage. You have heard it spoken of, I know. But perhaps you do not wish to undertake--"

"No, no, Miss, never would I let you go without me! Who'd look after you an' make you eat? And what be here for me? I've no family to keep me here. Nor nothin' else, Miss--only John Jacob. And that great dolt I found a-flirtin' with Miss Susan's maid but yestermorn."

"Then if you are certain?"

"Certain, for sure, Miss Anne."

"Then take an extra valise from the box room and pack it for yourself—but secretly, remember! Put it with mine in the dressing room. No one must see them, Dulcie. Put nothing but clothing and necessities in mine--I will pack what keepsakes I care to take in the little trunk my father gave me."

"Miss Anne, when are we leaving? *How* are we leaving? For well I know, Lady Catherine don't know naught of this!"

Anne looked quickly at the clock. "I have not the time to tell you now, Dulcie. Tonight when you dress me for dinner, I promise I'll tell you the whole. But now I must go back downstairs. Try hard to do all I have asked you! And let no one know."

As Anne started toward the stairs, Dulcie was bustling off the other way toward the backstairs to the box room, her freckled face transfigured by the devotion of a soldier marching off to war. With a small smile of ironic appreciation, Anne thought, *She is just the comrade for our battle plan.*

Approaching the small drawing room, Anne felt her heart pounding so hard she had to pause for breath. Over and over she murmured her talisman: *I am not alone. I am not alone.* When her tumultuous pulse had subsided, she walked into the room with every appearance of ladylike calm.

Sir Crawford was leaning on the mantel with his back to her, moodily nudging a log of the pile that had been laid for lighting. Hearing her footsteps he turned, met her gaze with infuriating aplomb, and gestured toward a settee. "May we be seated while I speak to you, Miss Anne?"

He looked annoyed when Anne chose a highbacked chair, but moved to seat himself on the settee, which creaked a protest as he leaned forward to speak. Anne had decided that she would say as little as civility allowed, so she folded her hands primly in her lap and directed a gaze of cool inquiry at her suitor, who seemed to feel the awkwardness of making a beginning.

"Miss Anne, I wish to apologize for my behavior last night. Suffered a momentary . . . ahhh . . . momentarily forgot who my companion was. Certainly will never happen again." He looked uncertainly at Anne who was wondering if the assurance that he would only force his attentions on females to whom he was *not* proposing marriage was supposed to mollify her.

"I was certainly surprised and dismayed by your manner toward me, sir. How my behavior might have provoked it remains unknown to me."

Sir Crawford regarded her narrowly, looking more ill-tempered by the minute. "I make no claim that your behavior was in any way responsible, ma'am. Fault was entirely mine. May I count upon your forgiveness?" He clearly did not doubt her acquiescence.

Anne was tempted to utter a resounding negative, but prudence dictated otherwise. She rose. "Shall we simply agree to draw a curtain of memory over that disturbing incident, sir? And now if you will excuse me--"

"There are other matters I wish to discuss with you." The color rose in Anne's cheeks at his peremptory tone as he continued. "I most ardently desire you to become my wife, Miss Anne. Surely my slip-up last night does not put my suit beyond hope? I give you my word as a gentleman that no action of mine will mar our engagement, should you so honour me."

I hear no guarantee of his actions after marriage, Anne thought instantly. *But why should he make any such promises? I will have no recourse then. He can do with me as he pleases.* As she met his hard brown eyes, Anne felt a sudden choking rage rise within her such as she had seldom felt before. For a moment she was quite incapable of speech and then a remembered voice overrode her fury. *Do nothing to anger them, Miss Anne, or to call attention to yourself.*

Digging her nails into her palms to gain mastery of her emotions, Anne forced a civil smile. "I have hardly had time to think of your very flattering proposal, Sir Crawford. I wonder if we might speak more of it tomorrow morning when I will be perfectly at leisure. I have promised several of our guests to take them on a tour of the conservatory directly." She drew a deep breath and forced out the words. "Perhaps you would care to join us, sir."

The remainder of the morning in the conservatory, its moist heat augmented by Sir Crawford's determined proximity, seemed interminable; luncheon stretched even longer. Finally the hour arrived for afternoon callers. Ten minutes after the hour of two, Povey announced Mr. and Mrs. Collins and Lieutenant Collins. Lady Catherine looked displeased, having clearly intimated to the cleric and his wife that, with Rosings so full of more exalted visitors, the Collinses' presence would be superfluous. Indeed, the apologetic look on the parson's face and his shamefaced greetings made it clear to Anne that her friend had had to exert his utmost persuasive powers to convince his reluctant relations to call.

Ten minutes after the Collinses' arrival, Anne stood and excused herself. As she moved toward the door, Lady Catherine questioned sharply, "Where do you go, Anne?"

"Merely to the library, Mama. There is a book whose illustrations I wish to show one of our guests." Before her mother could inquire more closely, Anne fled the room, hurrying down the hallway to the library, only to lean breathless against a pedestal holding a truculent-looking bust of Milton.

What if he is not able to get away? Anne worried frantically. *What if one of them accompanies him?* To calm herself, she picked up a volume at random, sat down, and found herself regarding the odes of Horace. Leafing through them soothed her although she could make no sense of the pages, and she was able to greet Lieutenant Collins with tolerable calmness when he appeared in the doorway and closed the door firmly behind him.

He offered her his swift, engaging smile as he approached the sofa where she was seated. "Are you still of the same mind as you were this morning, Miss Anne? I fear to influence you into actions which you may later regret."

"If our plan succeeds, Lieutenant, I will regret nothing. If it does not--well, I do not see how my situation can worsen."

His eyes met hers in a steady, measuring gaze before he nodded briskly. "As you say. Then let us arrange our little scene." He seated himself closely beside her and reached out a hand to hold the edge of Horace. "Remember, Miss Anne . . . it is only a suspicion we plant. Say nothing that might incite your mother to desperate measures such as locking you in your room."

Suddenly speechless with apprehension, Anne nodded.

Collins laughed as he took in her solemn face and enormous eyes. He gently brushed her cheek with the knuckles of one hand. "What a serious face is here! I assure you there's no need for such apprehension. Think of it as merely a light flirtation to while away a rainy afternoon. No more."

"I have not . . . I do not know *how* to flirt, I fear."

"What slowtops they must be in Kent to leave to me the pleasant task of teaching you," he replied teasingly. "Now, let's see. First, you must lower your eyelashes, while peeping at me around your fan."

"I do not have a fan," Anne laughed back at him, relaxing under the spell of his kindness and charm.

"No fan! Shall we make do with old Horace then?"

"You wish me to flutter my eyelashes at you behind Horace? Indeed, sir, I can hardly lift him," Anne protested.

"No, Miss Anne. I wish you to require my help in turning the pages. I seem to recall from what schooling my tutor could beat into me that old Horace is remarkably heavy going."

Lieutenant Collins' hand reached out to touch Anne's on the page. Large and brown against her slim white one, it felt firm and warm, but radiated nothing like the heat that had so repulsed her in Sir Crawford's plump hand. This warmth was altogether different. If she had thought in advance about the prospect of being touched by his hand, Anne would have imagined that it would be comforting. But it was not. The sensation of his hand lying over hers, his fingers lightly curled to encompass her slender fingers, set her pulse to jerking. *How strange*, she thought. *It is the lightest of touches. Why should it send such sensations throughout my whole body?*

Anne was also remarkably conscious of the lieutenant's gaze, which was not directed toward the book held between them. His dark grey eyes were on her face. When his gaze dropped from her eyes to her lips, she felt as though he had actually touched them, and she nervously bit her bottom lip, suddenly unable to think of anything to say because she was shocked to fine herself imagining how that firm, smiling mouth would feel pressed against her own.

For his part, Philip had intended nothing more than to set a believable scene for whatever audience would shortly arrive. That amiable objective began to transform into another desire entirely when he touched Anne's hand. He saw the colour leap instantly to her cheeks, and her grey eyes widen in response to his touch. He found his gaze drawn to the pulse in her throat. He had never been attracted to voluptuous women, and Anne's slender grace had excited his admiration from their first meeting. From his intention of providing no more than the pretense of flirting, he found himself imagining how it would feel to press his lips to just that point on her throat and feel it flutter against his tongue. If nothing more than the touch of his hand on her fingers had provoked her blood to stir--

At that moment his thoughts were interrupted by a voice that thundered from the door of the library. "Anne!

80

What is the meaning of this? Lieutenant Collins!" Had it not been for the fear he sensed in his companion, Lieutenant Collins would have been highly amused, for Lady Catherine's astonished visage could not have been any more indignant if she had discovered her daughter sitting on his lap unclothed. Even the stiff brown waves of her elaborate coiffure looked outraged.   Peeping around her employer's shoulder was Mrs. Jenkinson, wringing her hands as she bleated, "Miss Anne! Miss Anne? Whatever are you doing here?"

Collins raised his eyebrows in simulated surprise as Anne snatched her hand away, leaving poor Horace to slide to the floor with a disapproving thud. "Is there some way I can serve you ladies?"

Lady Catherine's face assumed an alarming purple hue. "Serve . . . serve . . . you may unhand my daughter, sir, and leave this room. In fact, you may leave my house. On the instant!"

Allowing his expression of surprise to deepen, Collins arose from the sofa in an unhurried manner. "Your ladyship, I cannot understand the reason for either your apparent anger or your command. Miss Anne was merely showing me a book her papa was fond of. She felt the illustrations would be of interest to me."

"Illustrations indeed! You were holding her hand. Do you take me for a fool, sir?"

Anne felt it was time to make her voice heard. Plaintively she murmured, "Really, Mama, how you embarrass me. Of course the lieutenant was not holding my hand. The book is heavy and he was merely helping me to turn the pages."

At once Mrs. Jenkinson eagerly proffered, "Oh, certainly that explains the very odd appearance which--"

"Be silent!" Lady Catherine exploded. The thought crossed Lieutenant Collins' mind that she might expire of apoplexy any moment and save her daughter an uncomfortable journey. "*You* may be a credulous fool, Mrs. Jenkinson, in fact

I have taken you for one any time these ten years, but I am thankful to say that I am not!"

Turning her ire upon her daughter who sat wide-eyed and innocent, Lady Catherine commanded, "Anne, you will return to our guests at once and remain there. Do not think to pull the wool over my eyes, miss. I know arrant flirtation when I see it--although I hardly expected to be entertained to a demonstration by a De Bourgh! As for you, Lieutenant--"

Feeling the scene had climaxed most successfully, Collins bowed. "I take your meaning, Your Ladyship. A good day to you all, ladies. I regret the misunderstanding."

He turned to Anne and their eyes met in a meaningful glance. "I regret that my desire to see the book has caused you disquiet, Miss De Bourgh. May the remainder of your afternoon be more pleasant!"

Chapter 8

At quarter past midnight Anne sat anxiously on the window seat, clad in a heavy printed cloth dress that drooped sadly both at the neckline and at its unfashionably low waist. In considerable haste Dulcie had cut it down from one of her own, and Anne felt that any curious stranger they met on their way would scarcely be likely to connect its wearer to the errant heiress of Rosings.

At her mistress' insistence, Dulcie had stretched out fully dressed on Anne's bed although she had insisted that nothing could possibly induce her to sleep at such a time even though her tasks that day had been legion. Her gentle snores rose and fell, the only noise other than the steadily rising wind outside and the ticking of the clock.

For what was surely the hundredth time, Anne reviewed her mental list of things she could not leave behind. The small store of money she had managed to hide away, the jewelry she might need to pawn, her precious drawings, the best of her paints and brushes, the testament given her by her father . . .

A gentle knock interrupted her anxious inventory, sending her heart into her throat as she rushed to the door and peeped through a crack. Povey stood there, outlined by the dim light shed by the only two wall sconces left alight. The old man moved noiselessly into the room, closing it behind him as Dulcie awoke with a snort and sat up, blinking sleepily.

"Everyone is abed, Miss Anne. I waited an hour after the last guest went upstairs to come to you. I also took the precaution of patrolling the halls first." Anne breathed a sigh of relief at the butler's softly spoken words. She had felt that an early night for Rosings' guests would be likely after the excesses of the previous one, but one sleepless wanderer in the house would have brought their plans to naught.

"Dulcie and I will carry the valises and the little trunk downstairs now." Seeing rebellion in her eyes, the old man shook his head. "No, Miss Anne. Think, child. If Dulcie and I are seen carrying something through the house or even out of doors, who will think to question aught I do? But if you are seen, there could be no explanation." Reluctantly Anne nodded.

"And the big trunk is in your room?"

"Safe as a nun's hen, Miss Anne."

"I still don't like it," Anne whispered. "If it were to be found--"

"Miss Anne, we have no time for such megrims. The trunk is out of sight should anyone enter--which they will not, for no one enters my room until I order it cleaned." Firmly, Povey turned to the maid. "Come, girl."

The two of them picked up the small wooden trunk containing Anne's drawings and supplies and backed out the door as Anne held it for them. Waiting for their return, Anne wandered over to the window to stare out into the dark night. *Will Patchett look for me tomorrow? He and the others will miss their treats.* Unexpected tears dimmed her sight. She turned hastily and carried first one valise and then the other to the door. She picked up the white envelope on the table by her bed and tucked it into a pocket of her skirt to be given to Povey. Taking up the worn woolen cloak which had also been Dulcie's until Anne had given her another for her nameday, Anne settled it around her shoulders, tying it tightly closed at her throat and pulling up the hood over her deliberately tousled hair. By the time Povey and Dulcie returned, she was rearranging the pillows shoved beneath the embroidered counterpane. To anyone peeping through her doorway, they would present the appearance of the room's occupant, deeply asleep.

As both Povey and Dulcie picked up a valise, he

whispered, "Wait two minutes, Miss Anne, before you follow. Come through the side door and all the way through the apple orchard to the lane behind it. We will await you there." At Anne's nod, they were both gone.

In what seemed a mere breath of time, Anne was outside her door. She saw that Povey had now extinguished all but one badly flickering light. Anyone seeing her moving through the hallways would take her for a servant on some late errand--or for a ghost, Anne thought with a shiver. Clutching the banister, she descended carefully to the dark hallway below and then flew on winged feet down the south corridor, through the side door, and out into the windy night.

Little more than a mile away, Philip Collins stood at the head of the horse harnessed to the light farm wagon he had borrowed from his brother's neighbor, ostensibly to visit a friend in a neighboring town. William had tried to press the gig upon him, but the lieutenant had declined on the grounds that his friend Buseby was storing some articles for him that needed to be retrieved.

A noise from the wood on his left had the horse shying restively. Moving to quiet him, Collins first heard an odd rolling sound, and then the figure of a man appeared, pushing something in front of him, closely followed by two slighter figures. For an instant the moon's rays pierced the clouds and Collins recognized Povey, in surely the most unlikely posture of his many years at Rosings--pushing a wheelbarrow. Both Anne and Dulcie were straining to carry valises.

As the wheelbarrow rolled to a halt, Collins said, "Here Povey, hold the horse and I'll see to the baggage."

Straightening painfully, the old man came to the horse's head while Collins walked quickly to Anne. Her face looked woefully white in the hood's dark shadow but she smiled valiantly up at him, saying gaily, "Good evening, Lieutenant-- no, I believe I should be wishing you an early good morning."

Appreciating her attempt at insouciance in circumstances surely frightening to a gently bred girl, Collins replied cheerfully in a low tone, "And a very good morning to you, Miss Anne. Here, let me take that." Swiftly the small trunk and both valises were stowed in the short bed of the wagon, leaving very little room to spare. "Now may I help you and your maid up?"

"In just a moment. Go ahead and put Dulcie up, please."

"I fear you will have to ride in the back," Collins explained apologetically to Dulcie.

"'Tis no matter to me, sir. Won't be the first time." As Collins helped her to settle on the blankets he had thoughtfully placed in the wagon's bed, Anne walked past him to the old man who stood smoothing a hand over the horse's neck.

"Povey . . . " The words Anne had framed in her mind for this occasion deserted her as she looked up into the old man's lined face. She tried again to speak, but was horrified to find herself shaken by a small sob. In a moment Povey's free hand had come out and gently gathered Anne to him; for an instant her muffled head rested on his bony shoulder as she fought tears.

"No fret, Miss Anne," he whispered softly in accents far less refined than the world was wont to hear from him. "I've no doubt Lieutenant Collins will see you safely on your way to Pemberley, and sure Master Fitzwilliam will see that no harm comes to you after that. And 'twill not be long, mayhap, before you're able to come back home. Now go. No need for words between us, child."

Anne nodded, speechless, a tear glinting in the moonlight, as she moved away before turning hastily back to say, "Povey . . . .will you leave some nuts and kitchen scraps for Patchett from time to time on the branch outside my room? He may . . . he is ac--accustom--"

Her voice broke and the old man answered gently, "You may be sure I will, Miss Anne."

She found Collins beside her and felt his wordless

sympathy in the clasp of his hand as he drew her to the vehicle's side, carefully lifted her onto the seat, and handed her two blankets. After helping her to sit on one and draw its ends over her legs and lap, he wrapped her shoulders in the other, vaulted into his seat and picked up the reins as Povey moved to stand beside him. "Take care of them, sir."

Steadfastly, Collins met his eyes in the dim light and replied, "You have no need to worry, I promise you. I'll see them safe on their way." He reached down to shake the old man's hand, clucked to the restless horse, and the little wagon moved off into the darkness.

For a short period Lieutenant Collins did not speak, feeling that his companion needed time and silence to master her distress. He heard no more sobs, and glancing at the quiet figure beside him, saw that she was sitting straight against the rough boards comprising the back of the seat, staring into the darkness ahead. "You need to keep the blankets wrapped warmly around you, Miss Anne. The night is a cold one. We'll land in the basket if you take ill."

Anne turned her head to smile at him. "No fear of that, sir. I am seldom truly ill." But she began to wind the blankets more tightly about her as she spoke.

"My brother has told me that your constitution is so delicate that you are often unable to come downstairs."

"Lieutenant, I fear I must sink myself beneath reproach by admitting that the flaws in my constitution spring largely from dislike of company a great part of the time."

Collins laughed. "Miss Anne, no one would suspect that beneath that innocent exterior you are such a little rogue! However, having sampled the company of Rosings, I must admit that I well understand you subterfuge." After a pause he continued more seriously, "I fear you'll find our journey tedious. I couldn't procure a more suitable vehicle without arousing suspicions later, and I'm afraid to travel faster with so little light from the moon."

"I think myself very well placed, sir."

Collins looked down into her face. "You think yourself well-placed to be traveling through cold and darkness in an old farm wagon in the middle of the night? Miss Anne, I say most sincerely that I admire your courage. It's the quality I value most in the world, and I have not found it predominant in your sex."

"Perhaps that is because women are not often called upon to display that virtue when most of us have husbands or fathers or brothers to protect us."

"Perhaps you are correct. When did your father die, Miss Anne?"

"When I was eight. He rode out to aid a tenant whose family had been ill and was caught in a hard rain as he returned. He never recovered from the chill he took."

Rebuked by the sorrow in her voice, Collins said gently, "Forgive me for stirring bad memories."

She shook her head. "It comforts me to speak of him on the rare occasions when I may. He was very dear to me. My greatest pleasure as a child lay in accompanying him on estate business." Even in the darkness, Collins could hear a smile. "Sometimes he only *pretended* to have business to transact. He would take me off with him and we would fish. Or to the wood to learn the names of the birds and trees and flowers. It was he who taught me to draw. He had a talent for it himself, but he felt that mine was greater, so he insisted on hiring a master for me."

Anne leaned her head against the back of the wagon as she allowed her mind to drift back to happier years. "Mama thought it a needless expense because I was so young, but Papa prevailed for once. Mr. Lawrence came to me on Tuesday and Thursday afternoons, and I used to think I would never live through the mornings, waiting for him."

"You were so fond of him?"

"Oh. . . I suppose I liked him well enough, but it was the instruction he gave that made me long for the hours I spent with him. He was actually rather choleric in disposition and very strict, but I don't know that I could have had a better master." Sadness crept back into her voice. "Of all the things that Papa gave me, I think none was more precious."

"I believe that I have made you sad, though you deny it."

"Truly, I love to speak of him. It makes him seem—still alive, in some way. But Mama feels that remembering him lowers my spirits, so she frowns if I talk of those years. Dulcie never knew him, and of course I cannot be often conversing with Povey."

"So you're never allowed to speak of him?"

"Oh--to my cousins occasionally. Due, I think, to having no son or nephews of his own, my father was particularly fond of Giles and Fitzwilliam--that is Colonel Fitzwilliam and Mr. Darcy, you know. When they were boys visiting Rosings, they would accompany us on our outings."

"And so you grew fond of them?"

"Very fond, although as we grew older, all of us were careful to keep any hint of that affection from our behavior before others."

"Because--?"

Anne laughed with a touch of bitterness. "You have met my mother, Lieutenant. In her estimation, only a Fitzwilliam was suitable to marry her daughter. Darcy was her choice because of his much greater wealth. She was intent enough upon that object without any show of feeling from us to incite her further, I assure you."

"She was so set upon a dynastic marriage for you?"

"She---oh, it's so hard to explain Mama to someone who only sees the facade she shows the world. I know that her veneration for the Fitzwilliams and the De Bourghs makes her almost a figure of fun. But I sometimes think that Mama is at war with the world and sees in the family her only allies--and my only safety. I truly think she trusts no one outside those two families. That is why my cousin Darcy's marriage caused her such grave hurt. Somehow she sees his marriage as a betrayal of the family, and nothing is more important to Mama than the Fitzwilliams."

A short silence fell. Collins was reflecting upon Anne's words, and the lady's train of thought became obvious in her next shy speech. "But . . . we speak only of myself, sir. What of your own family?"

Collins roused himself. "There's little of interest to tell, I fear. My father, as you know, was a cousin of the lady who married Mr. Darcy. There was a breach between the families because my father felt he had been unfairly treated in the disposition of some family property. And indeed, he had good reason to feel such pecuniary concerns, however founded or unfounded they might have been. I am one of eleven children."

"Good heavens!" Anne exclaimed. "But oh . . . how enjoyable it must have been to have grown up always with companionship and affection. Do tell me of them."

"The eldest are my twin sisters, Harriet and Fanny. Both of them are married now, as is my sister Maria. Fanny married very well indeed and has become quite my mother's favorite, in consequence. Her husband, Richard Treatham, is the heir to an Irish estate and title. My mother now lives with them, and I think if she survives to see Fanny's husband assume the title, she may promptly expire from the joy of it."

Anne's laughter joined his. "Then your father, too, is dead?"

"Yes, it was only upon his death that William dared to extend the olive branch to the Bennet family. With rather clandestine motives, I am sad to say."

"Indeed?"

"He wished to acquaint himself with the property which he will one day inherit—and he also wished to wed one of his cousins. In fact, he made an offer to Miss Elizabeth Bennet."

"Goodness gracious, I never knew that. Really, I think your brother and Miss Elizabeth would have been most ill-suited."

90

"I can have no opinion since I have not met the lady, but it has been my observation that he and Charlotte suit very well indeed."

"And the rest of your brothers and sisters?"

"My older brother Rupert died of a childhood illness. I cannot remember him, but I think he must have been a saint."

Anne looked at him in surprise. "A saint?"

"A paragon of all virtues, apparently, for Mama throws him in our faces every time one of us steps beyond the line!"

Joining his laughter, Anne snuggled into her blankets and asked, "And next came . . . ?"

"I was born next, to be followed by yet another set of twins, my brothers, Harry and Cedric."

"Two sets of twins! That must surely be most unusual."

"Not in the Collins family, Miss Anne. Nearly every generation of our family boasts at least one pair."

"And after Harry and Cedric, there came three more children? I trust no more arrived in duet!"

Collins laughed. "No more. There are Theodore, Decima, and Alice. They are all in the schoolroom still."

Anne sighed. "I envy you."

"To be candid, I don't know them as well as I would like. I spent long periods of my childhood with the maternal uncle for whom I was named. He remained a bachelor and is the owner of a small property in Cornwall, in addition to some mining interests there."

"And your parents gave you his name, hoping he would leave them to you someday?"

"You are very astute, Miss Anne. In fact, my uncle purchased my commission in the Navy, his nearness to the ocean and sea-faring men having given him much respect for that branch of the service."

"He did not wish to keep you with him then?"

"Oh no," Collins chuckled. "Not when I was young and 'bumptious,' as he phrased it. I'll need to learn more of his affairs soon, though. I'm sorry to say that he's not been in prime twig of late. In fact, we spoke of my selling out after my next tour when last I visited him in the summer. I have as yet made no definite determination, but that's the option toward which I lean at present."

"I envy you that also, Lieutenant. To be able to choose . . . to say, 'I will continue my naval career' or 'I will sell out tomorrow.' That is a freedom only men can know."

"I fear you're quite correct, Miss Anne. With the protection which women claim from the men of their family comes a loss of independence that must surely grate upon the intelligent and self-sufficient among your sex."

Pulling up the horse, Collins turned to his companion. "Can you hold the reins for a moment? I wish to examine that signpost at close range. I am tolerably sure that the road to our left leads to Brompton Little Hays, but I prefer to make certain. A wrong turn at this point would land us at *point non-plus*."

After a cursory inspection of the somewhat decrepit sign, the lieutenant quickly re-joined her on the seat; in the stillness brought about by their cessation of movement, a curious sound rose and fell at intervals from the wagon bed. "What in blazes is that?" he queried, gazing over his shoulder.

Anne giggled. "Only Dulcie. I have never known her to miss an hour's sleep even in the most uncomfortable of circumstances."

"You must surely have the right of that, ma'am! Anyone who could sleep in the back of this jouncing wagon could sleep in Bedlam. I thought we had somehow acquired some fierce nocturnal animal as a traveling companion!" Anne laughed again and he looked down at her. "Here, you are about to lose the bottom blanket." He reached around her shoulder to rescue the errant blanket and wrap it more closely. Briefly free of the banks of clouds, the moon shone down on Anne's face, silvering the curls that fell loosely around it. Both were suddenly aware of their proximity on the narrow seat in the darkness with his arm curving around her shoulders.

92

Reacting without thought, Collins leaned closer until his lips nearly brushed her face. His hand came up to touch her cheek, and he thought that he had surely never felt anything smoother or softer. Her skin looked like pale porcelain in the moonlight, but it felt like living silk.

I should move away, Anne told herself. *I should say something to break this spell. Anything.* But it was sweet beyond belief to feel his strong warm arm around her shoulder and his fingers gently stroking her face. She lifted it to him in the moonlight and every good intention Collins had formed vanished on the instant.

His kiss was light, the merest touch of his lips to hers. *It is the way a butterfly would have felt, had it lighted there,* she thought dazedly. The pressure increased slightly as she felt his fingers sliding through her hair to cup her head. Then she felt his lips open and his tongue gently stroke across the seam between her own closed lips. With a little indrawn breath, Anne moved then, but not away from him. One hand slid up to lie within his coat. She could feel his heart racing beneath her open palm and she pressed it unthinkingly against his shirt until the heat of his skin warmed her cold hand. She felt him quiver and the arm behind her head grew taut, but the kiss remained a gentle breath of tenderness on her mouth. As he moved his head to slant his lips over hers, the pressure left and then returned like the breath of life returning to her body.

For the moments that he held her, Philip Collins was conscious of nothing except physical sensation. The strands of her hair were satin twining through his fingers. Her breath was sweetly minty, and from her body emanated the enticing fragrance of some lightly-scented soap with a spicy touch of carnation combined with a scent that he could only identify as Anne. Most of all, her mouth--smooth and full and very slightly wet as though she had just touched it with her tongue-- enthralled his senses; the shock of feeling her lips move against his blotted everything else from his mind. He knew nothing beyond the combination of Anne's obvious innocence and her unexpected response to his touch.

Without realizing what she meant to do, Anne opened her lips and felt his tongue meet hers in the softest of caresses, which managed still, to burn like living fire. His hand, hardened by the exigencies of life aboard ship, moved beneath her cheek to stroke her throat, his palm caressing the nape of her neck as his thumb rubbed gently over the pulse. The contrast between the roughness of his fingertips and the tenderness of their touch sent an ache through Anne's body which she had never felt before. It seemed to impel her to touch, to taste, to melt against his heat as two burning candles will meld into one.

It was the horse which ended the kiss. Feeling the complete loosening of the reins, he whinnied impatiently, eager to return to a warm stable, and jerked his head, causing the reins to shoot out of Anne's right hand into the floor of the wagon. They would have ended in the road between it and the horse had not Collins lunged to catch them.

Furious with both his clamorously unrepentant body and his lack of control, he guided the horse to the left and sent it down the road at a much brisker pace, for this surface was wider and smoother, and the moon's light still bathed the landscape.

Blowing out his breath and moving uncomfortably on the hard seat, Lieutenant Collins finally said stiffly, "I can think of no excuse for that breach of propriety, Miss Anne. Or call it rather a breach of trust. None exists. I have proved myself no better than the man from whose attentions I am removing you. I can only apologize for it and assure you it will not happen again."

Silence greeted the apology. *She has lost all trust in me*, he thought. *And who could blame her? She will want me to take her back home now. And if we are caught, what a mull I will have made of this whole business.* After a very long moment, a small voice beside him asked softly, "You are not about to tell me that you forgot who your companion was, are

94

you?"

"What?" he looked at her in disbelief. "Of course I knew who my companion was. I was very much aware of it! That awareness was the exact cause of the occurrence, ma'am!"

There was no rationale for the glow of happiness that consumed her, Anne knew. Had she not been outraged and horrified at exactly the same indignity offered her by Sir Crawford Daviott only last night? At least he had made her an offer. But she could not muster one spark of maidenly indigonation against the joy that her companion's words engendered.

When Anne's silence continued, Collins drew the horse up and looked at her uncertainly, straining to see her expression in the darkness. "Anne . . . Miss Anne. Do you want to continue? We are more than halfway now, and I swear to you--"

At that moment a noise from the wagon's bed startled them both. Dulcie's voice asked sleepily, "Be we there yet? Miss Anne? Have we stopped? Where are we?"

Anne looked directly into her companion's self-condemning eyes and replied briskly, "No, not yet, but it is not too far to go. Drive on please, Lieutenant."

The remainder of the cold journey to the posting inn passed more easily that it might have since Dulcie managed to slither through the accumulation in the wagon bed until she could easily talk to Collins and Anne.

Once he realized both girls could hear him, and that his more than momentary lapse from the behavior expected of a gentleman had been, if not forgiven, at least overlooked, Collins began to remind them of the cautions he had already expressed to Anne about their forthcoming journey.

"My friend Buseby's manservant placed your names on the waybill yesterday--Rachel and Hannah Ackers. There are many of that name hereabouts and your presence will occasion no surprise. Threshett mentioned to the innkeeper in passing that one of the girls is a little simple. That will be your excuse to say little, keep your face down, and avoid contact with anyone else, Miss Anne. Allow Dulcie to speak for you both."

To his surprise, Anne laughed. "Lieutenant, after the events of the past two days, I shall have little difficulty in behaving as a simpleton, I assure you."

Uneasily Collins wondered just which events prompted her laugh, but resolutely plunged on with his instructions. "We will, in all likelihood, arrive before the coach. We will remain back in the shadows until the current passengers disembark. They will be wanting breakfast. Once the coach is empty, I'll secure your luggage. You, Dulcie, will go inside to receive your tickets. Try to keep your hair out of sight as much as possible--it's a telling mark of identity. And speak in the broadest accent you can manage."

Dulcie giggled. "Why sur, b'aint t'way I do be talkin' naow broad enow?"

"Exactly," Collins replied with a grin. "While you are inside, Miss Anne will seat herself in a corner of the coach. The reason is that she's so backward, you understand? Far too shy to speak to anyone unless she must."

"Aye, I understand right enough."

"As soon as we arrive, I suggest, Miss Anne, that Dulcie pull your hair back under your hood completely out of sight."

"Very well . . . although we dressed it loosely because I never wear it that way."

"It is too . . . too . . ." For a moment Collins stumbled since the only words that occurred to him to describe the shimmering fall of hair were wildly inappropriate.

"Noticeable?"

"Yes," he seized on the adjective with relief. "Far too noticeable."

He wondered if he imagined the amusement in the maid's voice when she demurely agreed, "Just as you say, sir. If you lean back your head, I can manage well enough, Miss. I've a brush and hairpins here in my reticule."

Collins began to wish he had waited to bring up the subject of Anne's coiffure when the shining mass of silver was unloosened over the back of the wagon seat, and Dulcie stood to re-arrange it. Instant images of Anne, clothed only in that silken cloak, invaded his mind. It was as though he had actually seen her, standing beside her bath like a slender white sapling transformed into womanhood by some god, lifting the weight of hair up to be tied out of the way of the water, her breasts rising sweetly with the motion until they resembled rounded, rose-tipped fruit ready to be--with an overwhelming effort of will, he forced the picture from his mind and continued.

"Your first stop will be Dartford, which you should reach mid-day tomorrow. There will be an express coach waiting. You will have to travel through the night tomorrow night. Or rather," he corrected himself, "tonight since it is morning already. I want you to reach London as soon as possible, so I did not book accommodations for you to sleep. You'll be exhausted, I know, but I fear it can't be helped."

"We shall do very well," Anne responded immediately. "I assure you that Dulcie will not lose a wink of sleep, sir, whether we lie over or not!" They both laughed at Dulcie's indignant snort.

Perhaps she does not truly hate me after all. Collins felt as if his neckcloth had been suddenly loosened. "Your passage is paid through to London. For safety's sake, I wish you to switch stagecoach lines there. I recommend Batson's out of the East India Yard. I've written it down here, along with the name of a small, but very respectable hotel in which you may quite safely spend the night." For a moment he fumbled in his breast pocket before handing Anne a small packet.

"You must remember on the afternoon of your arrival in London, to send Dulcie in a hackney to Batson's before six to put your names on the waybill. I also gave you there a sum that should be sufficient to see you from London to

Derbyshire. Your stage will depart early the next morning, so you must be up betimes. "

"But Lieutenant--I certainly never intended you to pay our fare. I have money here in my reticule. I even have some jewelry to pawn, if necessitated. Indeed, there is no need for you to expend your funds! You have done too much on our behalf already."

"Miss Anne, allow me to perform this small service for you." Understanding her rebellion, he spoke softly but forcefully. "Whatever amount of money you can have brought on such short notice can't be much. You will not convince me that your mother keeps you in lavish funds."

The silence from both girls which greeted his observation told him that his remark had hit home. "It's very possible that you will need the sum you brought. The amount I'm giving you is quite trifling. Enough to pay your fare to journey's end, along with meals and lodgings on the way from London to Derbyshire. Once you've settled at Pemberley, you can repay me, if you insist."

When no reply came, he continued, "Miss Anne, you don't know what exigencies might arise . . . now do you? It's Dulcie's well-being as well as your own that you need to consider. Think how you'd feel if she came to harm from the lack of a few pennies in your pocket. I am persuaded you can see the prudence in keeping your own money for emergencies."

Anne's voice was so soft that he had to strain to hear it. "You are very persuasive, Lieutenant, but you must know it is not right for me to take money from you."

"Now, haul sail!" he replied in a strong brogue. "'Tis the cap'n as gives the orders on this ship and midshipmen like you two must hop to and obey!."

"'Tis only sense he be speaking, Miss Anne," Dulcie chipped in, thinking to herself that the lieutenant handled her mistress to a treat, and also that it was a great pity he must leave them so soon.

"Then I think I must listen to sense and follow the

captain's orders," Anne replied at last. "But Lieutenant--or *Captain*, I should say--allow me at least to tell you this. You mentioned earlier that courage is the trait you most admire. I, too, recognize its claim to prominence in the catalogue of virtues, especially for one in your profession, but I must beg to differ."

Collins turned to face her and saw, even in the darkness, the shine of tears in her eyes.

"The virtue I most admire is kindness, and I have found such depths of that quality in your nature that I can only say that you have earned my deepest gratitude. In the midst of battle, anyone can be brave, but very few would have recognized my plight, and even fewer would have sympathized or offered me any aid in a situation so likely to bring them censure or embarrassment."

A long moment of silence ensued. The lieutenant's voice was matter-of-face when he spoke. "I believe I see the lights of the posting inn up ahead. We will pull up as soon as we're close enough and I'll reconnoiter a bit." But his hand had found Anne's in the darkness and pressed it to his lips.

Chapter 9

Light shone from the rear of the Blue Heron, indicating activity in the kitchen, but the rest of Brompton Little Hay's high street lay in peaceful darkness. A small brick church surrounded by an irregular wall stood a short distance away, and Collins drew the horse to a halt on the far side of the wall away from the inn.

"I think we cannot have more than an hour to wait," he told Anne and Dulcie. "I judge it to be nearer five than half past four if the moon doesn't lie, and six was advertised as departure time."

Anne turned her head. "Dulcie, lie back down. You cannot perch there like a bird on top of the trunk for an hour."

"Well," Dulcie looked longingly back into the wagon bed, "p'raps I'll just lay down and wrap up to get toasty warm again. But I shan't be able to sleep this time!"

"Of course not," Anne replied gravely. She slanted a mischievous glance up at her companion, thinking he would share her mirth, but she could see no humor in his expression. "Lieutenant, you are looking very grave."

"I don't doubt I am. The closer the time comes for you to leave my protection, the more apprehension I feel. Would that I could accompany you!"

She patted his arm soothingly and he was grateful for the implicit trust in the gesture. "We have discussed that possibility already. Without you to draw them off tomorrow, I should not get a day's journey beyond this point before my mother caught me up. However hard Povey tried, he could not reasonably misdirect them for long. And reflect that we will be on the public stage. What harm can come to us there?"

"It's not your journey on the stage which worries me.

100

Travel by stage may not be genteel, but it's quite safe these days. I should not otherwise have countenanced it. It's your stop in London that harrows me, Miss Anne. You've never been alone in the city, nor has Dulcie. Any number of mishaps might occur."

"Lieutenant Collins. You have so far paid me the compliment of believing that I am an intelligent and resourceful woman, an encomium that no one else has bestowed upon me. Do not rescind it now." She looked up to see his brows still drawn together in a frown. "You have written out most explicit instructions, and I promise I shall faithfully follow them. If the worst should come and we are stranded in London, I have simply to make my way to Fitzwilliam House in Upper Grosvenor Street where I have visited before. My aunt and uncle will certainly take us in. If they happen to be not at home, the servants will. They know me well."

He sighed. "Too late now to repine. But I shall be most thankful when I receive news that you've reached Pemberley in safety." She smiled up at him and he resisted the temptation to brush his fingers down her cheek as he had done at their last stop.

"The other thing that worries me is your trunk. I arranged only for two valises, for I felt that your dearth of baggage would deflect suspicion if inquiry is made. No one could expect Miss De Bourgh to be making a long journey with nothing but a valise. I hope your trunk is so small that its addition at this point will pose no problem."

"Oh, I hope so too!" Anne cried in distress. "I know you told us to bring only a valise, but I could not leave behind the trunk's contents. Their importance to me does not lie in mere sentiment though there are several things inside that it would wound me to lose. My drawings are also there and I am hoping . . . that is I had felt there might be a chance . . . "

When she floundered to a halt, he looked down inquiringly. "A chance of what?"

"I fear you will laugh at me. But, indeed, perhaps you are the very person with whom I should discuss a . . . a hope I have."

It took all the iron control that service in the navy had brought to keep Collins from taking her hand. "I certainly shall not laugh. You may tell me anything, and I shall be gratified by your confidence."

Anne took a deep breath and spoke rapidly. "You recall that you spoke to me of Mr. Reece? You said he had published some books of engravings. I had thought that perhaps I could sell some of my sketches to a publishing house. I have seen books such as you spoke of--indeed, I own several--and they have not seemed so *very* much better than mine. Or . . . or do I only imagine that, sir? Pray be candid!"

Collins saw the hope that shone in her eyes, obvious even in the moonlight, and his hard-won control vanished as though the last seven long years had never been. Gently he possessed himself of her hand, holding it between both of his own. "The only manner in which your imagination is working, Miss Anne, is in helping you produce works of art so perfectly executed that they rival any hung by the Academy. I think your ambition to publish your work is both laudable and practical."

"I know you flatter me, sir, but if even part of that is true, then perhaps I have a chance to sell them to some firm in London. I'm sure they would not bring in much--but perhaps enough so that I need not be totally dependent upon Darcy until I am five and twenty."

"Until you are five and twenty?"

"My father left a sum in trust for me, quite apart from what I might expect from Rosings. It is not a great amount, but if I observe strict habits of economy, I could maintain a small establishment in the country."

"It would mean a very different way of life from anything to which you have been accustomed at Rosings," Collins replied doubtfully.

"I assure you that I would not regard it. Although I should hang my head to sound so ungrateful for all the luxury that has surrounded me, Lieutenant, I tell you truly that I would welcome the freedom of such an existence. But a year and two months seems a woefully long time to hang upon my cousin's sleeve."

"Miss Anne, I would not let such a thought worry me for a moment." A note of sadness entered his voice in spite of all that he could do to sound reassuring. "I have not one doubt that you will form an acquaintance with some fortunate gentleman who will make all these worrisome details irrelevant long before any such length of time has passed."

"Some fortunate gentleman who wishes to possess Rosings?" Anne murmured bitterly.

"No," he replied passionately. "Trust me when I tell you that you mistake the matter. Don't judge all men by Sir Crawford. Your cousin Darcy will present you to gentlemen who won't care a rush for your inheritance--or anything else except winning your favour--and possessing the *owner* of Rosings." He squeezed her hand before releasing it. "Once you have established yourself in your cousin's household and begin to meet his friends, you will see. The young bloods will say you are *something like* once you are out of your mother's shadow. Now I think I'd better walk down to the inn. The stage will be arriving any minute."

It's good that the street is so windy and cold, Lieutenant Collins thought grimly, as he neared the inn. *It may serve to wake me up. What kind of bubble-headed fool forms an attachment to a girl so far above him that she might as well live on the moon? It is not I who will be the one for whom she lets down that glorious hair each night. But I am not wrong to feel that we would have been very well suited. That, at least, I have. We could have painted together . . . fished together . . . sailed . . . walked on the shore and marveled at the shells. I could have taken her to Italy and Spain . . .*

103

Stop, fool! She has allowed you to serve her and that should be enough. It will have to be.

Could he have meant himself when he spoke of the fortunate gentleman who will wish to win my favour? Anne shivered in spite of her blankets and stared up at the sky, where once again the moon had totally disappeared as though in disapproval of her thoughts. *But why did he look so sad if it was of himself he spoke? I should not imagine things--as I am all too prone to do. He is kind and he is a gentleman and he could not see me forced into marriage with a swine. To see more in his chivalry is foolish beyond permission.*

But the kiss--what of the kiss? argued her heart. *He was embarrassed by it. That was obvious. It was merely the result of the romantic situation in which we found ourselves. I must not make more of it than the impulse of a moment. Gentlemen do not view such things in the same light as ladies do. He is my friend. He has risked much to save me from Sir Crawford. With that, I should be content.*

By the time Collins had spoken with the guard about stowing the baggage, Anne had visited the necessary behind the inn and, well-wrapped against the cold, was safely tucked into a corner of the coach. The lieutenant swung himself inside and sat down beside her. "Miss Anne, I'm sorry that I must tell you they cannot take the trunk. They are contracted for a heavy load of baggage at your next stop."

Anne stared wordlessly at him.

"But how will this plan serve? I'll take it with me to Buseby's and we'll find somewhere to hide it. I give you my word it will be quite safe. Once the hue and cry has died, I'll take my leave of William and Charlotte, retrieve the trunk, and bring it to you at Pemberley. It won't be a long delay before you'll have it with you once again."

"Lieutenant, after all you have done for me, how can I possibly ask you to undertake a long journey solely to deliver my trunk?"

"Quite easily. It provides me what I most desire at the moment." He smiled at the question in her eyes. "A good excuse to visit you in Derbyshire. I shall be able to see for myself how you go on."

Unable to think of words to express either her gratitude or her happiness, Anne surprised even herself. Untucking her hand from the blanket, she reached up to touch Collins' cheek. The instant he felt the gentle caress on his face, he turned his head to kiss her fingers passionately, then bent to touch his lips to hers. But the kiss was not gentle this time. It held the urgency of his worry for her, the force of his desire for her, and desolation of spirit at her leaving. Time seemed to stop for Anne as the kiss deepened, and the quickening that had begun deep within when he had first kissed her stirred anew. His mouth seemed to devour Anne's entire consciousness. Rosings, her mother, Sir Crawford, even the precarious situation in which she found herself evaporated in a wave of fire that consumed everything except her awareness of Philip's hand cradling her head, his lips kissing her as if he could never taste enough of her mouth, and his blood beating in a fierce and primitive rhythm with her own.

When he lifted his head, she murmured a little cry of protest and her other hand came up to clutch his coat; breathless and burning for more than the taste of her lips, Collins knew that had they been alone, regard for neither chivalry nor propriety would have been enough to make him leave her. But Dulcie was approaching with a cup of tea and a hot brick and there was time only to say good-bye.

Minutes later he watched the coach set off through an early morning mist on the road to London.

Arriving at Oliver Buseby's comfortable two-story hunting lodge, Collins wearily stabled the tired horse when no stable hand appeared. The trunk he carried into the tack room where he covered it with several horse blankets and a saddle.

Although near the hour of ten, the lieutenant placed no confidence in his friend's wakefulness, but his manservant would be about.

As he had expected, the door was opened by Threshett, a short, whip-thin man whose eyes announced that they had seen all the world had to offer. In Buseby's service, Collins reflected, he probably had.

Invited into the little-used parlor, Collins declined. "I'll speak to you in the library instead, Threshett."

"Certainly, Lieutenant. Shall I bring you some refreshment there?"

"Not at present, thank you."

With the library door safely closed, Collins said at once, "Look here, Threshett, I need a favour. Your master will endorse my request, I'm sure--if he ever gets out of bed."

Threshett smiled primly. "I'm sure I shall be happy to accommodate you, Lieutenant."

"I hope so. Some time this afternoon, a party of people will, in all likelihood, arrive here. I think that one of them will be my brother, another will be Lady Catherine de Bourgh, and I have not the least idea who the rest may be."

"Indeed, sir. Shall I lay in more supplies?"

"Hardly. I wish you to inform them, if they inquire, that I arrived here in time for dinner last evening, spent the night here, and have not left the house since my arrival." Collins frowned. "The horse will be a problem. If I bribe the stableman and Buseby's groom, can they be trusted to keep mum?"

"Of that I have no opinion, sir, but the need will not arise. The stableman has traveled into Sussex to attend the funeral of his father. And Maynard has not yet returned with the new hack Mr. Buseby purchased in Ireland."

"Oh, excellent! But the cook would certainly know I was not here last evening."

Threshett regarded the lieutenant in surprise. "The *cook*, sir? You think these . . . persons . . . are likely to question

Mrs. Ruddy?"

"I fear it is quite likely."

"Then I fear, Lieutenant, that *they* are quite likely to find a rolling pin about their ears for their pains. Mrs. Ruddy has been out of reason cross since the last revival, sir."

"Revival?"

"She being of the Methody bent, sir. The last preacher who spoke to her Meeting convinced her that she is labouring in the tents of the Ungodly, and she is wrestling with her soul in regard to the matter."

Collins regarded him in fascination. "Why does she not give in her notice?"

"Because the Ungodly pays better than most hereabouts, sir. Worrying over it has quite cast her into the mopes. In short, Lieutenant, if they are impertinent enough to penetrate into our kitchen, I doubt these visitors you expect will get a word out of her--unless it comes from the Old Testament, sir.

Collins grinned. "That should be of great benefit to them. And I know I may rely upon you, Threshett."

"I should hope you do, sir. Who brought you off safe from that scrape in Naples? But may I ask why we expect these inquisitive persons to descend upon us?

"Of course you may," Collins replied with a yawn. "They think I've eloped with the heiress of Rosings Park."

Threshett blinked. "Indeed, sir." He paused for a thoughtful moment. "Might I suggest that if you have need of the clergy, Mrs. Ruddy can put you in contact with any number of them."

Collins' grin widened. "I am indeed grateful, Threshett, but alas, my heiress has departed."

"On the stagecoach to London perhaps, sir?"

Collins chuckled. "There were never any flies on you. Thank you for your help with that, by the by. It was invaluable." He yawned again. "Lord, I'm for bed. I'm as sleepy as a horse. But it's imperative that I speak to Buseby as soon as he awakes. Will you call me then, please?"

"Certainly, sir." He looked at the lieutenant's stained and muddy footwear in deep disapproval. "If you will leave your boots outside the door, sir, I shall see to cleaning them."

At Hunsford parsonage, Mr. William Collins had just bent to the task of pulling up dried bean vines and corn stalks in his kitchen garden when he heard the sound of a carriage at his front gate. Hearing his wife's call, he rounded the house still clutching a handful of vegetable detritus where, to his great astonishment, he beheld Sir Crawford Daviott handing Lady Catherine de Bourgh out of her traveling carriage.

Grasping his stalks like some strange bouquet, Mr. Collins advanced hastily toward his patroness. "Lady Catherine! What an unexpected honour! Pray forgive my gardening attire, dear lady, and you sir, and step--"

"Where is your brother, Mr. Collins?" snapped her ladyship without vouchsafing so much as a greeting.

"Where is . . . Philip is visiting a friend near Marley Vale, Lady Catherine. Why--"

"Visiting a friend, indeed! Your brother, Mr. Collins, is in company with my daughter. They have eloped, sir!"

Both Mr. Collins and his wife gaped at their visitors in amazement. For the first time since she had met her husband, Charlotte saw him totally speechless, his mouth working like a landed fish.

"But why do you believe Miss De Bourgh has eloped with Lieutenant Collins?" Charlotte was the first to recover power of speech.

"Because," began Sir Crawford, finally entering the lists, "when Miss Anne did not come down to breakfast, and Lady Catherine sent her dresser upstairs to discover why, she discovered only an empty bed!"

"And what else do you suppose she found?" demanded Lady Catherine, her voice rising dangerously. "*My* daughter left a stack of pillows in her bed! And neither Anne nor that red-headed hussy of a maid anywhere to be found! Where do you suppose she learned such deceit as that? From your encroaching brother, that is where, sir! *Weaseling* his way into Rosings! Pretending to *admire* Anne's pitiful attempts at drawing! Holding her *hand* in the library!" Lady Catherine's acerbic tones rose with each accusation until they reached such a thunderous volume that a curious passerby on the road stopped to listen.

Charlotte said quietly, "Your ladyship, might Miss De Bourgh and her maid not simply have walked out into the Park and lost track of time? It is, after all, a fine, sunny day."

"And taken all her clothes with them, Mrs. Collins?"

Stymied, Charlotte looked at her husband who made a gallant recover. "Lady Catherine, I assure you that, wherever Miss De Bourgh may be, she is not with my brother. He had announced his intention of visiting his friend Mr. Buseby before ever he met Miss De Bourgh. Besides, you surely do not believe an attachment could have been formed in such a short period of time?"

"We shall see," Lady Catherine announced in forbidding accents. "With such a Captain Sharp as your brother has shown himself to be, I shouldn't wonder if an innocent like Anne was taken in! Why, they may be halfway to the Border by now while we stand here idly! Put on your coat and get into the coach. You shall take us to this . . . this Mr. *Buseby's* house."

Charlotte had to remove the cornstalks from her husband's frenzied grasp before he shrugged hastily into his coat. As the coach pulled away, she could hear his voice earnestly assuring Lady Catherine that no Collins could be so lacking in gratitude for the many favours she had showered upon the family as to raise his eyes to Miss De Bourgh.

At one in the afternoon, the London coach stopped for the passengers to refresh themselves at a small inn called the Royal Garter. Anonymity had not been difficult for Anne to achieve, for only two other passengers rode on the inside of the coach, and one of those snored vigorously throughout the morning hours. Dulcie, wide awake and in fine spirits, entertained the other, a thin, bespectacled young man with shirt points so alarmingly high that he had to turn his entire body to converse with her.

Behind the cover of her hood and a blanket pulled up to her chin, Anne also pretended to sleep, although she was actually enjoying the story Dulcie was embroidering for the enchanted Mr. Hatwell. By the time the coach entered the inn yard, she and Dulcie had acquired a wealthy farming father, a sadly deceased mother, one brother in the army and one in holy orders, and a sister looking forward to the birth of her first child somewhere in Southwark. Mr. Hatwell exhibited a lively interest in the details of Oscar's meteoric rise to sergeant, Percival's likely move to a more lucrative parish upon its incumbent's demise, and the more unpleasant details of dear Sophronia's confinement. Anne could see that he was rapidly working up the courage to ask to call upon them once they had all reached London, and she felt a good deal of sympathy for the young man, not only for the heartbreak likely to ensue from Dulcie's enthusiastic deception, but also for the sad ache he was likely to have in his neck by journey's end.

Dulcie shot Anne a warning look as they disembarked, and Anne suddenly realized the shrewdness of her strategy. No one at the Royal Garter would have cause to remember two girls traveling together. She remained seated as Mr. Hatwell tenderly helped Dulcie descend. He paused to throw a doubtful look in her direction, and Anne heard Dulcie murmur confidentially in his ear, "Don't pay Hannah no mind. She be a little touched, ye might say, sir. If ye offer her your arm, she'd be like to scream the place down." Mr. Hatwell cast a worried glance over his shoulder and quickened his step. "She'll come in her own good time, an' if not I'll fetch her out a bite."

She towed Mr. Hatwell determinedly away, followed shortly by the fat somnolent gentleman who, suddenly awakening with a wheezing grunt, heaved himself out of the coach, taking no notice at all of its remaining occupant.

When the guard looked inquiringly into the coach, Anne accepted his help to descend and then walked down the side path by the inn. Her early morning experience at the Blue Heron had taught her where the necessary would be.

As she picked her way around the back garden to the little wooden structure located coyly behind a tall hedge, Anne wondered, as she had many times in the last six hours, about the reactions to her flight at Rosings. For all her determination not to be forced into marriage with a man she found odious, she could not but regret the worry her mother would certainly feel. But as she resolved to drink only a sip of tea during this stop, her mind was not upon the inhabitants of Rosings or the probable furor she had caused there; she was wondering what Lieutenant Philip Collins was doing at that moment.

Had Anne but known it, she was the topic of conversation between Oliver Buseby and Philip Collins at that very moment. Having slept soundly for two hours, Collins had arisen to join his friend, who was magnificently arrayed in a burgundy dressing gown with velvet facings, in either a belated breakfast or an early luncheon, depending on how one wished to regard it. Supplied by the evangelical Mrs. Ruddy with a lavish spread including half a ham, a lordly sirloin of beef, crisply fried trout, and a vast array of side dishes, their hunger was soon assuaged.

"And so, dear boy, what the plot boils down to is this," Buseby proclaimed in a magisterial manner. "You have landed yourself in the suds because of a pretty face."

"I suppose her face is well enough, but it didn't figure it my actions, Oliver. Damn it, you could not have left a delicately bred young lady to be mauled by a wrong'un like Daviott, could you?"

Buseby thoughtfully considered another slice of toast. "Don't try to gammon me, Philip. Well enough, you say? A

111

man don't risk getting mixed up in the affairs of a runaway heiress *and* being held to account by her fire-breathing mama for the sake of a face that's *well enough*." He waved his fork at his friend. "Now tell me the whole. First, describe Miss Anne to me."

Collins paused to think for a moment. "That's no easy task. She is quite out of the common way. The first time I saw her she was sitting in an orchard with her feet tucked beneath her and the sun shining all around. I have never seen anyone so intent upon a task. She was drawing flowers which she called fairycaps, and I recall thinking that a most appropriate name for them. She is . . . she is rather small, I suppose, though not undergrown. Fairy-like is the word that occurred to me then, and it describes her very well. Even better--do you know the Irish term *fey*, Oliver?"

Looking rather more serious, his friend nodded.

"Fey is the word I'd choose to describe her. She has blonde hair, very long. Not *brassy* blonde--but not a tow-head either. Silver, I suppose you'd say. Her eyes are silvery as well. They are that very clear, crystal grey that have such depth one never seems to see to the bottom of them. And--"

Collins looked up at that moment and broke off as he met his friend's eyes.

Buseby carefully bit into his toast and chewed it slowly as he reflected on the black-eyed beauty who had done her best to ensnare Collins in Naples, the lavishly endowed Irish widow who had cast out lures in vain, and the chestnut-haired grand-daughter of an influential admiral, who had pursued the lieutenant to the point that he had retreated from London on a series of visits to his widely-scattered family. Then he said mildly, "I will refrain from inquiring how you know the length of her hair, dear boy."

"Good!" Collins snapped.

"However, I will ask you if the phrase *parson's mousetrap* conveys anything to you?"

His friend's laugh held no amusement. "You are faint

and far off there. No chance of such a thing even if she would look at me."

"No chance?" Buseby raised his brows in puzzlement. "Not as if your pockets were to let, Philip. If you had only your prize money to depend upon, the dibs might not be in tune. But surely your prospects from old Trevalyn make you an eligible *parti* for most young ladies?"

Collins' eyes met his friend in a long, direct look. "She will one day have nine thousand a year, Oliver."

"Good God! Nine thousand a year!" Buseby sat up straight in his chair and tossed the remains of the toast aside. "I can only say that I hope the dragon soon presents itself for slaying. You must lose no time in pursuing your fairy to Derbyshire!"

Buseby's wish was granted by mid-afternoon. He and Collins were in the stable, directing the stripling from the farm next door in the chores left undone in the wake of the absent stableman, when a traveling carriage swept up to the front gate.

Buseby murmured softly, "Let me, dear boy," and strolled outside to watch the occupants of the coach descend. He saw an anxious-looking man in a clerical collar and black coat leap out, followed by a stout, dyspeptic-looking younger gentleman with a flourishing mustache. Both of them turned to aid the descent of a well-upholstered lady in a bottle-green twilled traveling dress and enormous green bonnet with three purple plumes.

When the lady glared accusingly at him, Buseby strolled forward, executed an elegant bow, and murmured, "Good afternoon?" on a questioning note.

Lady Catherine had at first taken him for a servant, but a glance at his tightly-fitting coat of blue superfine and faultlessly tied cravat informed her that her prey was before her. "Mr. Buseby?" she demanded in a tone of angry accusation.

"As you see. I fear, however, that you have the

advantage of me, ma'am."

"I am Lady Catherine de Bourgh! I will trouble you only long enough to ascertain--"

At that moment, Collins emerged from the stable, staring at the three newcomers in patent amazement.

"William? Lady Catherine? What in thun--that is, what are you doing here? Good lord, has something happened to Mama? To Charlotte?"

"I knew you would be here, Philip," gasped Mr. Collins, sagging to the mounting block in his relief. "I *assured* Her Ladyship that you would be here!"

As Collins gazed at his brother, clearly bewildered by his answer, Lady Catherine advanced upon him. "No, Lieutenant Collins, nothing has happened to either of them. However, something most definitely has happened to my daughter!" As she spoke, Sir Crawford stepped belligerently forward. "*Where is she?*"

After several moments of silence pregnant with tension, Collins spoke in the tone of one trying to calm a dangerous lunatic. "I think you had all better come inside and tell me what has happened. For you know--I haven't the faintest notion why you're here."

Some of the steam seemed to seep out of Sir Crawford, while Mr. Collins appeared likely to burst into tears of relief at any moment. Only Lady Catherine's flag remained at full mast. "Don't expect to hoax me with your pack of lies, Lieutenant Collins! My daughter has vanished. She has *vanished*, I say. She disappeared at some hour before morning and I know of no one else who would have helped her to flee the protection of her family!"

"That is indeed distressing news, your ladyship," Collins said softly, "for I can only assure you that Miss De Bourgh is not in my company. You are welcome to inquire of my friend Buseby when I arrived here."

Three pairs of eyes swung in Buseby's direction. Leaning negligently against the gate, he carefully removed a horse hair from his coat sleeve and murmured, "Really, this grows more and more interesting. The lieutenant arrived some time yesterday evening. I feel sure I would have noticed if he had been accompanied by a young lady. We played cards late, Collins had the devil's own luck, and we both retired to bed, he a richer man and I, alas, a poorer."

Lady Catherine raised her parasol, and for a moment seemed likely to bring it down across Buseby's elegant head. "You--you *fribble*! I will not be taken in by some Banbury story you and that libertine have concocted! She must be here!"

Buseby sighed wearily. "Madam, if my word is insufficient, you are more than welcome to search the house. Or you may inquire of my servants as to my friend's solitary state when he arrived."

Lieutenant Collins stepped forward. "Lady Catherine, I assure you that my acquaintance with Miss De Bourgh is very slight. We hardly spoke of more than her drawings. Do you not think it likely that she has received help from some family member if she has left home? Some relative of yours perhaps?" He paused for a moment before asking quietly. "Or of her father's?"

Lady Catherine's mouth, which had opened to issue an instant denial of this possibility, closed with a snap as her eyes narrowed and a red tide surged once again up her neck and face. "She would not. She would not *dare*!"

"Who would not?" Sir Crawford demanded.

"Sir Lewis' sister, Lady Haveloch! I will not have her in my house! The only reason that Anne is occasionally permitted to see her is that it was her dear father's express wish. Indeed, I have not spoken to *that woman* these fifteen years. She would not dare to take Anne into her house!"

"Ah yes," Collins met Lady Catherine's gaze blandly, thinking that he had never seen a fish rise so readily to the bait. "I seem to recall Miss De Bourgh's mentioning to me that her Aunt Elinor would be traveling home past Rosings Park

quite soon. Is that Lady Haveloch's Christian name? I
believe your daughter had received that intelligence from a
letter--but my memory could be in error. It is lamentably poor
upon occasion." He paused for a moment of thought. "I must
say that Miss De Bourgh did not seem to hold her aunt in the . .
.ah . . aversion which you seem to feel, ma'am."

Fifteen minutes later the coach was on its way, post-
haste, to Haveloch Hall in Sussex. Lieutenant Collins, having
gratefully accepted his friend's offer of a sporting curricle, was
traveling back to Hunsford in the farm wagon of which he was
heartily tired. Beside him sat his exhausted brother, for once
too enervated to speak. Collins was grateful for the respite as
he made his plans. He would take his leave of Charlotte, return
to the lodge with Buseby in the curricle and leave his friend
there, and with any luck, reach London in time to see Anne
safely off to Pemberley.

◆ ❖ ◆

Chapter 10

By the time Anne reached London, she appreciated the luxury of the De Bourgh traveling chaise as she never had before. Four other passengers had entered the coach at the Royal Garter. Seeing them when she entered the hostelry, she had barely taken the time to consume some bread and cheese and a bare half cup of tea before scurrying back outside to claim her corner seat. The tedious journey had been made more so by constant buffetings from rain and wind that only abated as they entered the crowded thoroughfares of London.

When she and Dulcie stepped stiffly out into the yard of the St. George and Dragon, they huddled together against the side of the coach until the guard deposited their valises briskly at their feet. Looking about her, Anne thought the inn yard was the busiest place she had ever seen. Vehicles of wildly varying descriptions were arriving, being loaded, disgorging passengers, and leaving, while horses were led through knots of people, all of whom seemed to the bewildered girl to be conversing at the tops of their lungs.

Feeling Dulcie tugging at her sleeve, Anne turned. "Mr. Hatwell said as how we'd need a hackney coach, Miss." Roguishly, she rolled her eyes. "Seeing as how Sophronia's husband bain't free to meet us an' all. He said the cab stand be on the street behind this yard."

"Very well," Anne replied, trying to inject all the confidence she could into her voice. "Let's go at once." Her tired legs were trembling from weariness, and she had eaten no more than a few mouthfuls of food in forty-eight hours. On her thigh, the bruise incurred in her flight from Sir Crawford had begun to throb painfully from being pressed against the unyielding side of the coach by her efforts to withdraw from the fat man seated beside her. Clenching her teeth, she lifted the valise with both hands and trudged after Dulcie, dodging ostlers and hurrying passengers and skirting vehicles as she walked.

As the two exhausted girls rounded the gatepost marking the inn yard's entrance, an empty hack rattling past them on the street pulled up. "Mayhap sech as ye two ladies needin' a 'ack?" the driver inquired, tipping his hat politely.

"Oh yes, that we be," Dulcie exclaimed joyfully. "C'mon, Mi--Hannah." Gratefully, Anne set the valise down in the mud and extracted a sheet of paper from her reticule.

"Do you know the location of Batson's Coaching Line, sir?"

"Why, this'll likely be short shrift for me, missy." The driver favoured her with a gap-toothed grin. "Batson's be only a matter o' two streets o'er."

Anne smiled back at him, liking his merry eyes. "We only need to stop there long enough to be placed upon tomorrow's bill. Then we wish to go to the Hotel Montclair. Can you wait for us?"

"Easy as lookin' at ye ladies, miss." He sent a twinkling look of appreciation in Dulcie's direction. "And though it be Ben 'Edrick as sez it, 'at be very easy indeed."

A hitch in their plans occurred at Batson's, for the scheduled stage to Derbyshire had been canceled for the morrow, due to damage inflicted in an accident caused by an inebriated young man in a tilbury who had tried to pass on a blind corner.

Anne listened to a graphic description of the accident as she cudgeled her tired brain. *Should we stay in London another day or try to discover a different coaching line?* she wondered frantically. Her decision was finally made for her by her aching leg which threatened to give out altogether. She reserved an inside seat for herself and Dulcie in a coach departing at six in the morning on the day after tomorrow,

118

tucked the boarding passes carefully inside her reticule, and departed for the quiet hotel Lieutenant Collins had recommended, with the conviction that both she and Dulcie were quite likely to sleep the morrow through.

The next day saw Anne in a state of mind more conducive to seeing something of the Metropolis, even if that endeavour encompassed nothing more than window-shopping on the streets adjacent to the hotel. On the preceding evening, she and Dulcie had devoured an early dinner consisting of a hearty mutton stew followed by apple cobbler. It had been the cheapest fare on the menu, so after due deliberation, Anne had felt justified in paying six pence for the use of a large canvas bath and the services of a man-of-all-work to convey it and several buckets of water to their room where both she and Dulcie had luxuriated in hot baths, taking turns washing each other's hair. The bath had also had the happy effect of lessening the pain in Anne's sore leg.

Feeling once again clean and extremely grateful to be out of the swaying coach, Anne had snuggled into bed beside a protesting Dulcie, who had suggested that she make use of the lumpy armchair and footstool beside their modest fireplace.

"How foolish," Anne had muttered sleepily. "You could fit us two and Mrs. Harpress all into this bed with room to spare." They both giggled at the thought of sharing the bed with Rosings' amply endowed cook.

Anne had lain listening to the quiet susurration of Dulcie's snores, finding them a happy conclusion to the long day, for she drifted off to sleep remembering the last occasion upon which she had smiled at the sound. The memory led to the pleasurable consideration of both the kisses she and the lieutenant had shared and from thence to speculation about the lieutenant's present whereabouts, which in turn had led to deep, dreamless sleep.

Now with the sun fairly blazing through their single window, accompanied by the sounds of London, which penetrated even this quiet street, Anne allowed Dulcie to dress her in the one good outfit she had brought, a walking dress of dark sapphire grosgrain, complemented by a cream chip bonnet with sapphire ribbons. She had chosen both the pattern and the material herself as a gift from her aunt, and it flattered her slender figure to a far greater degree than that part of her wardrobe dictated by her mother's tastes. With the addition of a thin cream pelisse and little leather half-boots, Anne regarded her appearance in the mirror with approval, marred by only the faintest qualm. On this quiet, out-of-the-way street, surely the danger of meeting one of the few people who would recognize Anne de Bourgh was remote.

Fortified by tea, toasted muffins, and blackberry jam which Dulcie declared to be so far inferior to the jam of Rosings as to be unrecognizable as the same comestible, the girls sallied forth to conquer, if not London, at least a single street of that Metropolis.

An hour later they had not progressed more than fifty yards down the street, for Temptation had beckoned to each of them in different guises. Anne had spent forty minutes in a large, dusty used book store with two long shelves devoted entirely to books of engravings. Seating herself in a decrepit armchair, thoughtfully pushed into a space between two shelves, she had hungrily turned the pages in volume after volume, wishing with all her heart that she was already in possession of the small sum left her by her father. Could she but have bought the book of engravings of nautical scenes, she would have left the shop happy. Although its creator wasn't the lieutenant's comrade Mr. Reese, just holding the volume containing the coloured plates of majestic ships and ocean scenes made Anne feel closer to her friend.

Dulcie had at first hovered near her, but she was soon convinced that that her mistress stood in little need of her chaperonage as the store boasted few patrons at this early hour. Dulcie first allowed herself to drift away to peer out the single window onto the street; then she decided that no harm could come from discovering what stores awaited them further down their side of the street. Total dereliction of duty followed her discovery of the Ladies' Bazaar of Sundry Necessities and Luxuries, an establishment with four enormous plate windows displaying all manner of trimmings and fripperies, and holding pride of place on the next corner. Pausing only to rush back to the book store to inform her mistress of her whereabouts, Dulcie flung herself into the mass of ladies rifling feminine wares which she heard one of them characterize as *dagger-cheap*.

Left to herself, Anne became conscious of her surroundings only when she was addressed by a willowy youth attired in a longtailed coat, pantaloons of a delicate pale blue, and a neckcloth of gargantuan size.

"Good morning, miss," he drawled, startling Anne as he removed his beaver hat and bowed deeply.

"I do not think we are acquainted, sir," she replied in a civil but cool tone.

"I am only too aware of that sad fact," the unknown young man observed languidly. "But we could remedy that unhappy state of affairs if you will but consent to share a cup of tea with me. There is a small shop only next door where we could pursue our acquaintance. And I will be deeply honoured if you will allow me to add your book to the selection I am about to purchase."

"Certainly not," she snapped and stood, reluctantly replacing *Scenes from the Quarterdeck* on its shelf.

Without looking at him again, Anne hurried out of the shop and walked rapidly to the Ladies' Bazaar, hoping the set-down she had given her impudent admirer might restrain him from annoying single ladies in the future.

She found Dulcie jostling for place at a table displaying on its ample width every imaginable hue of green ribbon. She was determined to purchase a spool from the section of goods whose sign informed the public that they were shockingly reduced in price, but there her decisive powers had wilted. How could one decide between a Pomona green satin which would in all likelihood be of little practical use, but was mouth-wateringly soft to the touch, a spool of apple green with twilled edges which would refurbish her best bonnet to a treat, and a length of thin emerald green velvet which could not but be indispensable once winter was upon them? She and her mistress debated the merits of each until eventually Dulcie carried away the apple green and Anne the velvet, with the private intention of bestowing it upon Dulcie when they reached Pemberley.

Their next dilemma presented itself when they walked out the door onto the corner of the street. They could go left toward what seemed to be a quieter area or cross the street being industriously swept by an urchin in a red yarn cap. Anne went left for no more reason that to avoid giving a penny of their small hoard to the sweep, but she realized her mistake in no more than half a block. Both of the businesses they passed were still tightly shuttered. More than halfway down the block, they passed an empty lot and Anne paused on the verge of re-turning, when Dulcie pointed out that another corner was nearer and they could simple turn left again onto what looked to be a busier thoroughfare. They were approaching what appeared to be yet a third deserted establishment, enclosed in decorous black wrought iron and designated only by the name "Maxton's" on a discreet signboard, when three fashionably dressed men stepped into the street, turned in their direction, and stopped.

One of them, Anne saw at a glance, was the thin dandified young man from the book shop. In one hand he still carried *The Gentleman's Guide to Boxing*. On his left was another youth, quite as tall but considerably heavier and dressed in more somber hues, with a florid face marked by either smallpox or a very bad case of acne. His flat black eyes went at once to Dulcie and raked her up and down with an expression of lewd assessment. Anne's acquaintance from the book store grasped the arm of the third man, older, blond and handsome, who at once lifted a quizzing glass to his eye and languidly examined both two girls.

"This is the blonde Venus I described to you, Fulham. A pocket Venus to be sure, but a little goddess all the same, is she not?"

"Indeed," drawled the other, lowering his glass. "Accompanied--*deliciously* accompanied--by an attendant nymph."

"Fiend take it, there should be another. One of us will find our luck out today," the burly one remarked with a guffaw. "Fulham, I hope for once 'tis you."

Anne instantly withdrew her eyes from the older man's intent gaze and whispered urgently to Dulcie, "Back! Hurry!" But the girls had taken no more than two steps in the direction from which they had come when Anne felt a hand upon her sleeve. She stared incredulously up into the face of the blond man whom her recent admirer had called Fulham and jerked her arm away as Dulcie gasped a warning. Anne glared furiously, attempting to freeze him with her look. He only chuckled and reached out to cup her chin in his hand. "What an unexpected bonus for an early lesson at Maxton's. What do you say, my golden-haired goddess? Shall we deepen our acquaintance while your little friend entertains my companions?" His hand tightened cruelly on Anne's chin as she attempted to jerk it away, and his grip on her arm turned to iron. "I prefer more delicate ware myself."

"Well, I've no objection to the little red-headed game-pullet, but I'm damned if I'll share her with Draycott," objected the dark-haired ruffian.

Anne suddenly realized that a carriage had stopped in the street beside them. Thinking at first that a savior had arrived, she realized to her horror that it belonged to the three men who had accosted them. Unable to believe that danger had overtaken them so quickly on a public street in London, she felt herself being drawn toward the carriage by a hand placed familiarly just beneath the curve of her breast.

"No!" she cried out frantically. She lifted her free hand to beat against her attacker's chest. Looking amused, he released his grasp on her side to capture the hand that was striking ineffectual blows at him. She heard her reticule strike the pavement as it fell. Glancing down, she saw the spool of emerald ribbon tip from it to unspool in the muddy puddle where it fell. An arm came around her like an iron band, easily immobilizing both hers, and she felt herself lifted toward the waiting carriage.

Behind her, Dulcie screamed shrilly, the willowy youth cursed and his companion uttered a loud, braying laugh. "Damn the wench, she has a scream like a siren and a left like Gentleman Jim's. For God's sake, Draycott, stop moaning and take her other arm. Or let us go and share the other one with Fulham! This is no hour for a kick-up in the streets!"

Anne heard no more, for suddenly the man against whom she struggled seemed to be wrenched away from her as if by magic. She stumbled when he loosed her arm, breaking her fall with one hand. Hearing his body crash heavily to the pavement, she was trying to raise herself from the curbside when she felt an arm come around her shoulders once again. Thinking her assailant had risen, Anne hastily jerked off her glove, ready this time to claw his face. Her hand had already reached his cheek by the time she realized she was looking up into the face of Philip Collins.

Collins had reached Batson's shortly before six, having driven the horses at their top speed in his attempt to arrive in time to reassure Anne before she and Dulcie left London. Upon hearing of the mishap to the Derbyshire coach, he discovered, by the simple expedient of pretending to be their brother, that the girls had placed their name upon the bill for the following day.

His next stop had been the Montclair where he was assured of the residence of the Misses Rachel and Hannah

Ackers. Feeling that he had time to catch a hundred winks, he secured a bed, leaving a note for Miss Hannah informing her that her brother Philip had arrived.

It was ten by the time he rolled over and opened his eyes. Blinking, he sat up, wondering if Anne had been too exhausted by the last two days to leave her room.

A look at his face in the mirror was enough to make him summon the boots for shaving water, and it was half past by the time he inquired at the desk for his sisters. A look of ludicrous dismay appeared on the face of the rusty-suited keeper of the desk.

"Sir, sir, I do most profoundly offer my apologies," he cried fussily, wringing his long thin hands in agitation. "We had a disturbance this morning--a lady was taken ill, and a doctor had to be summoned. I fear that in the hubbub, I forgot your note. The two young ladies left more than an hour ago."

Seeing Collins' eyebrows knitting into a frown, he added hastily, "But they was only going shopping, sir. I heard one of them tell her sister as they would go no further than the end of this street. No doubt you will easily catch them up."

"I hope so," the lieutenant answered curtly, already on his way out the door.

Unsure which way to turn from the hotel doorway, he first went right, passing in succession a haberdashery, a lamp store, and a seller of second-hand furniture. Feeling these establishments held few lures for two young ladies, he retraced his steps and went left instead.

He discovered almost at once that Anne had lingered in the used book shop and knew himself upon the right track, for the owner remembered the blonde young lady who had lingered so long over one particular book.

"Certain, I was, she'd buy that particular volume, and it's been a bit on our shelves, I don't mind to say," the stout proprietor told him regretfully. "But left without it, she did."

Collins glanced at the book in question, saw its subject, and surprised his informant with a pleased smile. "I'll take it," he said quickly. "Wrap it for me, if you'd be so kind, and I'll be back for it directly."

Trying to subdue his mounting eagerness to see Anne with a cold mental dousing of common sense, he stopped to glance inside any likely business; eventually he made his way into the Bazaar. That reconnaissance took longer, for the narrow aisles were crowded with ladies, many of whom cast interested glances at the gentleman glancing down each aisle, but eventually he decided that Anne and Dulcie were not among its beribboned shoppers.

He had just emerged with considerable gratitude from the Bazaar's perfumed interior when his attention was attracted by a cry from the side street to his left. Hurrying to the corner, he looked in the direction from which the sound had come and froze in incredulous horror, hardly able to believe the scene before him. Dulcie was struggling furiously between two men while Anne was being half dragged and half carried toward a chaise drawn up against the curb.

Collins reached the struggling group in seconds, flinging himself at Anne's assailant first. With the advantage of surprise on his side, he grasped the man by the back of his coat collar with one hand, brought his knotted fist down with all his strength upon the forearm of the hand gripping Anne's arm, and jerked her attacker away. As the man staggered, trying to regain his footing, Collins stepped forward and delivered an uppercut to his jaw that sent him toppling backwards onto the pavement where his head struck the curb with a resounding thud.

The lieutenant saw at a glance that Anne was rising, having managed to break her fall with her hands. He paused only a second to assure himself that she was uninjured. Setting her on her feet, he gave her a gentle push back toward the street from whence they had come. "Run back to the store," he ordered sharply.

Without waiting to see if she obeyed, he turned to Dulcie and discovered that her attackers had, at least

126

momentarily, abandoned her as they moved toward him. The little red-haired maid stood with her back against a railing, hands pressed to a face so piteously white that her freckles stood out sharply. The willowy dandy he dismissed at a glance, centering his attention on his more formidable companion. In his eyes, Collins read pleasure at the prospect of a brawl and a look of steady appraisal that he knew from experience betokened a seasoned fighter. His erstwhile opponent was attempting to rise; Collins had no doubt of his ability to handle three gentlemen of the *ton*, but clearly, if Anne and Dulcie were to be removed before such a scene ensued as would draw much unwelcome attention, he must act quickly.

Taking a step backward, he whirled, knowing he must dispatch Anne's attacker before dealing with the greater threat. The toe of his boot met the blond man's chin in a crushing blow which Collins calculated would to send him to grass for the duration of the fight.

He heard both girls scream a warning and wheeled to see the thick-set man moving swiftly toward him, fists held in readiness. Instantly, Collins whipped off his hat and flung it straight into the other's face. Its stiffly curled brim struck him full across his left eye. Instinctively, his hands flew to his face. With lightning speed, Collins moved in to close range, buried a fist in what he judged to be a somewhat soft belly, and followed it with a punishing left which set the burly young man back on his heels. His opponent must have had some ring experience, perhaps in the establishment behind them, Collins thought, for he recovered and launched himself forward in a valiant attempt to mill Collins down. Stepping coolly aside, Collins grasped him by one arm and used his own momentum to heave him headfirst into the black iron railings with all his strength. He left the big man no time to recover as he jerked his body around in a half circle and drove the toe of one boot into his groin. When he doubled over with a howl of agony, the lieutenant finished him off with the same uppercut that had leveled his friend.

Turning to deal with the third in the group, Collins nearly laughed, for the foppish youth was beating a swift retreat to the waiting chaise, whose driver was gaping at them all in astonishment.

"Here," he called after the dandy vanishing into the coach, "you've left your book--and I judge that you and your friends have more need of it than I." Picking up *The Gentleman's Guide to Boxing*, which had ended on the sidewalk in the fray, he flung it through the coach door just before it was slammed shut.

Although the entire altercation had taken less than five minutes, Collins saw that a small crowd was beginning to gather. After retrieving his hat, he was moving to collect Dulcie and hurry her away when he realized that Anne had not followed his instruction to run to safety.

She was standing no more than five feet away, clutching her retrieved reticule, and she held out a small hand with its bloody palm uppermost as he approached. Grey eyes met darker grey as she smiled and whispered tremulously, "Good morning, Lieutenant. You seem to make a habit of rescuing maidens in distress."

Chapter 11

By the time Collins had assisted the two girls back to the Montclair, the after-effects of their attack had begun to set in. Anne was so white that even her lips were bloodless while Dulcie was fighting a losing battle with hiccupping sobs.

"Show us to a private parlor," he ordered the septuagenarian in the rusty suit, and in short order they found them-selves seated before a blazing fire with tea and brandy on the side table.

"Here, both of you need more than tea at present. You've had a considerable shock." He poured a measure of brandy into two glasses and set them before the girls, receiving the satisfaction of seeing, as Anne sipped, faint color begin to seep back into her face. Dulcie downed hers at a gulp and nearly choked as a fit of coughing competed with sobs to reduce her to wheezing gasps.

"You should approach a ball o' fire with a little more respect, Dulcie," he adjured her with a grin. Leaving her to re-gain her breath, he turned back to Anne. "Miss Anne, should I summon a doctor? Are you injured?"

Seeing his eyes directed toward the blood on her palm, she quickly shook her head. "No indeed, Lieutenant, it is no more than a scratch. It only wants washing. As soon as Dulcie is better, we will go upstairs to cleanse it."

Immediately he shook his head. "There'll be no fire in your room, and you are chilled."

"It is true that it was not so warm outside as the sunshine led us to believe."

"I shall be back directly." He reappeared in a matter of ten minutes or so with a maid bearing a basin of water and a roll of gauze. Directing her to put it on the table, he smiled at Anne. "I gave orders for a fire to be lit in your room. Will you trust me with your hand, Miss Anne? I was used to help the ship's surgeon on occasion, you know, and I became quite deedy at patching up the odd injury."

"Oh no! No, sir!" Dulcie hiccupped, rousing herself and standing, with the smear of tears still across her face. "I be quite able to tend Miss Anne!"

Anne smiled at her. "No, Dulcie, my dear. You have had as bad a shock as I. Why do you not go upstairs to mend matters a little?" She directed a significant look at Dulcie's hair, which had fallen down her shoulders on one side and at a long rip in the material of the fabric under her arm.

"Oh my!" she cried, suddenly realizing the appearance she presented. "Oh, I do look a sight."

"Stop at the desk and direct the clerk to send up some hot water and towels and a fresh pot of tea, Dulcie. You need not hurry."

"Take another ball o' fire before you go, if you like," Collins offered with no more than the faintest of smiles. "Your room should be warming by now."

"No, I thank you kindly sir, but I doubt but I could climb the steps if I'd another."

When she had gone, Collins seated himself nearer Anne and took the hand she unhesitatingly extended. Examining her palm, he saw that the scrape was deeper than she had implied, with gravel embedded in two places.

As he held her hand, a small pool of blood formed in her palm and his mouth tightened into an angry line. "If I thought there was any chance of those loose screws being still on the street or in Maxton's, I should return once I have you set to rights, Miss Anne. For the fright they gave you, they got off far too easily."

"Indeed, Lieutenant, the fate of at least two of them did not appear in the least easy to me! Even the one who escaped unscathed is likely to go in fear for days."

"The Bartholomew baby? By now he's likely under his bed with his manservant on guard with a blunderbuss." Rolling back Anne's sleeve, he regarded her small palm intently before removing from his pocket a small pen knife, which he proceeded to cleanse thoroughly.

"My goodness," Anne remarked in some trepidation. "You did mean you had become a surgeon's assistant! I trust I shall be able to sustain the surgery with fortitude."

"It will be a very minor operation," he assured her. Holding her wrist firmly on the table, he carefully lifted the gravels from her palm with the tip of the blade. As blood seeped from the cuts, he looked up to find her watching him unflinchingly. "I make you my compliments, ma'am. I assure you my comrades aboard ship make far more fuss for far less cause."

Immersing her hand in the water, he gently cleaned the bloody scrape. "This will sting a trifle," he warned before taking up the bottle of brandy and pouring a stream of brown liquid across her palm into the basin.

Hearing her sharp indrawn breath, he laid her wrist across the towel with his own strong brown hand cupped underneath. "Let it dry and I'll take the precaution of wrapping it in gauze to keep out the dirt. Then the 'surgery' will be all over--and not a whimper. Nor any vapours in the street, thank God. I could not have gotten you both back here without drawing a good bit of attention if you had given way. Pluck to the backbone, Miss Anne."

"Some pluck I may own to, but very little common sense, I fear. You must have wondered at me for venturing into the streets, Lieutenant Collins. I have been very seldom in London, and Mama was always used to insist that I never go out unless I was accompanied by a footman. I thought it foolishly pretentious, but I must admit her to have been justified. I never would have believed we could run into danger at such an hour with so many people about."

Collins squeezed her hand gently and reluctantly released it as he folded a bandage to press into her palm before wrapping it in gauze. "Don't blame yourself. It was no more than a piece of bad luck, Miss Anne. Had you stayed on the street outside or almost any of the others near it, you'd have been perfectly safe. A maid is enough of a safeguard in an area such as this."

"Then why . . .?"

"Did you notice the sign on the building you were passing?"

Anne knit her brow. "Maxwell's?"

"Maxton's. It's famous in some circles--or perhaps *infamous* would be a better word. A certain set of gentlemen, if one names them by station and not by character, are known to frequent it." He hesitated before continuing. "Perhaps it would be best if I leave my explanation at that. Many of its habitués are not men with whom even a lady is safe--and to give credit to three very ugly customers, I doubt they took the two of you for ladies."

Anne looked confused. "Because . . . ?

"Maxton's is not a place where any lady would be seen." He saw her distress. "But let us say no more about it. You made a very understandable mistake and it's over, with not much harm done. I shall be paying a call there myself in the near future, but not for the same reason as my recent sparring partners."

Anne's eyes flew to his face and read his purpose there. "Sir, I pray that you do not! As you said, no true harm was done."

"Except the harm of frightening a lady and offering her insult. Of ruining what should have been a carefree day for her. Of teaching her to be frightened of the streets of London and of men whose station in society should of itself be a protection to a lady and not a threat." For a moment such a fierce light burned in her companion's eyes that Anne realized she was seeing how he might look as he went into battle. Then, as he saw her expression, it faded and a smile once more creased his tanned cheeks. "Well, perhaps not spoiling all of it. Do you feel equal to going upstairs to check on Dulcie? The day is yet young, and I propose to escort you two wherever you choose to go, if you're not too undone by what has occurred to venture out again."

"I am quite recovered," Anne responded, standing at once. "I promise we shall not keep you kicking your heels for many minutes." She walked to the door and then paused, with her hand on the porcelain knob. Turning, she met the lieutenant's eyes. He thought she looked incredibly delicate, outlined against the dark wood of the door, one hand lifted to the slender white column of her throat, her eyes shining with crystal greyness.

"I know that expressions of gratitude are not something you seek, Lieutenant. But when I think where I might be at this present . . . still at Rosings knowing that my future held only Sir Crawford's attentions . . . or being carried away by that horrible man . . . Fulham or whatever his name was . . . and facing what he would have done to me . . . then I fear I must be selfish and relieve my feelings at your expense." Her eyes met his in a glance that seemed to him to create a tangible link between them, as though some precious strand of metal extended from his inmost soul to hers with a tensile strength not to be broken by the harshest storm. "I shall never forget what you have risked in order to help me . . . *me*, a stranger, to whom you owed nothing but common civility." She paused again and this time when she looked up, he saw a tear, the first she had shed throughout her entire ordeal, sparkling on her face. "You are so very kind and brave. I shall think of you with deepest gratitude until my dying hour."

Shaken, he could think of no reply. By the time he did, the door was closed behind her.

When Anne returned fifteen minutes later, she had exchanged the light pelisse for her cloak and repaired the damage to her hair. "I am afraid Dulcie will be unable to accompany us, Lieutenant. She is prone to severe headache from time to time," she looked at him with a twinkle, "and unlike those suffered by *some* persons, Dulcie's are quite real. Nothing will do when one prostrates her but several hours of absolute quiet."

"I'm sorry to hear of her indisposition, Miss Anne. I can see that a physician is called, if you feel the need."

"Oh no. There truly is nothing that helps--except solitude and silence." Anne paused and looked at him a little shyly. "Will it . . . would it be very improper of me to accept your escort alone? I do not know when I might again have a chance to visit London, and I saw very little of it when I made my come-out . . . "

Collins smiled at her, immeasurably relieved that she trusted him enough to make the request. "No doubt the *ton* would be shocked if they knew--but they won't know, will they? I fear we can't visit any fashionable locations, such as Gunter's, for instance, or any establishment where you'd be wishful to make purchases. It would be unwise to risk meeting anyone of your acquaintance."

"Oh, I've no wish to visit places I have already been and there is nothing I need to purchase. I know where I would like to go, if you will not think my request an odd one."

"My curricle is waiting outside." The lieutenant removed the cloak from her arm and wrapped it carefully about her shoulders. "You'd like to visit a place that I might think odd . . . " he mused as they walked through the hotel lobby and out into the street. "I shall hazard a guess--no one has taken you to see the Tower and you wish to be harrowed by the sight of the Green?"

Anne laughed as he assisted her carefully onto the curricle's high seat. "You are partially correct, sir. I have never seen the Tower. But it is not my first choice."

"Hmmmm." Vaulting into his seat, Collins accepted the reins from the groom he had hired. "My second guess is Westminster. You've long held a secret desire to place a flower upon Chaucer's grave!"

"The abbey, I have visited, and cannot say I wish to do so again. It is beautiful but . . . intimidating, is it not?"

"Vastly. One is oppressed by one's utter insignificance in the great pageant of history. And at this season, it's deuced cold! Well then, I have one shot left to my bow, and I feel I should aim it toward a less historical target. Let me see . . . I have it! You wish to try the maze at Hampton Court!"

Anne laughed. "Alas, your last arrow flew wide of the mark, sir. If it is not too long a journey, I would like to see the naval shipyards at Deptford."

Taking his silence for disapprobation, she looked anxiously up at him, "But if is too far . . . if it would be improper for me to venture--"

"No. Nothing could be easier. I was only surprised." The teasing note had completely left his voice as he met her eyes. "But why should you wish such a thing?"

The color rose in her face and her eyes dropped to her hands. "A whim, Lieutenant, no more. Your paintings aroused my interest. And it is not likely this opportunity will arise for me again."

That observation silenced them both, which may have been just as well, Collins thought, for he needed all his concentration to guide Buseby's spirited bays through the crowded thoroughfare of Watling Street. *And I need all my self-control to keep from hugging her,* he admitted ruefully. *With all of London to choose from, she wishes to see the shipyard. Why could she not have been a draper's daughter?*

It was Anne who broke the silence. "You have not told me if you spoke to my mother before setting out for London."

"I did indeed. She tracked me down at Buseby's lodge, just as I thought she would--accompanied by Sir Crawford and my unfortunate brother."

"Oh, poor Mr. Collins! What an awkward circumstance I have thrust him into."

"William will survive." Collins looked amused. "It's

Sir Crawford with whom we should commiserate. He looked quite distraught, poor fellow."

"I don't doubt it," his companion rejoined dryly. "Who would not repine at the prospect of losing nine thousand a year and Rosings Park? I am sure he ill at the prospect."

Collins glanced at Anne thoughtfully. "Miss Anne, I wonder if you view matters quite so clearly as you think."

"How do you mean?"

"I was present on the balcony three nights ago." He struggled to keep the edge of jealousy from his voice. "I didn't see a man with his eye fixed coldly on a future inheritance. I saw one who was shaken from a careful courtship to passion."

Anne remained silent. Unable to stop himself, Collins reached out to lightly stroke her gloved hand. "It wasn't Rosings which inspired that passion."

After a short silence, Anne said, "I wonder if Mama has yet reached Haveloch Hall?"

Tacitly accepting the change of subject, Collins replied, "If they didn't stop long on the way, I imagine they have. What do you think your aunt's reaction will be to your mother's arrival?"

"I am not sure Aunt Elinor will be even at home. If she is, I wonder if she will admit Mama to the house. They do not speak, you know, even if they encounter each other at some social function. It is quite awkward, for I am very fond of her. I am allowed to call upon her when we are in town because my papa wished me to know her." She paused. "By this time, Povey will have 'discovered' the letter I left and sent it after Mama. I hope . . . I hope she is not terribly worried!"

"She should receive it about the time you arrive at Pemberley." Seeing Anne's frown, he said lightly, "But let us not spoil the day. I can't but think your mother is receiving her just deserts, Miss Anne. To suggest a marriage for the benefit of one's child lies within the bounds of parental prerogative, even to promote one--but no parent, however sure they are of the soundness of their decision, should force a marriage upon that child." He smiled down into his companion's troubled countenance. "And you will very soon reach a safe haven."

Doubts plagued Anne but she smiled sunnily up at him, and this time she was the one to reach out and lightly brush his sleeve with her fingertips. "I feel safe enough now, Lieutenant. And as usual, you are quite right. Let us speak of other things. Tell me what I may expect to see at Deptford."

Two hours later Collins had shown Anne the purported location of the knighting of Sir Francis Drake by Queen Elizabeth, telling her the story from the perspective of a seaman as she listened with shining eyes. They had walked past the house where the playwright Christopher Marlowe was killed and eaten a late luncheon in a tavern where Collins had warned her not to remove her cloak to reveal the fashionable walking dress she wore beneath it. Anne had devoured the seafood chowder, fried flounder, and buttery batter bread ravenously, putting out her tongue and refusing to be abashed when her companion laughed at her appetite.

Now, walking down the long docks supported by his arm, Anne was gazing raptly at the great ships, imagining the joys and privations of living upon one for months on end when Collins suddenly halted.

"Ah, here we are," he said softly. Following the direction of his intent eyes, Anne saw merely another tall ship, its masts brave against the brilliant blue sky, and looked at him inquiringly. "Miss De Bourgh, may I present to you His Majesty's Ship . . . the *Cormorant*."

"Oh! Oh, Lieutenant Collins, you did not tell me that *your* ship was docked here." Collins could not but smile as Anne bobbed up and down on tiptoe in her excitement. "Oh, let us move closer! I wish to see her closer!"

"I trust you'll be able to see her quite a bit closer. It's nearly time for work to cease for the day. I can probably arrange for us to tour her briefly--if the notion suits you, Miss Anne?"

"If it suits me? You must surely know there is nothing I would like better!" Excited, Anne clutched his arm; looking down into her face, he thought he would never forget her aspect at that moment. Her cheeks were flushed with excitement, the brisk wind blew stands of silvery hair across her face, and her eyes glowed with happy anticipation. Even if some acquaintance of Anne de Bourgh's saw her now, he wondered if she would be recognized with no trace of Rosings' languid heiress remaining.

He thought of other women he had known, of days he had spent with them--and of nights. Some of them were more beautiful by society's standards than Anne, and many of them had exerted every charm to please him. But he had never yearned to take any of them in his arms and simply hold them close. He had never spent a day with one of them, clutching each hour jealously and knowing that tomorrow without her held nothing of pleasure or promise. *Why is it that I have only to look into her face to feel as if I have never known another woman? It is as though all the other times were nothing but random strokes of a brush, and now I am finally able to complete a canvas with colours I never knew before.*

Once aboard the *Cormorant*, Collins led his companion on a tour of the ship so rapid that it left them both breathless, for evening was fast approaching. Anne paced the deck from the foremast to the mizzenmast and stood where the gunners would peer anxiously through the smoke and hubbub of battle, listening as Collins eagerly explained that, while the *Cormorant* might boast only sixty-four guns, she was much more maneuverable than a seventy-four. Eventually he caught himself, looking guiltily at his companion. "But I've run on long enough, Miss Anne. What a gabster I am! You should have stopped me long since."

"And so I would, Lieutenant--if I had wished to do so. You have been most enlightening. Now when I see a report of some naval action in the *Times*, I will understand something of its import."

He could think of no reply, for her words had conjured up a picture of a future in which he would have no part. He cursed his artist's ready imagination, for he instantly envisioned Anne seated at a breakfast table, *en famille*, clad in a dressing gown, her hair tumbled soft and loose about her shoulders. She idly perused the morning paper, reading aloud bits of interest to the man across the table. *I will be nothing but a dim memory to her then. She will scan the naval news and for a moment, remember me and this day, and then her husband or child will claim her attention and my memory will be dismissed.*

In the sudden silence, Collins realized that he had missed her last words. He turned and said apologetically, "I beg your pardon?"

"Were you lost in the memory of some naval engagement, Lieutenant?"

He shook his head. "No, my duties claimed my thoughts for a moment as I was looking at the repairs done to that section of rail. It had become quite dangerous. What were you saying to me, Miss Anne?"

"I only asked how often you have ladies aboard during a voyage."

"Occasionally the captain's wife will accompany us on a peacetime mission. We have once or twice had special passengers, but ladies seldom grace our decks. Life at sea is a lonely business, and naturally tedious to those of your sex."

"Perhaps that would depend upon the lady."

"Doubtless you've the right of it." He smiled down at her. "I have little difficulty imagining you here with your sketchbook and brushes, as happy as a grig."

Before he could be besieged by visions of Anne, married to him and contentedly sharing his quarters, he glanced up at the sky. "It's time we were returning, Miss Anne. The docks are no place for you after night falls--and one adventure is quite enough for the day."

Anne looked surprised. "Do you know, I had forgotten

the danger Dulcie and I encountered this morning. The rest of the day has been so splendid."

He tucked her hand beneath his arm again and held it there as he began to steer her back toward the waiting dinghy, trying vainly not to look forward to the brief moments when he would hold her in his arms as he lifted her into it.

Back at the Montclair, Anne rejoined Collins in the dining room. "Dulcie is still asleep, and I think it best if I leave her so. By morning I trust she will have slept the headache away and be ready for some nourishing food."

"I hope so," he replied, frowning. "Another day's delay might be a serious matter." After a pause, he continued vexedly, "I wish I could escort you to Pemberley in a post-chaise. It would cut the time of your journey by a third."

"And arouse all manner of comment when I arrive," Anne reminded him.

"It would certainly do that. Every gabblemonger in town would soon know," the lieutenant agreed grimly. If it ever became known that Anne had traveled for a week in a man's company, she would be hopelessly compromised, her name the subject of scandalous *on-dits*. As much as he wanted to see her safely to her destination, Collins knew he could do nothing that would bring her such notoriety.

"We shall do quite well on the coach," Anne said before firmly turning the subject. "I must remember to leave word at the desk that we need to be awakened by five of the morning."

"I'll tap at your door. I've always possessed the happy faculty of awakening at whatever hour I desire."

The dining room of the little hotel was not crowded, and they had been seated at a secluded table where they chatted throughout a leisurely meal, experiencing no difficulty in finding topics upon which to converse. *Quite the reverse*, thought Anne, remembering with an inward shudder her come-out, which had been marred by her distressing inability to engage her partners in frivolous chatter under the critical gaze of her mother. *I do not need to search desperately for something to say. There is not enough time for all that I wish to tell him.*

"What is your favourite among the canvases you have completed, Lieutenant? Is it one of the ones you showed me at Rosings? I liked the dolphins very much."

"No." Collins gazed reflectively into his wine glass before replying. "I believe that the painting of which I'm fondest is a little fishing village in Portugal."

"What is its special merit?"

He smiled into her serious eyes. "It really has none, I suppose. I was able to paint it from life instead of from a sketch. I painted it shortly after dawn on three successive mornings during a shore leave I was fortunate enough to have. It shows a little dock where fishermen gather each morning before going out for the day's catch. They are overhauling their nets, talking about the weather and the day's prospects, doing exactly the same things that their fathers and grandfathers did before them. If one could go back in time a thousand years, those same fisherman would be there, living just the same sort of lives. Perhaps that's why I like the canvas so much. The greatest paintings of the ages attempt to capture a timeless scene. Without realizing it, I was striving to do the same."

"And where is the canvas now?" The words were hardly out of Anne's mouth when the horrifying thought that he had given it to some lady occurred to her.

Wondering why she suddenly looked so self-conscious, Collins replied, "It hangs in Trevalyn House—my uncle's house, you know, in Cornwall. He too has an affection for it. Indeed, I painted it with Uncle Philip in mind, for he spent some years in Spain and Portugal in his youth."

"I'm sure he has a great affection for you, also."

"He must, indeed, to have tolerated me all these years." Although he spoke lightly, Anne heard an answering regard for the old man in his voice. *How much I would like to meet him,*

141

she thought, and *to see Trevalyn House and the painting of the Portuguese fishermen.*

"And yours, Miss Anne?" Anne came to herself suddenly, blushing lest her companion have followed her thoughts accurately, to find Collins regarding her anxiously. "I think you are tired from the day's exertions, and I have kept you too long over dinner."

"Oh no, I was only imagining the felicity of traveling to other countries and finding many fresh scenes to draw. Truly, I am not tired. What were you asking me?"

"Merely what your own favourite work is. Perhaps the drawing of the mouse breakfasting which you have mentioned to me?"

Marveling that he would remember her careless comment, Anne said thoughtfully, "I don't think I have a single favourite work. There is a group of watercolours which I finished only last year. They show the lake at Rosings in different aspects through the seasons. I was satisfied with it when I finished the series, and I do not often feel content with my work."

They were the last to leave the dining room, having lingered long over dessert discussing the relative merits of Joscoe's coloured pencils over Timmons', the thickness and texture of various papers for differing subjects, and other artistic matters of absorbing interest. They mounted the darkened stairs together, still talking but in lower tones, and finally paused outside Anne's door.

Collins smiled down at her in the dimly lit hallway, inspiring in Anne a distressingly improper desire to reach up and trace the vertical crease in his cheek to the corner of mouth. *He is my friend--only my friend. I must not behave like some hoyden trying to leg-shackle him to me.*

"Good night, Miss Anne. I hope the latter part of your day made up for its beginning to some small degree."

"I hardly recall the morning, Lieutenant. When I think of this day, it will be the *Cormorant* I remember . . . and the sea gulls calling over our heads and the faces of the seamen in that tavern, and the patterns the rigging made against the sky . . . oh, so many details that I can scarcely wait to have my pencils in my grasp." Impulsively, she reached out a friendly hand. "Good night, Lieutenant."

As he enveloped her small hand in his, Collins felt a surge of such mingled tenderness and desire that his other hand unconsciously clenched on the door frame as he fought for control. Throughout dinner, indeed throughout the day, he had resolved over and over not to touch her again. For a long moment, neither of them moved nor spoke. Anne made no effort to move her hand out of his as she leaned back against the door and raised her face. Their eyes locked together in acknowledgment of the longing that had lain beneath every moment of the day they had spent together, longing that had grown all the deeper for having been unspoken and denied.

Then Collins lowered his head. Her heart leaped, but he only laid his cheek against hers. His arms came about her and gathered her to him, one hand gently pressing the graceful arch of her back, the other caressing the nape of her slender neck. A fierce heat rose within him. Although he burned to lift her into his arms and carry her the few short steps down the hallway to his room, the pressure of his arms remained light. He felt as though he had captured some rare wild creature, content to remain in his arms but so delicate that the lightest touch could injure it.

As he moved his cheek gently up and down, his roughened skin barely brushed her face until she moved her head slightly to the side and their lips met. He continued the slow movement, but from side to side now, his lips brushing hers softly, questioningly, until he felt her hands slide up his arms to his shoulders and around his neck. The touch of her cool slender fingers in his hair set his pulse to pounding. The feel of her breasts pressed against his chest through the thin material of her dress, the exquisite sensation of the whole slim length of her body yielding to his brought the inward flame to a

143

white-hot heat that nearly consumed the tenderness he felt for her. The picture of her in his bed, pale and slender, with her hair fanned out beneath her naked body, presented itself to him like a canvas he knew by heart and must possess.

But one rational thought remained, impervious to burning desire. *She is an innocent. She placed herself in my care.* Calling upon every vestige of self-control, he lifted his head and framed her face with both his hands as he gazed down into her eyes, shadowed and unreadable in the dimness of the hallway.

He allowed himself one small parting kiss on her forehead before he released her to open the door.

"Sleep well, Miss Anne," Collins told her. With a last upward look at him, her glance holding he knew not what emotions, she murmured a good night and slipped into the darkened room. He could briefly hear the sound of soft snores before he gently closed the door, waited until he heard the key turn in the lock, and walked down the hall to his room, hoping that it would be very cold indeed.

◆ ❖ ◆

Chapter 12

Anne and Dulcie reached Lambton in early afternoon of a day whose cool wind carried the hint of winter. They had traveled the final leg of their journey in a hired chaise which had taken the last of the money Collins had given Anne. She was very grateful to have still at their disposal the small sum she had brought with her from Rosings. She felt enough perturbation at the thought of what lay immediately ahead of her without appearing at the inn, lacking even the means to pay for a cup of tea.

The Derby Arms lay at the eastern edge of the town, about five miles from Pemberley. Anne could have directed the chaise to take her to the Darcy estate, but Collins had impressed upon her the importance of being publicly seen to arrive with only Dulcie as her escort. She vaguely remembered the inn from visits during her childhood. As she entered, the host came bustling toward her, and his name popped suddenly into her head.

"Good afternoon, Mr. McDonwald," she greeted him with a shy smile.

His bright button eyes went questioningly to her face. "And a good afternoon to you, Miss."

"I am Miss De Bourgh," Anne continued calmly although her heart was pounding. "My cou-"

"Miss De Bourgh! Of course, I remember you--Mr. Darcy's cousin. When last I seen you, Miss, you was no bigger than a hop o' my thumb!" As his eyes went past her, enthusiasm gave way to surprise when he saw only Dulcie, looking very small and insignificant between two modest valises.

145

Forestalling questions, Anne plunged smoothly into the story she and Collins had concocted. "My maid and I are come in haste from my aunt's home in London. Because of an accident to her carriage, I was forced to hire a chaise. We did not have time to wait for repairs, you see. We have been traveling for so long that we are quite done in and wish to refresh ourselves before appearing at Pemberley." Anne employed her sweetest smile. "Might you be so kind as to allow us to do so, and to bring us some tea while a message is sent to my cousin?"

If the publican saw anything odd in the fact that Miss De Bourgh seemed to have lost her aunt's postilions and most of her baggage, along with her traveling chaise, nothing showed in his rubicund face as he bellowed for the chambermaid to take Miss De Bourgh and her maid upstairs and look lively about it.

An hour and a half later, Anne was turning in at Pemberley's lodge and reflecting that the stop had been a good idea for other reasons than establishing her arrival *sans* any escort besides her maid. She felt nervous enough about her unheralded arrival without descending from the barouche, disheveled and thirsty. At least she had had a chance to comb her hair and wash her face.

What will I do if Mrs. Darcy doesn't wish me to stay? She can have no very pleasant recollections of me. During Elizabeth Darcy's weeks at the vicarage, she had visited Rosings several times. Anne had wanted to extend a gesture of friendship to the lively girl, especially after she had perceived her cousin's preference for her, but she had known that any kindness on her part would be instantly noted by her mother with the greatest disapprobation. She had, therefore, maintained the impassive facade behind which her true feelings so often lay concealed. *Whatever my reception, I will not go back to Rosings and Sir Crawford. If I must, I will find some genteel employment. Or perhaps I truly can sell some of my drawings--*

By the time Anne descended from the carriage, she had convinced herself that a cold welcome was all she could hope for. Her legs were suddenly shaking, and she paused for a moment to take a deep breath of the frosty air before she found herself caught up in a vigorous hug.

"Anne! Never have I been more surprised. How very good it is to see you." Anne looked up into Darcy's handsome face and saw that he was beaming with honest delight. Her relief was so overwhelming that her eyes filmed over with tears, obscuring the lady who waited just behind him.

"Miss De Bourgh, I am so pleased to welcome you to Pemberley." Elizabeth Darcy stretched out both hands in welcome. Her speaking dark eyes met Anne's frightened grey ones, and natural kindness overcame decorum. Instead of taking Anne's hand, Elizabeth put both arms around the shivering girl and also hugged her. With Darcy on one side of her and his pretty bride on the other, Anne walked through Pemberley's imposing front door.

"Mama does not understand why I don't consider Sir Crawford an unexceptionable husband, Fitzwilliam. Indeed, she feels that his offer is an absolute triumph for me. But I cannot marry him. I *cannot*!"

The three were seated in the Pemberley library before a roaring fire, Darcy in a large leather chair, Elizabeth in a smaller tapestried one, and Anne comfortably ensconced on a cushion on the wide raised hearth beside Finn, Darcy's Irish wolfhound.

"You took him into such dislike, Miss De Bourgh?" Elizabeth inquired gently.

"Please . . . call me Anne. I wanted to ask you to do so at Rosings, but Mama . . . " Seeing the shadow fall over the visitor's pale face, Elizabeth met her husband's gaze and suddenly began to understand details of her visit to Rosings that had been previously unclear.

147

"Anne, then." Elizabeth smiled encouragingly.

"I do dislike Sir Crawford very much indeed. I can hardly tell you." Anne paused for a long moment. Darcy started to speak, but subsided when Elizabeth glanced warningly at him. "On the evening after his arrival, Mama gave a dinner in honour of the Daviotts. She had arranged a small dance in the gallery."

Darcy raised his brows in humorous surprise. "How very unlike Aunt Catherine."

Anne smiled bitterly. "She intended it as a . . . a romantical setting for Sir Crawford to ask me for my hand. He did." The anger in Anne's voice surprised her cousin. "He took me to the terrace outside the gallery, Fitzwilliam. We were quite alone there. He--he embraced me and kissed me even though I was not--did not--"

Finding no words, Anne's voice broke off as Elizabeth leaned forward to touch her hand in silent commiseration. Darcy looked first stunned and then angry. Before he could express his outrage, Anne straightened and rolled up the sleeve of her unfashionable gown. Against the white skin of her upper arm, bruises stood out like dark stains. Elizabeth drew in a shocked breath. Her husband exclaimed furiously, "The swine! I can't believe he offered you such brutality, Anne. Did he think no one would call him to account?"

A sudden thought crossed his mind, and he stood up and paced to the window and back, so great was his agitation. "Surely you are not telling us that Aunt Catherine *still* wished you to marry him? Anne, did you not tell her of his ungentlemanly behavior to you? Did not you *show* her?"

"I did, Fitzwilliam, that very night." Anne paused for a moment and then also stood, striving for composure. She began carefully to roll her sleeve back down, keeping her eyes directed on the task. "She told me that she knows what is best for me. She said that all men behave so. That I would become . . . accustomed." Anne's voice wavered. She looked up and both Darcy and Elizabeth saw her eyes brimming with

148

unshed tears. "Fitzwilliam, she was so very angry when you married. I could not make her understand that no feelings exist between you and me other than the love of a brother and sister. She was determined to prove to you . . . she said . . . sh-she s-said . . ."

But the strain of the last week overwhelmed Anne and she could no longer hold back her sobs. Darcy moved instantly to her side and put a comforting arm around her shoulders as he drew her back down on the hearth and allowed her to cry out the misery and fear of the last week on his shoulder, Finn whimpering unhappily beside them. His eyes met Elizabeth's in the perfect understanding that Lady Catherine had been so furious that her nephew had flouted her will that she had been willing to sacrifice her daughter's happiness to salve her pride. Anne would not be returning to Rosings.

After she had taken her guest upstairs to rest, Elizabeth returned to the library to find her husband staring into the fire. He looked up as she entered and Elizabeth hesitated, for his eyes held an expression she had not seen there since months before their marriage. The combination of anger and disdain stopped her in her tracks, but to her immense relief it melted the instant his eyes rested on her. He held out his arms and she flew into them, feeling their familiar warmth close around her. He said nothing for long moments, merely embracing her, until she tilted back her head to look up at him. "Elizabeth . . . "

She waited but he said nothing more. His dark eyes seemed to be tracing the contours of her face in the firelight, and now she could not read the expression on a countenance that had become nearly as familiar to her as her own. "My dearest?"

"That might have been you, Elizabeth. If I had not managed to set things right between Lydia and Wickham . . . if you had not found in your heart the generosity to forgive my stupid blunders . . . it might have been you at the mercy of some rakehell like Daviott. If you had been forced to marry such as he . . . and I had known your situation was my fault . . . I could not have lived with the degree of self-hatred I would have known." His eyes were dark with the contemplation of what such a fate would have meant to them both; now she understood that the emotions that had earlier frightened her had been directed against himself.

"It could never have happened, Fitzwilliam." Her hand slid up his shoulder, fingers soothing his neck and cheek, before they began to play in his hair. "I knew already when Lydia eloped with Wickham that my heart was set upon you." She stood on tiptoe to press her mouth lightly to his. He felt her lips brush his and then return to deepen a kiss which, after months of marriage, still managed to send an aching hardness like liquid fire throughout his body. "It would not have mattered what happened to me after Lydia disgraced us all, my dearest. I would have given myself to none but you." Her mouth returned to his and he shifted to cradle her head on his shoulder, the kiss leading to a wave of passion whose depth threatened to drown awareness of their surroundings.

Darcy drew in a deep breath before he released her, remembering with difficulty that they stood in a public room likely to be entered by a servant at any time. He leaned over to gently nip her bottom lip. "I think our guest is not the only one who might benefit from lying down before dinner, wife."

Instantly her lips curved in the teasing smile he loved. "Indeed, husband? Well, I have many duties that call me at this hour, but I do recall promising to love, to honour, and to *obey*."

"And we have time enough before dinner to practice all three." Darcy tucked her hand under his arm as they walked out of the library toward the wide stairs.

Before coming downstairs from seeing Anne to her room, Elizabeth had spoken to her dresser, instructing Banks to solicit help in quickly cutting down one of her most simply-made evening gowns for their guest, whose baggage had gone astray. Together they chose a robe of celestial blue. Elizabeth

150

and Anne were of a height, and the dress would fit tolerably well, its owner thought, after the side seams had been taken in.

After her unprecedented bout of emotion, Anne slept soundly for over two hours, awakening only when Dulcie shook her gently by the shoulder. Having brought no evening attire, Anne had intended to sup on a tray in her bedchamber; when Banks arrived with the hastily altered dress draped over her arm, Anne was overwhelmed by her hostess' thoughtfulness.

Banks stayed until she saw the fit, frowning critically, but finally pronouncing, "It will do, Miss, until your own things arrive. The colour is excellent. It could have been chosen for you." She received Anne's thanks stoically and retired after adjuring Dulcie to come to her for anything her mistress needed.

Dulcie drew Anne's hair up into a loose arrangement, lightly curling several of the long silky strands before allowing them to fall to her shoulders behind. The two girls once more resorted to their experimental stock of cosmetics, applying them very sparingly to Anne's lashes and cheeks. Once again Anne was amazed at the way the merest touch of Dulcie's brush made her eyes leap into prominence.

"There now," declared Dulcie in very satisfied tones. "We'd be rightly in the briars if her Ladyship could see us now, wouldn't we, Miss Anne? But that's nothing we need worry ourselves about tonight!"

Amused by the note of triumph, her mistress regarded herself in the mirror before replying, "I like the style very much indeed, Dulcie. It is a credit to you. Thank you."

Just as Anne stood, another knock sounded at the door. Banks bustled in with a pair of dark blue kid slippers. "'Tis to be hoped they fit, Miss. I'm sure Miss Georgiana's would be far too big." Elizabeth's slippers also proved too large, but some judiciously placed tissue in the toes made them wearable.

Banks' eyes swept Anne from her shining curls to the

dainty toes peeping from beneath the silk dress. "And here is a final touch, Miss, that I made up from the pieces we cut away from the dress."

She gestured to Anne to sit again, and expertly threaded a celestial blue silk ribbon through her curls. Standing back, a rare smile lit her stolid countenance.

Touched by her kindness, Anne smiled back at her, the same endearing smile that had made the Rosings servants her willing slaves. "How very kind of you, Banks. With all your own work to do, you must not have had a spare second today. I do thank you for all your trouble.

"'Tis but a trifle, Miss." Banks vanished with a nod, but her approbation had been felt, and Anne carefully descended to dinner in her made-over dress and borrowed shoes, feeling that she would not present an entirely discreditable appearance at the Darcy table.

At the bottom of the stairs, she was informed by a footman that the master and mistress usually remained in the library until dinner was announced unless guests were present. She took comfort from his implication that she was a member of the family and approached the library with a pleasurable anticipation which heightened when she entered. Her cousin, Colonel Giles Fitzwilliam, was standing before the fireplace with Darcy, both of them deep in conversation as Elizabeth bent over needlework in her accustomed chair. Colonel Fitzwilliam's eyes lifted as she entered; he stopped speaking and stared at her, clearly taken aback.

Elizabeth glanced up with a flicker of amusement in her face. "Are you not going to greet your Cousin Anne, Colonel?"

"I am delighted to do so," he replied at once, coming to her side. Anne realized that his surprise had not arisen from ignorance of her presence at Pemberley, as she had first supposed, but from surprise at the appearance she presented.

He was an old playfellow and she smiled at him with none of the constraint that had marked her demeanour under Lady Catherine's watchful eyes.

"Anne, I add my welcome to Mr. and Mrs. Darcy's. You make a lovely addition to our family circle."

She laughed a little at his formality, her eyes dancing in merriment. "Oh Giles, you sound for all the world as if we were at some fashionable London squeeze with Mama peering over my shoulder. But thank you! I am so very glad to be here." She held out her hand to him in greeting, her customary shyness nowhere in evidence. "I did not know that you were also a guest at Pemberley. How merry we shall all be together! Indeed, I can hardly wait until Georgiana returns tomorrow."

Colonel Fitzwilliam took the outstretched hand, drawing her closer to kiss her cheek. "Darcy has been telling me of all you have endured in the last two weeks, Cousin. It is too bad of Aunt Catherine! Had either of us known, we would certainly have endeavoured to help you."

"I knew you would, Giles, and the knowledge was a comfort to me. But I also knew that if you helped me to leave Rosings, your parents would be most unhappy with you."

Fitzwilliam looked annoyed at her observation. "They could have rung a peal over me if they liked. But according to Darcy, Daviott's a regular wrong'un, and I hope I know my duty well enough to do it, regardless of my parents' opinion."

Seeing she had ruffled his feathers, Anne applied herself to smoothing them down. "Of course, Giles, and I knew it too. I even considering applying to my Aunt Elinor for assistance, but she has been unwell these last two years, and truly, I had no wish to bring my mother's wrath down upon anyone's head. Had I anywhere else to go, I would not risk exposing Fitzwilliam and Elizabeth to it, and to the world's censure for taking me in."

Darcy shook his head. "You make too much of it, Anne. You are come on a visit to your cousins. Why should that make any of us the subject of ill-natured talk?"

Reynolds appeared at that moment to announce dinner, and Anne and the colonel preceded Elizabeth and Darcy out the door. They made a handsome couple, the colonel's dark blond hair and deep blue eyes a complement to Anne's feminine fairness. Elizabeth had not failed to note the admiration in the look Anne's cousin gave her as they left the room, and she glanced archly up at her husband. "Do you know, I think perhaps Anne's presence here may not bring down upon your head the family disapprobation that you all anticipate."

Surprised, Darcy looked inquiringly at her. "But why? I assure you that my aunt will be livid when she discovers where Anne has found refuge, and her brother the Earl will think I've taken leave of my senses. I'm quite ready to face the music, but I don't delude myself that we aren't in for a most unpleasant scene."

"I know you don't, my love. But I still think there is a factor you have not considered." Elizabeth's fine dark eyes sparkled with mischief. "Let us see if dinner brings any clarification."

◆ ❖ ◆

Chapter 13

In the three days that followed Anne's arrival at Pemberley, she settled into a happy routine, disturbed only by the threat of imminent invasion by her mother. She had first been installed in one of the grand guest rooms, but after the first night, she had asked Elizabeth if she might remove to a smaller one. Her choice was a blue-papered corner chamber with much simpler furnishings, a small white brick fireplace, and two windows, one looking out toward Pemberley Wood and the other giving her a view of the gardens and terrace at the rear of the house.

Her thoughts sometimes strayed to Rosings when she sat in the window seats, but she firmly dismissed the image of a small befurred rodent waiting hopefully outside her window; Povey had never yet failed her and he would not forget his promise. The grief she felt for her mother's unhappiness could not be so easily dismissed, for too well she knew the love and worry that underlay the imperious command to marry into the Daviott family. Anne had always understood that her mother did not attempt to dominate the lives of those she loved from either cruelty or caprice, but because life had never taught her that her that she might be wrong. Pity, fear, anger, and love had interwoven her life with Lady Catherine, and Anne thought there could be no more unpleasant mixture of emotions. However, neither worry for her mother nor dread of her arrival at Pemberley could ruin Anne's pleasure in her first real taste of independence.

She awoke early each morning and lay luxuriating in her four-poster bed as she waited for Dulcie to bring her tea and build up the fire. She thought she would never come to take for granted waking to a day that held nothing distasteful in store. No slighting remarks were directed toward her tastes and inclinations, and she drowsed through no long, tedious hours listening to didactic pronouncements, eager agreement, or lavish flattery.

At Pemberley she was free to follow her fancy, surrounded by lively, intelligent people who treated her with affection and respect. And if a shadow fell now and then over the sun of her happiness, Anne took care to hide its blight from the common view. After all, she told herself firmly, she would be wickedly ungrateful to wish for one absent face, among all those that smiled at her at Pemberley, or to long for the sound of one particular voice in the chorus that spoke pleasantly to her each day. In short, she had no right to wonder about Lieutenant Philip Collins, to speculate on whether he would himself accompany her trunk on its journey to Pemberley, or to hope that if he did so, his visit would be more than the cursory one owed to civility. He had completed his chivalrous service in rescuing her, and it was time to dismiss him from her mind. The dismayed realization that his smile and voice and touch seemed to have claimed a permanent place there, she tried hard to ignore.

Anne had feared that she would be an unwelcome intrusion into the lives of her cousin Darcy and his new wife, who had scarcely been married a year. She found her fears groundless, mostly due to the presence of Darcy's younger sister Georgiana and their cousin, Colonel Fitzwilliam. If the newlyweds appeared quite late to breakfast, disappeared for hours after lunch, or retired early to bed, their three companions took no notice. Anne spent her days sketching a myriad of new scenes, working hard to complete a watercolour portrait of Elizabeth for Darcy's nameday, chatting with Georgiana and listening to her play the new pianoforte her brother had purchased for her, walking with Giles Fitzwilliam or riding with him on the gentle old horse which he laughingly characterized as a shuffler, or reading voraciously from the shelves of books in Darcy's well-stocked library. Sometimes she marveled at how her life had changed from days that stretched endlessly into utter tedium to ones so short she could not find the time to do all that she wished in the allotted hours.

On the second day after her arrival, she had stood for hours as dresses had been tried upon her slender frame and then had been either rejected or pinned, tucked, and marked for alteration by Banks, Dulcie, and the gratified seamstress from Lambton whom Elizabeth had insisted upon calling in.

"But I cannot accept so many dresses from you!" Anne had exclaimed, horrified.

Elizabeth had regarded her with sparkling eyes and leaned closer. "Let me explain to you just why you must do me this favour, Anne. Very soon, none of these clothes will any longer fit me. When they will do so again, they will be sadly out of fashion. You are merely helping me feel less guilty about the fortune Darcy insisted that I spend on them when we visited London."

Anne looked at her in confusion. "They will no longer fit?"

"Not for some months," Elizabeth rejoined teasingly.

"Oh! Oh, you are *increasing*!" In her delight at the news, Anne embraced Elizabeth spontaneously for the first time. "How excited you must be! How happy Fitzwilliam must be!"

Elizabeth glanced away, but not before Anne saw tears well up in her dark eyes. "Forgive me," Elizabeth murmured ruefully. "I'm a watering pot these days. Yes, I daresay he is pleased, but very worried also, I fear."

"Because he fears to lose you." Anne said softly, immediately understanding her cousin's apprehension.

Elizabeth nodded. "I've told him how foolish he is. My mother gave birth to five children in seven years, with few complications. I am as healthy as may be, and there's no need for him to torture himself with these qualms." She sniffed

157

indignantly, "And his apprehensions are quite spoiling my anticipation of welcoming a new little Darcy into our lives!"

"I shall give him a stiff scolding for his foolishness, you may be sure, Elizabeth!" Anne cried, and both girls laughed together before returning to the tiers of dresses.

Anne protested no more, not because she truly believed the lovely, expensive clothing could not be useful to Elizabeth again, but because she saw that her new friend delighted in giving the dresses to her. *This must be what it would have been like to have a sister,* Anne thought wistfully as she stroked a delicate cream lustring gown, trimmed with elaborate periwinkle beadwork. *Elizabeth and Georgiana mean more to me than a dozen wardrobes of beautiful gowns.*

It was the forenoon of Anne's fourth day at Pemberley when she and Georgiana were interrupted in the music room by the stately entrance of Reynolds. He politely waited until Georgiana paused in the difficult nocturne she was practicing before informing Anne that she had a visitor in the saloon. From his disapproving aspect, Anne feared that her mother or her emissary must have arrived to harry her, and she laid her book of poetry aside with some trepidation. To her great delight, she found Philip Collins in the lofty-ceilinged room, planted squarely beside her small battered trunk.

Heart racing with joy, Anne walked straight up to him, extending both hands, her face flushed with pleasure. "Lieutenant Collins! I am delighted to see you!"

Taking her hands, he enfolded them and resisted the temptation to kiss one of them. *Like some Bond Street beau on the strut,* he thought, irritated with himself. "And I am even more delighted to see you, Miss Anne--safe and looking very happy indeed."

"Thanks in great part to you, sir."

He waved away her comment with a disarming smile. "You may be even happier to see what I have restored to you. I vowed to deliver your drawings into your hands, but that has

158

been no easy task, I assure you."

Anne looked questioningly at him.

"The journey here was nothing, but I had to wrest the small trunk bodily from a very stocky footman outside, and I thought the butler was going to refuse to admit me with my burden. Your large trunk has been taken around to the back door. You should have seen me and Povey smuggling it out of the house at midnight. God knows what we would have said, had anyone apprehended us!"

"I see," Anne laughed. "Then I think you are very deserving of some refreshment to revive you after these epic struggles." She summoned Reynolds and requested a tea tray.

"Very good, Miss," he replied, eyeing the battered little trunk disparagingly. "Would you wish me to have the . . ah . . . baggage . . . conveyed to your bedchamber?"

"No, I thank you," Anne replied tranquilly. Returning to Collins, Anne seated herself on the sofa and motioned him to a place beside her. "You saw very few of my drawings at Rosings, Lieutenant. Would you care to look through some of the rest while we wait for tea? I will find your criticism most valuable."

Eagerly, Collins assented and helped her unfasten the tightly bound trunk. Hardly pausing when tea arrived, the two sat happily turning over the drawings, unaware of the passing of time.

"An excellent perspective here, Miss Anne," Collins commented, as he studied a view of the lake through a fringe of waving reeds.

"Thank you," she replied. "But I cannot find my favourite group. Surely I cannot have failed to include them!"

Before her companion could reply, the door opened and Collins looked up from a watercolour of a silver birch dripping with lacy ice, to find a slender fair man of military carriage, his hair cut in a fashionable Brutus, regarding them thoughtfully. As Collins rose, Anne glanced up from the portfolio she was opening, smiled, and greeted the newcomer without ceremony.

159

"May I introduce you to my cousin Colonel Fitzwilliam, Lieutenant? Giles, Lieutenant Collins has very kindly brought the trunk containing my drawing materials and some keepsakes I could not leave behind."

Fitzwilliam greeted him pleasantly enough, but Collins felt his surprise at finding his cousin seated so familiarly with a stranger. He became aware that he had been with Anne for more than an hour, considerably extending the time deemed appropriate for a call upon a lady.

Turning to her, Collins said quietly, "I have trespassed too much upon your time, Miss Anne." He saw the colonel's brows knit at his use of Anne's Christian name and his mouth thinned into a straight line. "I can only plead the pleasure that looking at your work has given me. It has been a rare treat."

"Oh, pray do not go, Lieutenant!" Anne glanced at the graceful pendulum clock ticking on the mantel. "It lacks little until time for luncheon. I shall inform my cousin Mrs. Darcy that we will have a guest if you will consent to stay. She is your cousin too, is she not? I know she will be delighted to meet you."

Seeing Anne's eager eyes and inviting smile, Collins thought there were few things he would rather do than share the meal with her. But then he glanced at Colonel Fitzwilliam who had moved closer to his cousin, his demeanour clearly protective. He did not voice a second to Anne's impulsive invitation.

"I believe that I must not impose," Collins said quietly.

"Then will you call again this afternoon? I would like you to meet all of my family here. Darcy knows that I am deeply in your debt, and he will wish to thank you himself."

Collins' hesitation gave the colonel the chance to say smoothly, "Perhaps, my dear Anne, the lieutenant does not have time at his disposal to call again. You must not press him to do what may not lie within his power."

"Oh," Anne exclaimed softly with reddened cheeks. "I did not mean--"

"Of course I shall call again, Miss Anne." Collins bowed over her hand and met Colonel Fitzwilliam's eyes in a long, direct stare. "I am pleased to have made your acquaintance, Colonel." He could not resist a parting shot. "Miss Anne has spoken to me often of her fondness for her *cousins.*"

Reaching the door, he glanced back to see Fitzwilliam taking his place upon the sofa beside Anne. He was already reaching for the portfolio she held. *And why,* he asked himself in bitter self-derision, *should that sight be a barb planted in my heart?*

Colonel Fitzwilliam sought out Darcy immediately after luncheon, finding him in the stable block discussing with his head stableman the addition of two birthing stalls. When the three men had exhausted every possible detail of this absorbing project, Fitzwilliam accompanied Darcy back to the library where he had expressed his intention of determining the cost of the stalls.

Closing the door, Fitzwilliam addressed Darcy immediately, for he knew the impossibility of distracting his cousin from work, once it was begun. "Do you have time to talk with me about Anne, Darcy?"

"Of course," Darcy waved him to a chair. "Are you dreading the descent of our aunt and possibly your father upon us? Do you know, I have wondered if you might not find it convenient to be called back to duty for a week or so. It's a curst awkward situation for you."

"I'm damned if I'll shab off!" the colonel retorted, resenting the allusion to his position as a younger son, dependent upon his father's generosity.

"I'm quite capable of taking Anne's part, fire-eater. Aunt Catherine can hardly drag her from Pemberley by force."

"Perhaps she will not make the attempt, Darcy." His cousin's brows rose, but for a long moment Fitzwilliam said nothing else. Then he continued, somewhat hesitantly. "I can

161

think of a circumstance in which Aunt Catherine might actually desire Anne's presence here."

"Well, I cannot. I can more easily imagine her arriving with a bride-gift for Elizabeth!" Seeing his cousin still silent, apparently searching for words, Darcy said impatiently, "Cut line, Giles. What is it you wish to say?"

"Aunt Catherine might be quite content to see Anne remain here because I am also here." He flushed as his eyes met Darcy's surprised ones. "She wished for a union between you and Anne. Well, God knows that's understandable, but after all, I, too, am a Fitzwilliam. And Anne certainly doesn't need to look for fortune in marriage. What could be more suitable?"

Striving to overcome his astonishment, Darcy said, "And this is a match you wish for? I have certainly never thought you to entertain any partiality for Anne."

Fitzwilliam's reply was nearly lost as he turned his back and bent to mend the fire. When it came, his reply was strained. "No, it was never Anne for whom I felt a partiality."

Darcy, stunned, wondered if he had read the other man's meaning aright; when the colonel arose, their eyes met again, and Darcy knew that he had not been mistaken. Neither of them had ever spoken of the colonel's decided preference for Miss Elizabeth Bennet's society before her marriage, but Darcy could not doubt the meaning in his cousin's brief, bitter comment. Finally he cleared his throat. "Do you think such a solution is fair to Anne?"

"I think we will go on well enough together, Darcy. I have a fondness for her, and she for me. I can, at least, deliver her from her mama's tyranny. Although I must say that her initiative in removing herself to Pemberley surprised me. I have sometimes felt these last few days that I never knew her."

Darcy remained silent until his cousin looked challengingly at him. "Well?"

"There was a time when I'd have thought you to have hit on the very thing. But that was before I knew the felicity

162

that comes from marriage to one without whom I would not care to exist." Darcy cleared his throat again and forthrightly continued, "And frankly, that's why I feel that both you and Anne deserve better than the milksop marriage you propose."

"Better me than some jumped-up, shabby-genteel tin merchant," Fitzwilliam snapped.

"What?"

The colonel smiled grimly. "You have not had the pleasure of meeting the brother of the vicar of Hunsford." Seeing Darcy still at sea, he continued, "Lieutenant Philip Collins. I found him seated most cozily beside Anne on the drawing room sofa this morning. He had been there, so Reynolds informed me, for more than an hour--having brought Anne's trunks all the way from Kent, Darcy--he could not trust them to a job-carrier apparently. Anne has informed me that he intends to sell out at first opportunity and take up his inheritance of some tin mines somewhere in the wilds of Cornwall."

Darcy frowned. "Anne told me that Lieutenant Collins conveyed her and her maid from Rosings to the nearest posting inn. It was a kind service, but surely you exaggerate the danger of an attachment. Lord, Giles, we are talking of the brother of that pompous toad-eater, Collins!"

"His brother is a man of a different stamp--as you are about to discover, Cousin. He will be your guest at tea in some . . ." Colonel Fitzwilliam's eyes went to the clock ". . . five and twenty minutes."

Darcy appeared as Elizabeth sat at her dressing table, allowing Banks to make minor repairs to her coiffure before her guests' arrival. Not only was Lieutenant Collins expected, but also the Satterlees, a brother and sister with whom Georgiana, Darcy's sister, had been staying. Among Banks' other invaluable qualities was an unerring instinct for when her presence was superfluous; she vanished the second the last dark curl was secured in place.

Leaning against the door, Darcy related his conversation with Colonel Fitzwilliam, more or less verbatim, omitting only the remark that had referred to his rapt listener. He had no wish to cause his wife distress. When he had finished, Elizabeth sat in silence. Seeing him raise his brows quizzically, she laughed. "I cannot say that part of your budget of news surprises me, Fitzwilliam."

He nodded. "I recalled your dark hints to me on the evening of Anne's arrival. You never miss a trick, my love." He leaned over to nibble beneath a particularly titillating curl. The perfume of her skin filled his nostrils and his hand moved below the neckline of her gown to caress the soft skin there.

"His admiration for her was obvious. I think you only overlooked it because you assumed that the colonel's attitude toward Anne mirrors your own. But I am certainly amazed that he thinks there is some attachment between Anne and a brother of Mr. Collins!" Catching her breath on a little gasp, Elizabeth twisted away to laugh up at her husband. "I can think of few unlikelier matches. And you must unhand me at once, or we shall disgrace ourselves by being late for tea. *Again*, Fitzwilliam!"

Elizabeth welcomed Philip Collins as a cousin, albeit one she had never met due to their fathers' estrangement, and was relieved to find him a profound contrast to his brother William. She saw a spark of mischief light his eyes and realized that her reaction had been obvious to him; that he found amusement rather than offense in it caused her to like him at once. She invited him to sit beside her, and they spoke first of Kent, of William and Charlotte and the prospective addition to their family, and then of the Bennet family, whom he had heard described by his brother.

She saw his eyes wander several times to Anne; he had spoken to her upon entering and received a warm greeting, but Colonel Fitzwilliam, seated beside her, had soon claimed his cousin's attention as he related some story which caused both

Georgiana and Miss Emily Satterlee to laugh.

"I believe that my husband and I have a great deal to thank you for, Lieutenant Collins." An upward look of her dark eyes drew Darcy away from Miles Satterlee and into the conversation. "Anne has told us how you aided her in acquiring a seat upon the stage. It cannot have been a comfortable position for you."

"A most trifling service, Mrs. Darcy. Its only discomfort derived from my worry about Miss Anne and her maid until I could retrieve her belongings and assure myself of her safe arrival here."

"My wife speaks for me, Lieutenant, when she thanks you for your care of my cousin." Collins nodded to Darcy as he met his appraising stare. "Had Anne written to me, I would have done my utmost to help her, but it would have been a dashed awkward business as my aunt and I are already upon uneasy terms. I can far more easily defend giving my cousin the shelter of Pemberley than I could have explained any agency on my part in removing her from her home."

Collins nodded. "That was Miss Anne's reasoning, sir. She had no desire to cause discord in the family."

"I can only be relieved that she didn't doubt her welcome here."

"She did not, Mr. Darcy. Indeed, she spoke most feelingly of the warm affection she has always felt for you and Colonel Fitzwilliam." As he spoke, Collins' gaze was drawn inexorably back to the picture Anne presented, clad in a simple primrose muslin gown, the color high in her cheeks, as she looked up, sparkling with animation, into her handsome cousin's face. He could not but be aware of what a pleasing picture they made, seated side by side in obvious amity.

Elizabeth felt a pang as she followed Collins' impassive stare. Having spoken with him for half an hour, she could now understand Anne's apparent liking. He possessed neither the easy charm of Colonel Fitzwilliam nor the good looks of her husband, but Elizabeth could not but acknowledge that the

165

intelligence and humor of his demeanour and the aura of masculine power that surrounded him made him a very attractive man. Indeed, it seemed incredible to her that he could be related to Mr. William Collins, a gentleman whom both she and her husband regarded as foolish beyond description. Any lady might be pardoned for trying to gain Philip Collins' notice, and Elizabeth was quite sure that he had bestowed far more than that upon Anne.

But they both must know that the Fitzwilliam family would never countenance a marriage between him and Anne. And she, poor child, is most unlikely to marry to disoblige her family. It would be bruited by the ton as the mesalliance of the season. No, Elizabeth thought for a bleak moment, *my own marriage certainly earned that distinction. But a union between a De Bourgh and a Collins might rival even that shock to polite society's sensibilities.* Her eyes met Darcy's and the empathy that had grown between them in the past months told her that his thoughts exactly matched hers. His thoughtful gaze moved from Anne to Collins before a slow smile assured Elizabeth without words that he cared nothing for popular opinion of their marriage, and her moment of sadness vanished like snow in April sunshine.

In the momentary silence, Collins stood and bowed to them. "It has been a pleasure to meet a cousin I have never known, Mrs. Darcy. And you, sir. I wish you both very happy."

Anne had looked up as he stood, and the others followed her glance as Elizabeth said warmly, "The pleasure has been ours, cousin. This meeting has been too long delayed and has proven too short once it took place. I regret that our fathers' disagreement prevented an earlier acquaintance between our two families. But now that that breach has been repaired, I hope you will wait upon us frequently while you are in Derbyshire."

Collins thought he was returning her smile, but his face felt so stiff the he could not be sure. The sight of Anne, clearly happy in her cousin's company, had told him all he needed to know. If not Darcy, no more suitable candidate for her hand could exist than her other cousin, whose admiration of her was so evident.

"You are too kind, Mrs. Darcy, but I shall be returning to London on the morrow. There is no more to keep me here."

He paused by the other group to say a few words, lightly pressed Anne's extended hand without looking into her face, and was gone, having seen neither the satisfaction upon the colonel's face nor the dismay upon Anne's.

Chapter 14

On a cool morning some days later, Darcy, Elizabeth, Georgiana, Fitzwilliam, and Anne were drinking tea when the visitor they had all been dreading arrived at the front door of Pemberley in a luxurious traveling chaise. Reynolds appeared and quietly announced that he had ushered Lady Catherine de Bourgh and Sir Crawford Daviott into the saloon.

Anne had thought she was prepared for the inevitable meeting with her mother; she had even convinced herself that it would be a relief to have the unpleasant scene behind her, for she had been dreading her mother's advent for two weeks now. However, when Reynolds' words fell on her ears like a summons to judgment, Anne felt the familiar rush of panic and the rising nausea that had always preceded those confrontations involving loud voices, angry words, and bullying assertions of her unworthiness. *And how much worse this argument will be*, Anne thought in sick dismay, *than any that has gone before. I think I could have borne Mother's disappointment and anger if only . . .*

Anne did not allow herself to complete the thought. Since Lieutenant Collins' departure, she had rigorously tried to banish him from her thoughts. She had no claim upon him, save that of friendship, and no right to expect him to remain in Derbyshire, dancing attendance upon her. His delivery of her trunks had been merely a means of assuring himself that the lady to whom he had offered a gentleman's aid was now in safe hands. He was back among his friends and family and must soon re-join his ship; Anne doubted that he spared her more than a passing thought. So she had drunk the bitter cup of common sense and tried to present a smiling face to the world.

Darcy quietly thanked the butler and told him to inform their guests that he would be with them directly. When the door had closed behind him, Darcy looked at Anne. "Do you wish me to speak to my aunt on your behalf, Anne? If you choose, you can go upstairs with Georgiana and Elizabeth until we have done."

For a long moment the girl sat with her hands clenched upon the arms of her chair. The memories of many humiliating and painful confrontations with her mother were passing through her head, none of which she had won. The temptation to avoid this one was overwhelming. Then she lifted a face which the others saw had completely lost its colour and said shakily, "No. I thank you, Fitzwilliam, but I shall certainly speak with her. I am no longer a child, and she has no power over me. Nor am I insensible of the duty I owe her. As for Sir Crawford, I have no idea why he should have come, as this business in no way concerns him." Anne's chin lifted. "And so I shall tell him."

The colonel also rose. "I will accompany you."

"I thank you, Giles, but no." Colonel Fitzwilliam stared at her, astonished at her decisive tone. "The only reason I allow Darcy's company is that I know she will demand to speak with him in any case. But if I cannot now stand my ground against Mama, then I must pack my bags and go back to Rosings."

"Oh Anne," cried Georgiana, who had feared her aunt since earliest childhood. "You mustn't say such a thing." Patches of colour flamed in her face as she rose to her feet, and stunned them all by saying fiercely, "I *hate* Aunt Catherine." Her eyes flew to her brother. "Fitzwilliam, you must not let her take Anne away!"

Considerably startled at such an emotional outburst from his usually gentle and reserved sister, Darcy replied, "Of course I shall not. Compose yourself, Georgiana--there's no need for such heat. Anne is of age and may certainly choose

169

where she lives. Elizabeth, why do not you take Giles and Georgiana into the library? We will not be long, I promise you." He paused only to brush his fingertips over Elizabeth's curls before holding the door open for Anne to precede him into the hall.

Darcy stopped as he and Anne approached the saloon and looked questioningly at her. Her eyes were enormous in her white face, and he saw that her teeth were actually clenched in her effort to present a calm demeanor. He feared the result of the coming interview, for he could not but remember the little girl who had shivered and wept for hours after a scolding by her overbearing mother. Pitying her distress, he said, "Do you need a few moments, Anne? We can sit in the small drawing room long enough for you to compose yourself."

Anne shook her head and met his eyes resolutely. "No. Let us get this over."

Lady Catherine was seated in a large chair in the saloon, her hands, curved like talons on the upholstered arms, seeming likely to shred the delicate fabric. One look sufficed to tell Anne that she had never seen her mother in the grip of such fury as now showed upon her rigid countenance. She did not rise at Anne's approach, but her hands tightened on the armrests until they showed white to the knuckles. Looking burly and ill-tempered, Sir Crawford stood tensely by the window glaring out onto the front lawn. He turned at their approach, his bulging brown eyes flying to Anne's face, and his heavy indrawn breath sounded loud in the silent room.

Lady Catherine said nothing, and Anne recognized the strategy of old. She expected her daughter to break down into excuses or entreaties in the face of her crushing silence; instead, Anne paused by a chair, leaned her arm upon its back, and said nothing at all.

It was left to Darcy to advance into the center of the room and greet his visitors. "Good morning, Aunt Catherine." His voice was civil, if cold. He glanced toward Sir Crawford inquiringly. After waiting in vain for an introduction from either Lady Catherine or Anne, the baronet said awkwardly, "Fancy we have not met, Darcy. Sir Crawford Daviott. Miss Anne's betrothed, you understand."

"Indeed?" Darcy raised his eyebrows in simulated surprise. "My cousin has certainly not informed me of a betrothal."

He glanced at Anne who said at once, "I can only think that Sir Crawford is hard of hearing, Cousin. I informed him quite distinctly that I would not accept his obliging offer. I have not since changed my mind."

The baronet flushed, but the color in his face paled beside the red tide that flooded Lady Catherine's. She sat bolt upright in her chair and hissed, "How dare you speak in that impertinent, brassy manner, Anne! And to stand there without so much as a greeting to your mother! I could not have thought it of you!"

Maintaining silence, Anne met her mother's livid anger with a look of cool composure, glad the chair's support concealed her shaking knees.

Darcy moved between his aunt and cousin and said coldly, "Aunt Catherine, I understand your desire to speak to Anne. You are very rightly concerned with her welfare. But as Anne's host and nearest male relative, it is incumbent upon me to inform you that you will either address her with civility or you will not do so at all." Meeting his aunt's shocked eyes, Darcy continued, "I am unable to understand why you feel that this conversation should take place before a stranger. Anne has refused Sir Crawford's suit in perfectly intelligible terms. I suggest that he wait in another room while we who are family discuss my cousin's circumstances."

Lady Catherine heaved her not inconsiderable bulk from the chair. "Indeed, nephew! Then let me inform you of why Sir Crawford accompanies me today. Remarkable though I find it in the face of such hurlyburly behavior as Anne has demonstrated, he stands ready to make good the offer he made her. And I may mention that it is the *only* offer she has received--or will receive after the news of her flight from home is known!" Her eyes went to her daughter and she said spitefully, "May I ask how you intend to support yourself, Anne? For you will have nothing from me--not one shilling. Do you plan to hang upon your cousin's sleeve for the next year? Until you receive the miserable pittance your father left to you? To rely on the charity of a man who cast you aside and married to disoblige his family? You, a De Bourgh?"

In the shocked silence which followed Lady Catherine's angry speech, both Anne and Darcy were unable to answer, she unspeakably embarrassed by her mother's crudeness and he so infuriated that he feared what reply he might make to the crimson-faced vulgarian before him.

"You are mistaken, Lady Catherine, on both the premises you have stated." So engrossed had the occupants of the saloon been that none of them had heard the opening of the door. They turned as one to see Lieutenant Philip Collins standing two paces inside the room with Elizabeth Darcy at his elbow.

Elizabeth glanced at her astonished husband and quietly explained, "Lieutenant Collins insisted on speaking to Miss De Bourgh at once."

"I apologize for my apparent ill-manners," Collins continued as Elizabeth turned to shut the door once more. "But when I heard at the inn that Lady Catherine was come, I felt my presence here necessary to Miss Anne."

"You . . . you impudent lying scoundrel!" Lady Catherine was shaking with such fury that she could hardly articulate her words. "You have the . . .the . . the unmitigated temerity to stand there telling me I am mistaken about my daughter's prospects when you lied to my face about helping her abandon her home to go jauntering about the country, exposing herself to the justified criticism of the world?"

"I did not lie," Collins replied calmly. "I told you that Miss De Bourgh was not in my company and she was not. I didn't say I had not aided her in escaping a situation that no young lady should have to face. I am proud to own that I helped her to reach her cousin, and I stand ready to serve her in any way she may require."

Sir Crawford came suddenly to life, lumbering menacingly toward Collins. "You damned prating coxcomb! Dare to force your way in here as though you have some right and speak such fustian to your betters! *You* stand ready to serve Miss Anne? Well, I stand ready to thrash your presumptuous hide!"

Collins smiled thinly. "Good morning, Daviott. How fortunate that you are here. I'm happy to be in the position of bringing you news of some friends of yours. From Maxton's."

Daviott stopped in mid-stride. "Eh?"

Darcy interjected sharply, "Maxton's?"

"Why yes," Collins replied softly. "Sir Crawford is a member there. Are you not, sir? I had occasion to drop in several days ago to look up a crony of his. A fellow by the name of Fulham." For a moment pregnant with meaning, his eyes met Anne's, before they returned challengingly to Daviott. "Fulham had insulted a lady of my acquaintance, you see, as had another friend of Daviott's--Jack Garner. I fear you will not find them ready to join you in your usual pursuits, though, Sir Crawford. Poor Garner had the misfortune to break his jaw and some ribs. And Fulham suffered a wound to his shoulder that is of some concern to his physician."

Collins paused, but Daviott made no reply. "I see that you are shaken by the news of your friends' misfortune, sir. So would I be if my pockets were as much to let as yours." The lieutenant smiled mockingly. "The play is deep upstairs at Maxton's, I hear. No doubt you would be able to give us more exact information on that point."

Lady Catherine finally found her voice. "I have no idea what the point of this maundering is, nor do I care. We are not here to discuss some set of rackety gamesters."

"No," replied Collins. "We are here to discuss only one

173

of them--the one you see standing before you." He glanced at Darcy. "It's common knowledge in London that, between cards and the horses, Daviott has run himself into the ground. Had you been near any of the clubs, you'd have heard it yourself, Darcy."

Eyes gleaming, Darcy turned to Elizabeth, still standing near the door. "My dear, would you summon Reynolds?"

When the butler appeared in a suspiciously short period of time, Darcy nodded grimly toward Daviott. "Reynolds, this gentleman is leaving immediately. If his baggage is in the traveling chaise, remove it. Have it and him conveyed to Lambton, accompanied by two footmen. I wish them to ascertain that he is on the next stage to London."

Looking for once at a loss, Reynolds replied, "Yes, Mr. Darcy." He glanced questioningly at Daviott, who stood for an uncertain moment, looking ready to mill Collins down. But when the lieutenant took a step forward, his eyes flat and coldly inviting, Daviott turned toward the door. "Be damned to you all!" he grated before slamming the door behind him. With a murmured excuse, Reynolds followed him.

Four pairs of eyes turned to Lady Catherine whose jaw had dropped in consternation. Feeling herself completely in error for perhaps the first time in her life, she said angrily to Collins, "I may have been misled in countenancing a betrothal to Sir Crawford, but that does not mean, sir, that *you* have any right to interfere in my daughter's affairs. No doubt you hope that casting these aspersions on Sir Crawford will result in Anne's flinging herself and Rosings into your arms."

Scarlet-faced, Anne cried out, "Oh Mama, how could you say such a thing? I am ashamed to own that I even know you, much less that you are my mother!"

Grateful to find a familiar and vulnerable object upon which to vent her disappointment, Lady Catherine rounded on her daughter. "Do you think he helped you to flee those who have your welfare at heart from some chivalrous motive, you little fool? See how fast he is to offer to *serve you in any way*

174

he may when I inform him that Rosings is not secured to you and will never be yours if you persist in this defiance. I'll lay odds that neither this fortune-hunter you ran away with nor anyone else will make you an offer when they know you will be a pauper." Lady Catherine's voice rose to a shrill crescendo of triumph. "You will see how long his offer to serve you will last when you are penniless!"

Elizabeth gasped, Darcy moved forward as though he would actually lay hands upon his aunt, but Collins spoke first. Such fury sounded in his low voice that the others were frozen where they stood. "As I told you when I entered this room, Lady Catherine, you are wrong in every particular you have stated of your daughter. She need not depend upon her cousin, upon me, or upon anyone else to support her. She is quite capable of doing so herself."

His eyes went to Anne, standing as though turned to stone by her mother's attack. "I had wanted to tell you this in private, Miss Anne, but I believe the time for my news is now. I returned to Pemberley to tell you that, on my way here the first time, I took the liberty of removing some of your sketches and watercolours from your trunk. I took them to a publishing firm that was recommended to me by a friend who moves in literary circles. It's called Reheuser & Pope, and I am happy to inform you that they wish to enter into a contract to publish a volume of fine engravings from some of your watercolours."

Collins smiled tenderly into Anne's incredulous eyes. "I showed them the series you did of the lake, illustrating its changing beauty throughout the year. They wish to call the volume Seasonal Musings of a Country Lady. If this collection is successful--as I am certain it will be--there will be others to come. I do not think their revenue will make you independently wealthy--but you need not depend upon your cousin for all your needs until the money your father left comes to you."

"I . . . you . . . " Anne smiled brilliantly at him through the tears that had welled up in her eyes. "There is no one else I

175

know who would have done that for me. No one who *could* have--for no one knows me as you do. I don't know what to say to you, Lieutenant. I have thanked you so many times already."

"Well I know what to say," Lady Catherine snapped. "Have you run mad, Anne? I can only suppose that you are deranged! It is natural enough that someone of this . . . this *person's* background should not understand the indignity of what he proposes. But you--a De Bourgh! It is not enough that you have run away from your home to go racketing about the countryside, causing God knows what gossip to spread about your flight! It does not suffice that you have flung yourself on the mercy of the man who has jilted you! You propose to disgrace our name by lowering yourself to trade and expect the world to ignore behavior that must forever forbid you to claim the character of a lady?"

"I have heard enough!" Collins thundered, startling them all. Face white with fury, fists clenched at his side, he strode toward Lady Catherine until he stood directly in front of her. "Of the females in this room, madam, it is not Miss Anne who cannot support the character of a lady! Nor is it Mrs. Darcy who, despite the station in which she was born, has proven herself in character and deportment to be most truly well-bred. It is *you*, Lady Catherine, who have disgraced not only the high lineage from which you so frequently boast descent, but also every principle guiding ladylike behavior."

Lady Catherine tried to reply but he swept on ruthlessly. "You offered your daughter to that drunken bully with no more morals than a back slum bravo for no other reason than to salve your pride. You refused Miss Anne's pleas for mercy with a callousness that the stable cat would not have shown its young. Can you, in all honesty, tell us that your love for your daughter was not superseded by your selfish pride and your anger against your nephew? And what was his crime? That he married for love instead of cold-heartedly pursuing money or social status like the rest of your heartless breed!"

Collins drew a deep breath and his glance swept over all four of his listeners, Elizabeth with her head now leaning against her husband's arm and her eyes shining, Darcy staring at him with astonished approbation, and Anne, her face glowing with vindication like, he thought in a sudden poetic fancy, an angel in a stained glass window. Last of all, his blazing grey eyes rested on Lady Catherine, silenced for once in her overbearing career.

"I repeat, madam, it is *you* who stand proven before us all to lack any of those attributes which constitute the character of a lady."

Chapter 15

In the aftermath of the lieutenant's startling announcement and even more surprising denunciation, Lady Catherine discomposed everyone by bursting into noisy tears. Anne went reluctantly to her mother, and Elizabeth quietly suggested that the rest of them withdraw. Seeing her husband's harassed expression and knowing well his distaste for household drama, Elizabeth halted in the hallway. "Darcy, I know that the colonel and Georgiana are very anxious. Why do you not go to the library and relieve their suspense? My cousin and I will sit in the small drawing room. Anné will wish to speak with him when she is at leisure to do so." She smiled warmly at Collins. "And we still have much to say to each other."

Darcy greeted this plan with relief, vanishing in the direction of the library, and Elizabeth accompanied Lieutenant Collins to the comfortable parlor where she often sat sewing or chatting with Georgiana and Anne. After they had seated themselves, she directed her dark eyes at her companion and he was relieved to see their familiar twinkle had returned. "Lieutenant, if I didn't fear to sink your opinion of me as *most truly well-bred*, I would venture to ask you a question. Indeed, I would ask you two."

Collins smiled back at her. "I think the high place you have won in my esteem will survive two questions, Mrs. Darcy."

"What is Maxton's?"

The lieutenant's smile vanished. "Your husband might have something to say to me if I answered that question truthfully."

"My husband will not know, sir. But surely you realize that I am dying of curiosity to learn the meaning of the words that made Sir Crawford turn tail and flee. Must I appeal to some other gentleman for clarification, Cousin?"

"Good lord, no!" exclaimed Collins, horrified. "I will say this much. The ground floor of Maxton's is a gymnasium of sorts. Gentlemen go there for practice in boxing, single stick, fencing and other such sporting pursuits. They also go to observe athletic exhibitions upon which they bet."

Looking into his listener's expectant face, he continued uncomfortably, "Upstairs are games of chance where play runs very deep. You understand that I speak from common report, my only personal experience coming from the visit to which I alluded."

"Nothing you have told me accounts for my husband's reaction, Lieutenant."

Collins sighed. "Mrs. Darcy, the third floor is reserved for feminine entertainment, the description of which is not fit for any lady's ears. That, in itself, is not so shocking. Such vice abounds in the Capitol. But I have heard it said that although some of the ladies are the regular dashers that one would expect--others who provide diversion are not always there of their own volition."

Elizabeth's hands clenched in her lap. "And was that the reason for your visit to Maxton's, sir--resulting in such serious injuries to the parties you named?"

After a moment of hesitation, Collins said reluctantly, "It was, ma'am."

"Anne is the lady to whom you referred, isn't she? It is Anne who would have found herself providing unwilling entertainment for these men." In her agitation, Elizabeth stood. "Lieutenant, my husband and his cousin should know of this."

Rising also, Collins replied earnestly, "Mrs. Darcy, I assure you that that communication would bring about exactly

179

the scandal I wish to avoid. If I had killed those two villains--
and I could have, for I have survived in parts of the world
where a man's life hangs by a thread and the gentleman's code
is unknown--then the reason must become known. And Miss
Anne's name would be dragged through the mud by ever tattle-
monger in town Therefore, my answer to you must be this
one: No. My actions in regard to Fulham and Garner are
unconnected to Miss Anne in any way."

As he spoke, Mrs. Reynolds, the housekeeper, entered
hastily with an apology for her interruption. Elizabeth rose to
accompany her to whatever domestic crisis awaited, but she
paused to give her cousin her hand and a speaking look of
gratitude and understanding. "I see that I leapt to an
unwarranted conclusion, Lieutenant. Thank you for correcting
my misapprehension. And pray forgive me for leaving you.
Anne should not be much longer.   I will send in some
refreshment, and I should myself return directly."

Anne was unsurprised to discover that Lady Catherine,
although chagrined at her misjudgment of Sir Crawford and
flustered by Lieutenant Collins' pithy summation of her
behavior toward her daughter, was adamant in her refusal to
allow Anne to remain at Pemberley. Half an hour of argument
and expostulation proved unequal to changing either of their
minds, and Anne finally rose to her feet.

"We move no closer to agreement, Mama, and I tire of
arguing." Seeing the familiar signs of wrath re-appearing,
Anne met her mother's gaze with an expression of steadfast
determination. "If I return to Rosings with you, there will be
no change in our relationship. You have never consulted my
tastes or desires, and you will still expect me to sit mumchance
while you ride roughshod over me! I will earn my bread,
Mama, before I tolerate such treatment again."

Seeing her mother's mouth open, Anne interrupted her.
"I hope you will consent to remain here at Pemberley until you
have recovered from your journey. But whether you do so or

not, I am determined to finish out my visit with my cousin. It may be that you and I can eventually agree upon a course of action, but first I believe we both require some period apart for reflection."

Lady Catherine could have looked no more shocked if one of the portraits on the walls had suddenly begun to speak; taking advantage of her surely momentary silence, her daughter said hastily, "I must go upstairs to dress for luncheon now."

Wilted from the ordeal Anne looked around for Reynolds to ask him if Lieutenant Collins was still in the house; instead, she discovered Colonel Fitzwilliam, who had clearly been waiting for her appearance.

He smiled at her in commiseration. "Poor Anne--what a turn-up! Darcy has explained to us what ensued, and I am only sorry I could not have had an interview with Sir Crawford Daviott before he departed. I hope I shall be so fortunate as to encounter him in the future. But now, putting aside unpleasant subjects, let me take you outside for a walk."

As Anne hesitated, he continued caressingly, "I fear this is one of the last warm days we may expect. You have not been your usual sunny self of late and I know your talk with your mother must have been very trying. The exercise will give you appetite for luncheon."

Anne could have wished her cousin at Land's End, for she wanted nothing except to find Collins and speak with him, but she recollected that she had brushed off Colonel Fitzwilliam's offer to stand with her in the dreaded confrontation with her mother, and her heart smote her. It would be too unkind to refuse yet another well-meant gesture, and surely Elizabeth would ask the lieutenant to remain for luncheon.

So Anne allowed her cousin to send for her pelisse and accompanied him outside where he directed their walk to the small garden where Elizabeth had caused to be placed a sundial inscribed with the date of her marriage. Already, ivy twined around its base. Anne walked to it at once, for it was a favourite with her, and stood tracing its lettering with one forefinger. "*I only count the sunny hours,*" she murmured, slanting a look of mischief up at her cousin. "If I truly follow this philosophy, Giles, this will be the first hour I count today, will it not?"

He did not respond with the smile that she expected. Instead, he caught her hand and held it within both of his. "I hope these may always number themselves among the minutes you wish to count, Anne."

As she looked at him, uncomprehending, he drew the hand up and kissed it. "There is a way out of this maze, you know. A solution that I hope may be as welcome to you as it certainly is to me. It will allow you to retain your right to Rosings and keep the goodwill of your family. And it will bring me great happiness. Will you do me the immeasurable honour of becoming my wife, Anne?"

Having finished his tea, Lieutenant Collins wandered to the window to look out upon the sunny prospect before him, noting the carefully planned gardens beyond which rose the first hill of Pemberley Wood. He was mentally transferring certain aspects to Trevalyn House, his uncle's property in Cornwall, when Anne appeared on Colonel Fitzwilliam's arm. Collins felt he should move away from the window, but no amount of military discipline could will him to turn his back. He had thought that Anne would come to him as soon as she left Lady Catherine, but she had clearly felt another call upon her time to be more pressing.

He tried desperately to hold back the crushing tide of disappointment as Anne and Colonel Fitzwilliam strolled along the cobbled pathway.

Anne owes me nothing but a thank you for showing her work at Reheuser & Pope, and it is quite likely that even that exertion on my part was unnecessary. She will not long stand in need of an income. Even though her cousin is a younger son, he will have enough to support them until Lady Catherine comes to her senses, and with this marriage, she will not be long in doing so. It is not even likely that the Colonel will allow Anne to publish a volume of her work. I must not allow her to be swayed toward me by a misplaced sense of gratitude-- the same emotion that probably accounted for the kisses she gave me.

As he stood musing, the lonely years of his childhood passed through Collins' mind. He had been the most observably fortunate of his parents' children, chosen early from them all as his uncle's heir, but that distinction had effectually estranged him from his immediate family. He had spent his formative years at the school paid for by his uncle or in that worthy's company. Collins could now appreciate the old man's fondness for him, but it was the affection of a deeply reserved bachelor who had not known how to show tender feelings for the little boy who shared his roof. Long years at sea had followed, first as a midshipman and then in a greater position of command.

From boyhood, art had become Collins' solace and companion, but always he had wished for someone with whom to share his innermost thoughts and desires. Physical passion with a woman had not been enough to dispel his loneliness or touch his heart, and he had resolved that he would emulate his uncle's example rather than marry a woman who held no place in it. *And now I have found her . . . and she is as distant from me as the North Star.*

As the comparison crossed his mind, he saw Colonel Fitzwilliam take Anne's hand. There could be no doubting the significance of the scene being enacted before him. For a moment only, his eyes rested upon the charming sight presented by the couple in the sunny garden, standing as though posed before the sundial, but he knew the tableau was indelibly burned into his remembrance. Pausing only to school his countenance to indifference, he breathed a silent good-bye and turned to stride swiftly out of the room.

183

Anne returned from the garden alone, so disturbed by the interview with her cousin that she ran upstairs to her room, rather than try to find Collins. Knowing she had only minutes to compose herself before the summons came for luncheon, she hurried to her washstand, pouring water into the basin there and splashing her hot cheeks with it. *Perhaps Mama is right and I am a fool. How could I have so mistaken the signs of Giles' regard? How could I have allowed him to offer for me? He will never, never wish even to be in my company again.*

She was seated at the window with her forehead against the cool glass, still bitterly reproaching herself, when a tap sounded at her door. Elizabeth entered, looking troubled.

"Oh no! Am I late for luncheon?"

"It's still fifteen minutes before the hour. I wanted to speak to you before you come down."

Colour flamed in Anne's face. "About Colonel Fitzwilliam?"

Elizabeth frowned. "No, my dear. I merely wanted to tell you that Lieutenant Collins asked me to give you this." She handed Anne an envelope. Eagerly, the girl tore it open to find *Reheuser & Pope, 414 Grelamer Way, London,* written on it in strong black script.

Confused, Anne met Elizabeth's eyes. "But why did he not wait to give me this at luncheon? Surely he is remaining?"

"No, Anne. He did not stay. He did wait for you for quite some time, but eventually he found me and said that he must go. He asked me to give you that address along with his very best wishes."

In her agitation, Anne stood. "You mean he is *going,* Elizabeth? Going away? But . . . I have not had even the opportunity to thank him!"

At that moment another tap sounded at the door, accompanied by Darcy's voice. "Anne?"

"Come in," Anne called, so agitated she scarcely knew what she said.

"I have just spoken to Giles. I thought you might wish

to talk to me, Anne. I didn't realize Elizabeth was with you."
Seeing his wife's questioning look, he said quietly to her,
"Anne has just refused an offer from him."

"Darcy, are you put out with me?" Anne turned from
the window where she had been striving to compose herself.
"Indeed, I could not accept him. Why, I feel toward him
exactly as I do toward you."

"I wish for nothing of the sort," Darcy returned calmly.
"I cannot feel that either of you holds sufficient regard for the
other to make a marriage between you advisable. I came only
to tell you that he will not be at the luncheon table, nor will
your mother be there to rip up at you. Although I asked her
most civilly to remain, she has already left for Rosings."

"Thank you. You are so kind. You are both so kind!"
Impulsively, Anne stood and hugged him. "But I fear that what
I'm about to tell you *will* anger you." Apprehensively, Darcy
met her eyes. "I must see Lieutenant Collins before he goes. I
should have gone to him immediately after I finished speaking
to my mother."

"And that is an action so terrible that I should be angry
with you?" he asked gently.

"Fitzwilliam . . . I intend to tell him . . . to say to him
that . . . " The colour that the cool water had washed from
Anne's cheeks flooded them once more, and she bit her
underlip before taking a deep breath and continuing, "I must
tell him that I hold him in . . . in tender regard. You do not
have to tell me how . . . how *brass-faced* that is! I feel it. He
is under no obligation to return my sentiments, but . . . " Anne
met first Elizabeth's eyes and then her cousin's, her voice
vibrant from the depth of her emotion. ". . . I cannot let him go,
perhaps forever, without knowing my heart."

In the silence that followed her declaration, Anne's eyes
went desperately back to Elizabeth. "Do you feel that doing so
is quite unforgivably forward?"

Elizabeth stood briefly silent as though in thought
before she stood and linked her arm through her husband's.

"Anne, I once came to this house, uninvited, with my Aunt and Uncle Gardiner. I did not admit to myself at the time the motive for my boldness in doing so, but I can state it now. I felt that I had lost Darcy's regard, and if I had to live my life without him--at least I would not do so without making a push to show him how much my sentiments in regard to his affection for me had changed. True, I was told he was not in residence that day, but my heart hoped otherwise."

Elizabeth's eyes met her husband's in a long look that seemed to Anne to hold too many emotions to be deciphered. To Anne's complete amazement, Darcy bent his head and kissed his wife soundly on the lips. Then, still holding her in the circle of his arms, he raised his head and smiled down at her. "Thank you," he said simply.

After a moment he released her. "My dear, I fear you will be lunching in solitary state today." Transferring his gaze to Anne, he said briskly, "Anne, I will have the phaeton at the door in fifteen minutes."

Lieutenant Philip Collins had, of necessity, become a fast and efficient packer. Within half an hour of his return to the Derby Arms, his bags stood ready to be carried downstairs. He was inclined to set out at once, as though watching the road unwind beneath the bays' swift hooves possessed some magical capacity for allowing him to mentally escape a scene so painful that he had downed several ounces of brandy in the taproom to dull its ache. However, he knew it to be foolish to set out immediately, having partaken of neither breakfast nor luncheon, and so had resolved to wait until he had eaten before departing.

Somehow it seemed that this sensible decision might serve to counteract the knowledge of his own foolhardiness and transform his state of mind nearer to that of the carefree Philip Collins who had decided on a whim to visit his older brother in Kent.

Stretching out on the homely quilt-covered bed, he

closed his eyes wearily. *It's only the freshness of the injury that makes it so unbearable. Time and employment will blunt its edge. I will not be forever in the mopes.* He had always been able to regulate his mind, to seal unhappy memories in some internal chamber and close the door upon them; part of his present unease came from his inability even to find such a place to stow his thoughts of Anne. He had often found relief for sorrow or grief in his favourite poets, and he allowed his mind to drift now . . . *For oft when on my couch I lie, in vacant or in pensive mood, they flash upon that inward eye that is the bliss of solitude, and then my heart with rapture fills . . .*

"Oh, God," he spoke his misery aloud, standing up to pace to the window. *What bliss can there be in solitude now? For how long will I see her face against my eyelids every time I close them?*

His artist's eye for detail was his enemy now for he could recall Anne in every aspect he had known her: leaning forward on her knees in the grassy meadow, teeth biting deliciously into her full underlip as she strove to capture the essence of some flower; pouring over his paintings and lifting her face to his like that flower turning to the sun when she was struck by some small, well-executed detail; meeting his eyes in the dim light on their cold journey to the posting inn, her hair hanging in loose curls silvered by the moon; turning to him in the stagecoach and raising her lips to his . . .

"Oh, the devil fly away with luncheon!" He turned abruptly and moved to where his bags stood against the foot of the bed. He could always stop later for some refreshment. Surely, putting some miles between himself and the face that had bewitched his senses and ravished his heart would help to banish it.

On the way to the Derby Arms, Anne sat with her hands gripped anxiously together in her lap, unable to imagine how she would find words for what she wanted to say even if she found Collins there. As she grew more and more nervous, she

187

turned to Darcy and asked with a shade of desperation in her voice, "Fitzwilliam!"

Her cousin transferred his attention from his horses to her. "Yes, my dear?"

"How did you tell Elizabeth that you loved her?"

Darcy was silent for a moment and then he surprised her by chuckling. "Very badly, on my first attempt."

"Your *first* attempt?"

"Yes, indeed. The first time that I made Elizabeth an offer was the day before I departed from Rosings on the occasion she was visiting Mr. and Mrs. Collins there. She heard me out before informing me that I was the last man in the world whom she could be prevailed upon to marry."

Anne stared at him in such astonishment that he had to laugh, albeit ruefully, at the memory. "Then . . . how did your marriage come about?"

"I asked her again when I visited my friend Bingley some months later. His house is in the village where the Bennets live. By that time I had had the opportunity to form a better estimation of her character. Indeed, I found that having my offer flung back in my face, however painful the experience, cleared up many of the illusions I had formed about Miss Elizabeth Bennet and the qualities she felt a prospective husband must posses."

"I can scarcely believe that you asked her a second time."

"Because you would have thought my pride would preclude a second offer?"

"Well . . . " Anne blushed. "To be frank, yes I would have thought it."

Her cousin looked at her kindly. "Elizabeth has taught me many valuable things, Anne, which my parents, although very good in their way, neglected. One of the greatest is that I now judge a man more by the content of his character than by his pocket book or his station in society."

He glanced at her quizzically as he continued. "I have

learnt to laugh at myself."

"I have seen that, Fitzwilliam. How precious a thing is the laughter you share with Elizabeth. Even a stranger may understand one's sorrow and sympathize, but I think it very rare to find someone to laugh with." She was silent for a moment, her thought turning again to Lieutenant Collins before she banished them. "And perhaps you have learnt to be happy, Fitzwilliam?"

"Happier than I ever dreamed possible. Until I met Elizabeth, life seemed largely a matter of duty. I was raised in the knowledge that one day the lives and fortunes of all who live on this estate would depend upon me. My father also taught me that maintaining the honour of the Darcy name was of paramount importance. Those beliefs combined to instill in me a sense of my own superiority to others which society with my chosen friends did little to mitigate."

"Surely you are too harsh!"

Darcy shook his head. "Not until Elizabeth refused me did I examine my own character. Socrates said that the unexamined life is not worth living. I read that in the schoolroom but had never applied it to myself until then. When I took serious stock of myself, I found a man I could not like, Anne, any more than she could, for he was too often proud and over-bearing, often above being pleased by his company, and far too likely to consider his birth and breeding an excuse for any conceit."

He paused for a moment before saying gravely, "I have a reason for saying this to you now, Anne. The faults I found and have sought so hard to correct in my own character are ones that belong to our family. I might almost say they are bred into us. In your dealings with Collins, do not let the Fitzwilliam pride stand in the way of achieving an understanding with him if he is the one man in the world who will make you happy."

Reaching the inn, Darcy lifted his cousin down from the

phaeton and accompanied her inside where the innkeeper rushed to greet them. Learning that the lieutenant had signified his intention to leave after luncheon, Darcy dismissed MacDonwald after telling him that they would await Collins in the small private parlor. Once installed there, Anne turned to her cousin. "Fitzwilliam, will you perform for me one more kindness today? Return home now and share your luncheon with Elizabeth."

He looked at her in astonishment. "I cannot leave you here alone, Anne."

"You can. It is what I wish you to do." Seeing him begin to protest, she laid an imploring hand on his arm. "If all goes as I hope it will, Lieutenant Collins will drive me back to Pemberley. If it does not . . . " she faltered, "well . . . it does not signify. I will send a groom with a note for you." Seeing him wavering, she asked softly, "Were others by when you settled things with Elizabeth?"

"No, Anne, but--"

They were interrupted by the opening of a door. A stout maid in a mobcap hastily apologized and withdrew after retrieving a serving platter from the sideboard.

"Please, Fitzwilliam." She looked at him imploringly.

Wondering why he had always found it so difficult to refuse Anne, Darcy decided it must be because her entreaties were few. He thought of Collins' face when he had looked at Anne, laughing up at Colonel Fitzwilliam. He remembered the day Elizabeth had gazed at him with flushed cheeks and confessed how much her sentiments had changed since the first time he proposed. "As you wish, Cousin. Collins should be down momentarily."

After he had left her, not without a worried backward glance, Anne wandered over to the room's single window, trying to think of how to begin what she must say to Collins. Whatever expressions of civility or gratitude began her interview with him, she must eventually come to the point. Other ladies would probably be able to bring about the desired result through coquetry or oblique innuendo. Anne, a stranger to both, could find no words to express her feelings. *How can I say that I have felt his touch on my skin, his lips on mine, that I have hugged those few brief moments to me every time I lay down to sleep since I left London? The way the sun plays on the different shades of gold and brown in his hair, the trick he has of looking so solemn just before he smiles, the crease in his cheeks when he is only thinking of smiling . . . these and a hundred other things are as familiar to me as my own body, as dear to me as each breath I breathe . . .*

Once again the door opened, and Anne's heart leapt so painfully that one hand went to her breast. And once again it was the serving maid, who looked at her inquiringly. "Please, miss, was you wishful for me to bring you some refreshment?" Mutely, Anne shook her head and the girl retreated. *Oh, how can I talk to him with someone popping in and out every five minutes like a jack-in-the-box?*

Anne knew which room belonged to Collins; he had laughingly complained that he was tucked beneath the gable over the inn yard, where he heard every arrival and departure. Without giving herself time to acknowledge the total impropriety of her intent, she left the parlour. Closing the door behind her, she moved swiftly down the hallway behind the public rooms, and flew up two flights of stairs, to find herself breathless and terrified, outside the attic bedroom on the inn's eastern side.

Chapter 16

Hearing a timid tap on his door, Collins assumed that the maid was summoning him to the luncheon he had bespoken. Still undecided whether to eat before leaving, he swung open the door to be confronted by the last sight his tired eyes expected. In the dimly lit hallway, Anne de Bourgh stood hesitantly on the threshold to his room, clutching her pelisse around a thin muslin dress of the softest blue and looking at him with such trepidation in her wide eyes that he exclaimed impetuously, "Anne! How do you come here? Is something amiss at Pemberley?"

She seemed to recover her breath as he drew her into the room and replied hesitantly, "No, nothing. I merely . . . I had no chance to speak to you before you left, and Elizabeth told me . . . " She looked up at him in imploring dismay. "She said that you are leaving today! I could not let you go without saying. . . without trying to explain to you . . ." Her voice trailed off as the impossibility of what she had come to say to him overwhelmed her.

With great effort, Collins recovered his composure. "Here, let me take your wrap. Come close to the fire." He helped her remove her pelisse, careful not to touch even her hand, and tossed it over the end of the bed.

"You wished to thank me for presenting your work to a publisher? There was no need to exert yourself, Miss Anne. The task took only a few hours of my time, and I enjoyed boasting that I know the creator of such fine watercolours. Indeed," he joked, striving for levity although he had never felt less light-hearted, "I considered claiming them for my own, for

I can tell you that the gentlemen who reviewed them were most impressed! But, alas, I didn't feel I could live up to the expectations they have roused."

She had walked to the fireplace, standing half turned away from him, and she met his attempt at humor with only a faint smile. "I do most truly owe you thanks, Lieutenant, for that and all else you have done. The length of time expended in my behalf is no measure of the importance of the service. I wonder if you realize--no, I think no man *can* realize--what you have given me."

Their eyes met in wordless communion.

"What has been most lacking in my life is self-respect. I was never more than a cipher at Rosings, a pawn to be moved here and there by my mother's will. I so hated the scenes . . . the constant admonitions and scoldings . . . the overwhelming knowledge that I had failed her if I did not behave always in a manner befitting a Fitzwilliam and a De Bourgh . . . that I reacted just as my father did. I gave in to her whims and withdrew behind a wall of indifference. Indeed, I carried pretense even further and feigned illness, hiding in my room where I kept the world at bay. I was a coward, a contemptible creature afraid to venture so far as to express an opinion contrary to hers."

He could not bear the self-contempt in her voice and moved to her across the room. "When the right time came, however, you didn't bow to her wishes."

"Because of you." Anne's wistful voice shook him as no naval engagement ever had. They were standing inches apart, and he once again experienced the curious sensation of sinking into her crystalline eyes, as though his soul were no longer his, but intermingled with hers, never to be his own again. "You told me once that you prize courage above all the virtues, but it was not my courage that spurred my flight from Rosings, Lieutenant. It was yours." A fugitive smile quivered on her lips. "I only borrowed it, you see."

He wanted to enfold the hand partially extended to him,

but since she had entered the room he had fiercely reiterated to himself that she was betrothed, would soon belong to another man, and he knew himself too vulnerable to her to chance even a touch so brief.

"And then you handed me the greatest gift of all. You offered me the chance to become independent of everyone--of my mother or of any husband she might have chosen for me. I will be unable to command the luxuries of life, but with the money I can make from my drawings, plus the little my father was able to leave away from Rosings, I am sure that I can get on well enough."

She smiled up at him, but her joy and triumph were diluted by fear, for he had made no move toward her. "You cannot know, Lieutenant, how it feels for me to need no longer the shabby stratagem of ill health or delicate nerves or any other! You have given me the freedom to be myself, Anne de Bourgh, and to be proud of that person--a stranger to me though she is at present!"

Collins smiled back at her, his heart glad even though he knew that he was imprinting one more haunting image in the volumes of memory. "Then I can only say I am very proud to have given you the right to choose for yourself, Miss Anne. And I wish you very happy in that choice." She looked a little puzzled as he continued with supreme effort. "Indeed, I wish you both happy."

She tilted her head, bewildered. "Both?"

He could not make himself smile again. "I'm afraid I've stolen a march on you, but it was quite unintentional. I was in the small drawing room earlier today when you were outside with your cousin. I couldn't doubt that he was making you an offer."

"I see." Relief began to steal over Anne. "You did indeed see such an offer made, sir. I suppose you could not deduce that it was refused."

Thunderstruck, Collins stared at her. "You refused him? I had not thought it possible. Marriage to Colonel

Fitzwilliam will bring you all that you could desire--affection, a high position in society, the approbation of your family, even Rosings, in all probability."

Anne nodded and then took a long breath. If she did not say what she had come to say now, she never would. "It would have brought me all those things, and certainly they carry great import. But there was one element lacking in a marriage between myself and Colonel Fitzwilliam, you see, and I knew that all the felicity of the others could not combine to outweigh its absence."

He took her hand now, curling his fingers around her slim, cool ones as his eyes questioned hers.

"I don't feel for Giles what I should feel for my husband." She drew a deep breath, feeling there would never come a more propitious moment for what she must say. "There was a time when I wouldn't have realized something to be lacking." Bravely she gazed into his eyes, grey meeting grey in a clash like silver lightning, bright and dark. "But I know it now--and I fear, sir, that it is too late to *un-know* it."

"Anne!" He caught her other wrist and pulled her to him, releasing her only to slide both arms around her and hold her fiercely against him. For a long moment he felt every inch of her body through the fine muslin, her small high breasts, the delicate cage of her ribs, her slender waist, and the warmth below it, heating his blood instantly to a white-hot pitch. He drew back after a moment of absorbing the rhythms of her body and drew her chin up so that she shyly met his eyes.

He saw the dark blood dyeing her cheeks to crimson before she lowered her face again, her shining, loosely dressed curls hiding her expression from him. "Anne, tell me the whole! What is it that would be missing from your life if you marry your cousin?"

She looked up, her face still flushed with lovely colour, uncertainty plain as her little white teeth caught her underlip. The sight released the last of his inhibitions, and he spoke passionately, feeling a desperate relief at finally saying the

195

words. "You must know that I adore you. How could you not? Three times have I violated the laws of honour because I was so bewitched I could not keep my hands from you. My life has been a living hell since I was forced to leave you. There has not been an hour, hardly a minute, that I couldn't see your face in my mind's eye, hear the music of your voice, feel your hand on my cheek as it was when you said good-bye to me in that curst stagecoach! I love you, Anne. I didn't think I could love a woman. I passed a loveless childhood and had come to believe that love can only be learned, that it was too late for such lessons to make any impression on me."

Anne's face was transfigured by wonder. "And you too came to feel its absence?"

"Not until I stood one day in an orchard and watched a fairy reproducing her magically coloured world on paper for us mere mortals. Then I knew love, and God help me, I thought I'd learned the lesson too late. Anne," she heard the entreaty in his voice. "Is it love that you knew would be absent if you married anyone but me?"

Vision blurred with tears of happiness at the shaking tenderness in his voice, Anne reached up to touch the crease in his cheek as she had once touched him in the darkness of good-bye. This time joy flooded her being as she traced its length down to the corner of his mouth. "I love you too," she said simply. "So much that I could find no words to tell you. I came here today because you are leaving, and I love you so unbearably that I had to tell you--to beg you not to go or to take me with you wherever you are going. Pride doesn't matter or propriety or obligation or any other stuffy, meaningless word-- not beside my love for you."

He needed to hear no more to catch her up in a fierce embrace, his lips meeting hers like fire consuming fire, not a gentle caress but an expression of his burning need for her. Her lips opened, yielding to the demanding pressure of his, and he turned his head to slant his mouth over hers, his tongue licking her lips, her tongue, and the sweet recesses within before sucking her into his mouth, holding her flesh in a gentle love-bite that pierced Anne to the innermost core of her body.

After a moment Collins raised his head, shaking it as though her kiss had been red wine of which he had drunk too much. "Anne, you do realize what you're giving up? Your mother may not forgive such an unequal marriage. I could not bear you to look at me one day and see only the reason your inheritance is denied you."

"Philip . . . why, it is the first time I have spoken your name!" The joy of it lit her face. "Darling Philip. I care for Rosings because it holds the memory of my father. Because the people of Rosings have cared for me and I thought to return that care some day. And I must tell you that I fear for my mother if there is a breach between us, for underneath the layers of worldly foolishness and pride, she loves me. I have always known that. But for myself, I care nothing . . . an old name, an old house, the heavy weight of the world's expectations of who Anne de Bourgh should be . . . they mean less to me that your little finger."

"You will not be a pauper, my darling. My wife will not be able to command the luxuries of life, but we shall be perfectly comfortable. I promise that you shall lack for nothing that lies within my power to give you."

For a moment Anne's eyes dropped and then she raised them and whispered softly, "And if all that I desire stands before me now?"

His finger traced a lingering passage over her eyebrows, down her cheek, pausing to caress the little indentation beneath her lip. Drawing her once again into his arms, he kissed her forehead, her eyes, her cheeks, her throat, pausing to lightly lay his tongue on the racing pulse there and feel her heart's blood beat against it. Finally, he took a deep, shaky breath and stepped reluctantly away from her. "I think, my darling, that we'd better leave this room--on the instant! Shall we go downstairs and discuss our plans over luncheon? It will not equal the fare of Pemberley, I'm sure, but I have been informed that Mrs. MacDonwald's chicken Mornay is not to be despised."

At Collins' urging, Anne ate a large portion, both of the chicken and the baked egg custard that accompanied it. "You seem even more slender than you did in London, Anne. It is like holding a little wood sylph in my arms. I know how you dismiss any anxiety for your health . . . but have you been unwell these last two weeks?"

Anne showed her lover a laughing face as she sampled the syllabub. "I have been pining, sir."

He captured her hand, lifted it, and kissed it before curling her palm inward and returning it to her. "And so, ma'am, have I," he replied feelingly. "For a moonlight fairy whose silver hair wrapped its tendrils around my heart. But let us talk about the future instead of the past, Anne. When do you wish to wed?"

"If we do so soon, would you wish me to remain here at Pemberley during your next tour of duty?"

"Ah, I have not told you. So much has happened, my love. I spoke to my captain and received his kind leave to sell out at once. I was not leaving for Deptford, you see, but Cornwall. The reports my uncle sent me of his health alarmed me, and I feel his need of me directly. So you need only consult your own wishes in regard to setting a day."

A troubled look dimmed her radiance. "It is all so awkward that I hardly know what to reply."

"Then here is my suggestion. You must tell me if it's not what you wish. I can procure a special license and return here within a week if I leave today. Do you think Mr. and Mrs. Darcy would oppose a plan for you to be married from Pemberley?"

"A week?"

"That is too soon, my darling?"

"No . . . oh no! I am only accustoming myself to the thought. In seven days, I will be *Anne Collins*." Her voice invested her words with such wonder and happiness that he rose and came to kneel by her chair and take her hands in his.

"I promise you shall never regret it, Anne. I will teach you what I know of painting, and show you new worlds to draw and paint, and I shall love you each moment of the journey. There will not come a day of my life that I do not cherish the treasure I hold."

At that tender moment, the mobcapped serving maid thumped through the door with a tray, causing Collins to rise hastily with a stifled curse before he joined Anne's laughter. "Dash it all! Perhaps I had better wait for a more favourable time to tell you this! At all events, we should go speak to Mr. and Mrs. Darcy. I have every reason now to wish to be on the road as soon as may be."

◆ ❖ ◆

Chapter 17

Elizabeth helped Anne choose a fabric and design for her wedding dress, aided by Banks' keen eye and Georgiana's eager interest. Now she stood in her little blue bedroom at Pemberley, attired in a dress which could not be called pink or peach or coral, but seemed a delicate mixture of all three hues. The muslin was so fine that Dulcie had declared that it would slide through the band of Anne's diamond engagement ring, which she had teasingly claimed that her mistress regarded no more than a hundred times a day. The gown's only trimming consisted of fine seed pearls, sewn lovingly by Dulcie one by one, swirling around the low square neckline and the hem of the column skirt, with silver ribbon tying closed the tiny puffed sleeves and securing the high waistline beneath her breasts.

Collins' one request regarding their wedding had been that Anne wear her hair down; defying fashion she had done so. Banks had directed Dulcie in brushing the entire shining mass up into an intricate weaving at the crown of Anne's head, secured by a pearl aigrette. From there it fell in a sheet of silver-gilt far down her shoulders, with one long lock curled to lie over her breast and tendrils dancing at her temples. She had refused the jewelry which both Elizabeth and Georgiana had offered, determined that she would begin as she meant to go, without depending upon her wealthy relations for more than their affection.

Eventually Banks was satisfied with the coiffure and took herself off, leaving only Anne and Dulcie in her room; looking down at the springy red curls bent over the fastening of her little silver shoes, Anne thought how many times in the past she and Dulcie had been shut into her room with a hostile world on the other side. Now she reached out to brush an affectionate hand over the carefully arranged curls. Dulcie looked up quickly, and their eyes met for a long telling moment. Instantly, Dulcie sprang up. "Now, Miss Anne, your face and hair be fair perfect an' . . . an' we must have no haverin' or 'tis going to the lieutenant with teary eyes you'll be an' 'twouldna do at all."

"It would not," Anne smiled back at her, swallowing the rising tears. "I only wanted to speak to you of a plan I have-- for when we reach Cornwall."

Dulcie's brown eyes sparkled. "I've worked with Banks for hours, Miss Anne. You wouldna thought she'd be so like to help me to look at her, would you? But so many tricks that fine ladies use, I've learnt. Why, Miss, it's lampblack that they use to darken their eyes. And so many other things as Banks has taught me--just wait 'til you see! "

"I don't want you to be my lady's maid, Dulcie." Anne met her shocked gaze steadily as Dulcie gasped. "I want you to be my companion."

"Your *companion*? Like ole Mrs. Jenkinson was? But, Miss, I havna the manners nor the turn of speech for any such thing!"

"I think you have not realized how much you have improved over the years, Dulcie. When you strive to do so, you can sound as much a lady as you please. And Dulcie," Anne leaned over and kissed her check, "it is only your speech that you need to change. Your character and behavior have always been that of a lady."

"I woulna wish to be an embarrassment to you, Miss Anne, as you meet your new relations."

"Lieutenant Collins has told me that we will be living in some isolation, Dulcie. There will be only his old uncle and the servants in the house. My husband will be very busy at first, learning his uncle's business, and you and I will have the time to work on such trivialities as genteel speech and manners. But I can tell you now that those things matter little compared to having a friend upon whom I can depend."

Anne squeezed her hand. "And that you have always been to me, Dulcie."

Seeing her little maid still hesitating, torn between joy and fear at the prospects before her, Anne said firmly, "I need you, Dulcie, and all will be well. You'll see."

A tap sounded at the door. Seeing Dulcie still sniffling, Anne went to the door to find Elizabeth standing there, a grave-faced Elizabeth who said quietly, "Anne, my dear, there is someone who wishes to speak to you." She hesitated and then added reluctantly, "Your mother."

The girl stood frozen for a moment before crying out, "Oh, I am so glad!"

Elizabeth let out a little breath of relief as Anne demanded eagerly. "Where is she?"

"I am here, Anne." Lady Catherine's bulk appeared beyond Elizabeth's shoulder. "I wasn't sure that you would see me." For a long moment, both women stood motionless before Anne opened her arms. In an instant, Elizabeth had beckoned to Dulcie, standing speechless with mouth agape, and closed the door behind them.

Anne was the one who broke the embrace. "Mama, I am so glad you came to be with me today. I love Philip and I dreamed of marrying him from the day we met--but I could not totally rejoice in our happiness without you to share it."

Lady Catherine hesitated and for a moment Anne feared that she was about to launch on a last-minute effort to dissuade her. Then her mother lifted her hand, and Anne saw that she was holding a long perfect strand of rosy pearls. "How like your dear father you look today, Anne. I wish he could see you. He would have been bursting with pride. But at least I can give you the gift he would have given, could he have seen this day." Tears glistened in both of their eyes as they met for a long moment of remembrance. "Lift your hair, my child, and let me fasten them."

As Anne stood before the mirror, her mother fastened the De Bourgh necklace around her neck, and their eyes met again in the mirror, happily acknowledging that the pearls, a last gift from Sir Lewis, had transformed Anne from a beautiful bride--to the perfect bride.

"Philip, wilt thou have this Woman to thy wedded Wife, to live together after God's ordinance in the holy estate of Matrimony? Wilt thou love her, comfort her, honour, and keep her in sickness and in health; and, forsaking all other, keep thee only unto her, so long as ye both shall live?"

As the ancient words of the marriage service flowed over them, Collins looked down into Anne's upturned face. *Of all the men who have ever stood ready to fulfill those vows, there can never have been another who knows so well the treasure he is receiving.*

"I will," he promised in a steady voice, forestalling his nervous friend Buseby, attired for once in a subdued dark grey coat, from reaching out to nudge him.

"Anne, wilt thou have this Man to thy wedded Husband, to live together after God's ordinance in the holy estate of Matrimony? Wilt thou obey him, and serve him, love, honour, and keep him in sickness and in health; and, forsaking all other, keep thee only unto him, so long as ye both shall live?"

To obey . . . to serve . . . love, honour . . . keep only unto him . . . how has it come about that those are the only things I desire?

Her voice rose confidently, audible throughout Pemberley's little chapel. "I will." In the deep silence, she heard a little sniffling sob and recognized it for Dulcie's.

The rest passed in a haze as Darcy stepped forward to place Anne's hand in Philip's, as a wedding ring was slid onto that hand, as she looked up, grey once again meeting grey in a look of shining joy as he promised tenderly, "With this Ring I

203

thee wed, with my Body I thee worship, and with all my worldly Goods I thee endow."

Then they were walking back down the aisle, arm in arm, Mr. and Mrs. Philip Collins, and Anne realized for the first time how many people had lent their support to the new couple by appearing: Colonel Fitzwilliam, his older brother and wife, and their parents, the Earl and Countess in the pew with Lady Catherine, Georgiana and Elizabeth, all of whom were dabbing away tears; her Aunt Elinor beaming at her through more tears, seated beside both her daughters and their families; three couples who, her new husband whispered, were his sisters and their husbands; some figures in Naval uniforms, a few beside smartly dressed wives; other faces, passed too quickly to recognize; and then, near the back of the church was Dulcie, tears streaming down her face, as Threshett, allowing himself a prim smile, passed her his immaculate handkerchief. Beside them sat Mr. and Mrs. Reynolds, Banks, and various Pemberley servants, beaming upon the new couple.

Finally, there stood Povey, bony shoulders straight in his best coat, old blue eyes bright with a mixture of tenderness and pride. Astonished, Anne halted, flinging out her free hand in an impetuous gesture, and Collins grinned at the upright old man.

"I do believe we brought it off, Mr. Povey. Join us as we sign the register. The bride would like you to be the first to felicitate her."

So it was that Anne stood between her oldest friend and her newest as she wrote *Mrs. Philip Collins* for the first time.

When the couple emerged from the church, Anne looked up and saw that the sun still hid behind the clouds of an overcast day. Seeing the direction of her glance, Collins smiled. "Don't fret, sweetheart. We shall make our own sunshine. I'll take you to Spain and Italy and Portugal and Greece and we will paint our memories together. When we're old and sit by the fireside, those sunny hours will hang upon our walls."

Reader's Digest

(ISSN 0034-0375)
PO Box 6095
Harlan, IA 51593-1595

PERIODICALS SUPPLEMENT

As their guests began to trickle out onto the church porch, Anne looked up into her husband's face and asked him seriously, "And you will teach me how to paint the dolphins' colours?"

"Among other things, my love."

Before the tolerant eyes of the wedding guests, Philip Collins picked up his bride and kissed her fiercely, one hand tangled in her long silver hair. "Among other things."

Made in the USA
Lexington, KY
07 April 2013